D1012546

IT'S JUDGMENT DAY

The blood-drenched monstrosity standing before her could not be the man she loved. It was a dream, or a punishment from God, or a demon made flesh. But not Jake. Not Jake.

Then it smiled at her, and Emmy knew that smile. It was the one he used to charm, to smooth over the rough spots. It was the one that she had fallen in love with.

And the voice, as it spoke, was his, too.

"Look at you. My little Bible baby." He stretched out the last words affectionately, just as he reached out with gore-matted arms. "Don't be scared. It's all right. You knew this would happen.

"Come to me..."

As if in a dream, she took another helpless step. The smell got to her, the closer she came. Emmy held her breath and forced herself closer, tears streaming down her chin.

Then he closed the distance, grabbing her up in a huge embrace, squeezing so hard that she wheezed and turned as red as the blood on his hand, now painting her face and hair...

Other *Leisure* books by John Skipp:

THE LONG LAST CALL

JOHN SKIPP
AND CODY GOODFELLOW

JAKE'S WAKE

LEISURE BOOKS NEW YORK CITY

For Stephen Walter,
The one and only Jake.

A LEISURE BOOK®

January 2009

Published by

Dorchester Publishing Co., Inc.
200 Madison Avenue
New York, NY 10016

ISBN 10: 0-8439-6076-0
ISBN 13: 978-0-8439-6076-1

The name "Leisure Books" and the stylized "L" with design are trademarks of Dorchester Publishing Co., Inc.

Printed in the United States of America.

10 9 8 7 6 5 4 3 2 1

Visit us on the web at www.dorchesterpub.com.

ACKNOWLEDGMENTS

Because *Jake's Wake* started out as a motion picture, and it takes a shitload of people to make those things, John Skipp would like to effusively thank: the very brilliant Laura Bahr (for working on the screenplay with me from the very beginning, embodying Emmy on both the page and the screen, and in the process, giving kisses to the missus); Steve Walter (production partner, prime mover, and villainous muse extraordinaire); Damon Packard (editor, sound designer, visual fx whiz, and one-man encyclopedia of film); my wonderful stars Alisha Seaton (Evangeline), A. K. Raymond (Esther), Peter Pano (Eddie), Kerr Seth Lordygan (Christian), Garrett Liggett (Mathias), Steve Stone (proto-Jasper), John McLaughlin (Jasper), Dierdre Lyons (Lorna), Ursula Vari (Natalya), Cyanne McClairian (Crissy), Cheryl Lyone (Sugar), Frank "Fuk'n Frankie" Pestello (as, you guessed it, Frankie), and that Goodfellow guy (for whom Gray was created), all vastly enriching our sense of who these characters might truly be; production partner and line producer Ed Polgardy, who pulled and held the team together; Laurence Avenet-Bradley, who shot it beautifully; Rob Winfield, who sprinkled CG magick; Marianne Walter, who made up both the living and the dead; and Mike Gaglio, Chris Garcia, Lou Garcia, Annette Garcia, Jesse Anderson, Tim Keegan, Isabel Ferrer, Paul Gebeau, Michael Su, Dan Martone, Laura Martone, and Dani Cahn, for making it happen behind the scenes. I'd also like to thank my beautiful family; the short-lived tribe at Brilliant Drive; Scott Bradley, who bailed me out when the floor caved in; my friends at JR Media; our agent, Lori Perkins; Don D'Auria and the Leisure machine; the dearly loved and lost Ms. T; everyone else I love; and finally, Jane Hamilton and Max Cirigliano, for giving me a home at last.

*   *   *

Because it takes a village to raise a village idiot, Cody Goodfellow would like to thank: Adam Barnes (if I had to fight for my own work as vigorously as he has done, I would have quit before I got started); the Punk Horror family, David Agranoff, Paul Stuart and Gabriel Llanas; our webmaster and Furry Community liaison, Travis "Funky Trunk" Hoecker; our digital witchdoctor, Rob Winfield; Darius Shahmir, Benji Gillespie and Ian Hannin, for putting sex in the Champagne Room; Ryan C. Thomas, for putting the raunch in *Ranch & Coast*; Green Party candidate Peter Shenouda; my first, favorite and most feverish fan, Eunice Magill; Jeromy and Claudia Cox; Curt Benedetto and Kristen Tinderholt of Frock You Vintage, for dressing me like a grown-up; my funky Dutch unclefucker, Ron McPhee; my brother, Matt Carter; my brother by another mother, Aaron Costello; my brother in excess (and ex-wives), Steve "Tweak" Cordova; tech support guru and Honky Propulsion Systems CEO, Chris "The Stormin' Mormon" Frandsen; Del and Sue Howison at Dark Delicacies; Alan Beatts and the alluring, enduring staff of Borderlands; Ed "Big Daddy" Bove, Cathy Down, Nancy Dietermeyer, Jeff Gelb and the Mediabase Militia; the inestimably awesome Ray at Copy Hub (because if you live in the 818 and get your copies anywhere else, I will fight you); and most of all, my lovely and vivacious wife Victoria, for copyediting with benefits, and everything else.

JAKE'S WAKE

Prologue
Sugar Turns To Dust

One minute before the knife went in, Jacob Connaway was up to his nuts in glory.

It was Saturday night—nearly one A.M. (*Amen!*)—and as usual, he had scored a sinner to save. A saucy little number named Sugar—hot, tight, and hammered in every sense, already drinking off a lifetime of abuse at the ripe old age of twenty-three.

He could smell her damage from the moment he opened the pool hall door, then zeroed right in. And sure enough, she was ripe for the plucking. She wore fuck-me clothes on a fuck-me body, with a fuck-you attitude that was purely for show.

When he got up close, she had fuck-me eyes.

A total paint-by-the-numbers seduction.

It had taken an hour of drinks, sweet-talking, and Jesus to get her out to the parking lot. Another fifteen minutes of lewd jokes and groping to get her into the car. At that point, with less than an hour until showtime, his crib in Joshua Tree was out of the question.

So it was either her place in San Bernardino, or a cheap hotel with cable. But even cheap hotels cost money.

One fifteen-minute multiorgasmic finger-bang later, they were on their way to her place.

So there was no way anyone could call it rape, when they got there just in the nick of time, and he hustled her down to the basement rec room, turned the TV on. Tuned in Cable Access Channnel 23, serving the whole Inland Empire.

Skootched up the nearest chair.

Ripped her panties off from underneath her skirt, despite her sudden protestations.

And took off the belt, just to let her know he meant business.

There was panic in her eyes. And self-loathing. And hunger. All of them as naked as her ass had just become. They masochistically commingled as he whipped her around. Bent her over the chair. Dropped his trousers. Spat in his hand. Juiced her up, just in case (though she was wet as could be).

And slid himself up to the hilt.

When his theme song kicked in, Jake was slamming away, with that godly feeling already comin' on strong.

Closer to Jesus than even he knew.

But the demons were closer still . . .

"Oh, god," Sugar moaned, and then again, harder, transfixed by the helplessness, pleasure, and shame. He had her ass in the air, and was banging it hard, with her face so close to the TV screen that she could feel the static electricity off the glass. Feel it tug at her hair, and tickle her skin, sparkle off of the tears streaming down her face.

For Sugar, the situation was as typical as it was retarded: so hot, so destructive, so completely insane.

She wanted to ask her herself *how did this happen*, but the answer was *same as it always does, stupid. Get drunk. Get in a fight with Frankie. Go do something to make him crazy . . .*

Only this time, it struck her, she might have finally gone too far.

The preacher on the screen looked the way she'd always seen him on late-night cable, at the end of the drinking day: rugged, handsome, persuasive, and powerful. Like a barbarian turned Old Testament prophet turned rock star at a fashion shoot, with his wild dark Jimmy Page locks sweeping over the broad shoulders of his impeccably tailored suit.

She'd always figured he'd be very large in person, just from the way he filled the screen, with the billowing digitally enhanced blue sky behind him. A giant among tiny believers, standing on a freshly conquered mountaintop, delivering his sermon to all who had ears.

She stared into the eyes of the man on the screen. They were beautiful, deep, dark, scary eyes, in riveting counterpoint to his wide, boyish smile.

"Oh my god," she whimpered again, drawing the notes out, almost ululating at the pounding from behind.

The man on the screen nodded and grinned at the raucous applause that greeted him now, as it always did. These people clearly loved him. How could they not? The sound of it flooded her ears as she grunted and moaned.

"Shhhhh!" hissed the harsh voice behind her. The music trailed off.

And the sermon began.

"Let me tell you something, people," said the man on the screen. His voice was sonorous, sexy as hell. *"I'm a sinner. Lord KNOWS I'm a sinner! I have broken the laws of God and man so many times that it's a wonder I'm still standin' here today!"*

Televised applause and hoots of audience approval filled the room, nearly drowning out her own mounting groans.

"I have stared death straight in the eye. Felt its gaze down to my soul."

"OHHHH . . . ! Oh god, oh god . . ."

"SHUT UP!" roared the voice from behind her, slamming into her so hard that her forehead smacked the screen.

"Felt the full force and fury of Judgment Day howlin' like a hurricane inside me, rattlin' around in my bones, as if to say, 'Jake? This time, there is gonna be hell to pay!'"

And then, God damn it, she began to cum hard, as if *she* were the one with the hurricane inside her, obliterating thought in a shattering crescendo, ripping her apart with jagged, painful spikes of bliss. It blinded her, deafened her, wiped the universe clean. She couldn't see the TV right in front of her eyes, and felt more than heard herself screaming.

Next thing she knew, there was a hand over her mouth, and the world came back in violent focus. She bit down hard, pure animal now, heard him yelp as the hand yanked away. But the fucking barely broke its rhythm, and the hurricane was far from done with her.

She didn't hear the door at the top of the stairs open, any more than the man on the screen: the man who was about to make her go off again, whether she liked it or not.

So far as they knew, they were alone in the world.

She had totally forgotten that Frankie might come home.

Frankie Tatum had a lot of faults. He talked over people. He got angry quick. He was diabetic, so he shouldn't drink or do speed, but he drank and did speed anyway. Those things all sort of ran together, and, with rare exceptions, made Frankie all that he was.

He also had a tendency to act first, and think about it later, if ever. Which accounted for his list of regrets.

But if there was one good thing about Frankie Tatum, it was probably this: he really loved his Sugarplum.

So it was one thing to know that she would run off

and grudge-fuck her way into his deepest, darkest place. It had happened before, and would happen again. After today, maybe even tonight.

But to hear her doing it right here, in their home, right in front of him . . .

From Frankie's drugged-out point of view—quivering with rage, at the top of the stairs—there was nowhere to go but down.

And so he went, hunting knife already in hand, one thunderous step at a time, the world a rush and a blur that converged on two shapes before a TV set where that preacher Sugar thought was so hot bellowed out his bull-shit about a so-called loving God.

"And HERE'S THE MIRACLE, brothers and sisters! The thing I'm here to tell you, one and all, today!"

And Frankie was crying, oh yes he was, one wracking sob for every moan and thrust of the rutting couple before him. Not a speck of hesitation as he brought the blade up.

"THERE IS NO DEATH!" roared the voice on the screen. *"Do you hear what I'm sayin'? THERE IS NO SUCH THING AS DEATH!"*

Then the blade came down.

And changed everything, forever.

A split second before the knife went in, Jake was shouting along with his TV self while the jism pressure mounted. He could feel it swimming up from the soles of his feet as he looked from his face to her ass and back again.

" 'It's a lie that Satan taught you!' " he howled. *" 'It's a joke that isn't all that funny!'* AHH, FUCK . . . !"* Almost getting off more on himself than this sweet, twisted lit-tle girl before him . . .

. . . and that was when his own penetration began, right between the shoulder blades, cold steel sliding in so fast that he didn't even feel it happen, the blade was just suddenly *there*, inside him, all the way in and almost through his chest, point grinding against the back of his breastbone.

Jake howled, his cock forgotten as his ruptured heart-meat started squirting instead. He started to spin, and the knife pulled out, blood gutters letting the steel slide smoothly back into the open air, glittering black in the blue TV light.

"And right behind it is the SECRET TRUTH that Jesus has been tryin' to tell you the whole time!"

Then the knife came back, gutting him this time, carving his insides and spilling them out in the open. He bent over as if to catch them, dimly aware of the woman who scrambled away from him, hysterically screaming.

And over it all, the sound of his own voice.

"Christ has promised us life everlasting. It's in the Book. In black-and-white."

The knife pulled out, went in again.

"NO!" Sugar screamed, was not the only one screaming.

Jake felt blood squirt out of his mouth and staggered back, then collapsed to the floor, hitting it hard and yet barely aware of it. His perception was a crumbling mosaic, life dissembling into death one broken shard at a time.

"Omigod, Frankie, I'm sorry, I'm so sorry . . . !"

From his perspective on the floor, he could see Sugar wrap herself around Frankie, sobbing and clutching him tight. The killer just stood there, swaying, unsteady, then dropped the knife, sobbing, letting her kiss the tears from his face.

"All we have to do is pledge our souls to him . . ."

Jake hissed out another thick mouthful of blood. It was the only thing that didn't feel cold. He could feel the warmth drain from his face, his shivering limbs and ruptured torso.

"Pledge our souls . . ."

"I love you," Sugar said, but not to him. "Look at me. I love you so much. Look at me, baby. I'm so sorry . . ."

Look at me, Jake tried to say, but he couldn't do it, and they didn't care. He faintly heard Frankie slap her, heard her sudden yelp of pain, but found himself staring straight up at the crappy stucco on the ceiling.

". . . all our hearts, and all our souls . . ."

He had always expected a motion picture at the end. *Jake's Greatest Hits*: a biblical travelogue, in Cinemascope and Technicolor.

But there was no vision, no thought, no revelation. Just the numb wash of shock, like an icy gray tide, slowly drowning out his pain.

". . . to that DIVINE RESURRECTION!"

And that was when Jake's demons appeared.

It began as a flicker at the far end of the room, like a strobe light from another, even uglier dimension. A crackling in the air that made his short hairs stand on end.

Something was taking shape there, with the body
(jake)
of a woman, flicker-flashing
(jake)
in and out of the darkness.
(jaaaake)
It whispered to him as it writhed upright, like some malformed exotic dancer, hips undulating obscenely, arms snaking through the air. Too many arms. Two, four, six
(look at you)
and then they were laughing, the three-demons-in-one: almost solid now as its spectral body crouched, nearly squatting, as if to shit or give him birth . . .

. . . and Jake couldn't feel his fingers or toes, but he could feel his balls contract in terror. It was the only emotion he had left, and it screamed through every still-working nerve in his body.

Worse yet, it screamed through his soul
(and your life everlasting)
with horrible recognition
(everlasting jaaaake)
and before he could blink, the three-faced demon was upon him. Leaning over him. Leaning down close
(in everlasting judgment)
with all of its six flickering eyes so knowing
(death everlasting)
knowing him, as he knew them.
(but only for the blind, jake, does death never end)

Jake's own eyes were glazing over, smoke-clotted windows between this world and the next. But he could see the demon smiling now, and knew that it hadn't just come to claim him.

His great work was only beginning.

The miracle had finally come.

Part I
Old Home Night

Chapter One

Three nights later, and the chill autumn wind prowled over a desert painted silver by a brooding half-moon. It simmered like a window fan set angrily on low, fretting at chimes and whirligigs on porches, then gusted up hard enough to rattle windows in their frames and bow the jagged crowns of Joshua trees and yucca plants, roaring in across the empty California desert as if looking for a place to hide from whatever chased it.

A storm was coming, but nobody had the slightest clue how bad it was going to get.

The news of the day was focused elsewhere, loaded with the same domestic absurdity and foreign atrocity as ever, fodder aplenty for arguments that the world continued to chase its own tail, or charge straight off a cliff.

For those looking for signs of the end times—aside from the wars, floods, famines, hurricanes, earthquakes, tsunamis, conspiracies, scandals, UFO sightings, soaring oil prices, homosexual agendas, and polar ice caps melting—there were more than a few bits of good news.

A "rather popular" Shiite cleric—whose name reporters dutifully mangled with every repetition—was killed by a suicide bomber in Basra, along with two

dozen of his followers. After loudly denouncing the sec-
tarian violence and American occupation of Iraq, he
foretold his own death, but proclaimed that "I will be the
last to die."

The assassin who made the cleric a martyr was dis-
guised as an Iraqi policeman. His prophecy held true for
three eerily quiet days, until this morning, when an IED
outside Kirkuk flipped a Humvee filled with marines.

In other news—and a stunning reversal of centuries-
old doctrine—the Catholic Church issued a digital papal
bull closing the limbo loophole, retroactively consigning
untold millions of pagan babies to the fires of hell.

This, combined with their admission that life on
other planets did not contradict biblical infallibility—
since extraterrestrials would be "God's children, too"—
begged the question: what *else* did the pope suddenly
know that he wasn't letting the rest of the world in on?

And in New Zealand, global warming had finally
given comfort to bereaved humanity, or at least some
closure, as a melting glacier off Baffin Island disgorged
the frigid remains of a Kiwi survey plane and its crew,
given up for lost in 1964. Loved ones and descendents
gathered on a chartered ship to watch as the wreckage
thawed in the summer sun, then tumbled into the sea.

Signs and portents. But mostly smoke and mirrors. For
gloomy true believers and faithless curmudgeons alike,
the real indicators never appeared as mainstream news.
They were tiny details, stuck between the cracks of con-
sensus reality: hidden in sacred texts and environmental
reports, research dug from the *Fortean Times*, or the rant-
ings of little-known small-town cable access prophets.

For most people, the only news that mattered was the
substance of life that impacted them directly: money,
jobs, friends, and loved ones. The world was too big,
too unwieldy to fathom. The question was, "How are
you today?"

On a desert road in the Southern California night, a white sedan passed a billboard asking WHAT WOULD JESUS DO?

The frightened people inside asked themselves the same question. It was a personal question, which they kept to themselves.

The desert, as always, was full of secrets.

But the storm was blowing in.

Chapter Two

Esther's house—formerly the Weston-Partridge Free School and Homestead—sat alone on ten acres surrounded by no one. It looked like a single-level ranch-style house that had been blowtorched by hippie witchcraft until it was pliable, then awkwardly stretched to twice its normal length.

Esther's parents had built it in 1971, shortly after their groundbreaking scholastic treatise, *Know Your Self, Grow Your Self*, hit the best-seller charts. This had allowed them the luxury of giving up on fighting the system from within, pioneering radical alternatives instead.

Clearly, the architect they conspired with had some radical alternative theories on quality, as well, because the place not only looked wrong, it was wired wrong. It was plumbed wrong. They had endless fucking problems all the time, only some of which were ever truly fixed.

The result was, the house had patches on its patches, one quick save after another, like a perpetually leaky vessel that somehow managed to stay afloat.

But they were cheerful people, her parents. Eternally

optimistic, even when they were fighting: with the house, with disease, with her, with each other, with the county or the culture at large. They were mellow, stoned, passionate, rigorously well-meaning take-it-as-it-comes sort of people.

And they had always made her crazy.

In their heyday—which neatly paralleled her developmental years—the Weston-Partridge Free School and Homestead had been vibrant with the songs and laughter of children, the exchange of information, the cultivation of exciting young lives. Rarely more than two dozen kids at a time, and once as few as six, all given the kind of attention that rich parents paid thousands for, at private academies.

And it was all very sweet, but of course it died, as the eighties brought an end to hippie homeschooling, and the Reagan years brought corporate bottom-line hardball back into vogue. The kids stopped coming, the books went out of print, her father passed away. And then her mom, not far behind.

But the land and the house were paid for. And they'd left a generous trust. At least their lawyer wasn't stoned.

Relics of those days still remained in the yard—a derelict wooden carousel, a rusted-out slide, some monkey bars—a playground ghost town where she once played, then dreamed of bringing back to life with her own children—

The paint had faded and begun to peel. The grass had gone brown. The old oak tree that everyone used to climb on had been struck by lightning and driven insane, its longest half-severed limb still stretched out twenty feet alongside the stone fence that bordered the property.

The rambling front of the house was entirely dark, but halfway down, the fitfully flickering light from the hallway glimmered through narrow ceiling-level windows. And around at the back, there was the shy, yellow glow of a porch light. A beautiful stained glass window set into the front door.

And dark curtains, concealing the picture-window walls of the living room.

Behind them, a fire was burning too hot.

While secrets and worse fluttered between the shadows and the flame.

Eddie Echevarria knelt before the roaring fireplace, wiping the sweat and dark bangs from his forehead, warming himself from the chill outside and watching the raw primal power of dancing energy in its purest state.

Eddie was in awe of flame. Not in some twisted, pyro way, but with the kind of love and fascination that the cavemen must have felt when they learned that they could make that sort of magic with their own two hands.

Fire *was* magic, and the fireplace was an altar, where a handful of properly stacked chunks of dead wood, some good kindling, and a couple balls of newspaper could transmute single-handedly into proof of a living God.

To watch shapes transform in that red-yellow dance, sheering away into sharp charcoal outlines of themselves that radiated both heat and light—disintegrating into something both hotter and higher than themselves— was more than *un pocito* like watching human beings rise above themselves under stressful situations.

And dear God, they were under some stress tonight.

Eddie was thirty-six, just slightly younger than Esther. He had devotedly cared for the family, and for Esther, for nearly eighteen years—five times longer than her marriage—and he had no intention of quitting. Especially now.

He turned to look at her pinned in the stark kitchen light, leaning over the counter that linked it with the living room where he knelt, thinking thoughts high above his station and half expecting to wake up to something worse.

She was chopping something—cheese, from the sound of the knife on the wooded cutting board—with metronomic precision.

She looked, as always, beautiful and frail: too skinny for her own good, if the truth be told. She had pale, regal features and fine ash-blonde hair that cascaded in lush ringlets when set free; but tied back now in elegant fashion, it lent her an air of poise she could almost hide behind.

Her black dress was designed for mourning, with spaghetti straps slung just low enough to set off her slender neck and accentuate her modest cleavage. Needing to feel both beautiful and powerful tonight, she had asked him to help pick out the dress.

Not a problem, as far as Eddie was concerned. But it also revealed how tight her shoulders were, how stiffly she carried herself as she tried to hang on.

And the drinking helped only up to a point, which was closing in fast.

Something clearly had to be done.

"Esther," he said, just loud enough to be heard without startling her.

"What?"

"Come look."

She looked up and smiled thinly. "It's beautiful. Now could you help me . . . ?"

"No, no. *Uno momento.*"

Her voice wound high and taut. "Eddie."

"Please. Put the knife down and come here."

Then he winked at her, lightly slapped his fingertips on his thighs, and said the word she liked to hear. *"Querida."*

Esther paused, knife quivering in her white-knuckled hand.

She found herself stuck—as was so often the case, these days—in this horrible moment of hesitation, between what she thought she ought to be doing, and what she *knew* she ought to do.

It was the old head-versus-heart argument she'd always had, only now it was shared, and so alien, precisely because it was how it should be. She lived in her head, as usual.

And Eddie, God bless him, was the heart.

Esther had been slicing sharp cheddar cheese into neat, symmetrical cracker-sized slabs. She already had far more than was needed—lord knew hunger was the furthest thing from her mind—but the process was somewhere between Zen and fixation. Something she could do right now. Something with actual results.

Meanwhile, her mind was racing, not meditative at all. More like the restless wind outside, disturbing everything while settling on nothing . . .

But her mind finally found a safe harbor, and came to rest on Eddie, solid and kind.

Just looking at her, with only love in his eyes.

It was embarrassing to be seen that clearly, that knowingly, and not feel judged. Embarrassing to be caught freaking out. But also unspeakably heartening.

Because the fact was that he really cared. *Really cared.* Even with all her faults, her stupid decisions and horrible mood swings and many, many weaknesses.

He cared enough to help her through. To hold her close. To back her moves.

He cared enough to make her feel like a beautiful woman, and more . . . a beautiful *person*.

And there he was, smiling as if to say that she had already won.

If only that were true . . .

Esther looked down at the knife in her trembling hand, then looked at the veins in her paper-thin wrists. Cheese, shmeese. She could slice through those things in an instant, and all of this would be done.

Instead, she put down the knife. Grabbed her scotch. Swigged hard. And exited the kitchen, stage left.

Eddie looked up at her and smiled as she came to kneel beside him, sipped, set down her glass. He was strong and compact, and he hugged her well, looking so handsome in his dress shirt and jacket. As if he had been hired to work this event. Which, in a sense, he had.

She sighed, jittery, settled into his embrace. Closed her eyes, then found herself staring into the fire.

"Oh, Eddie," she almost moaned. "You know they're going to be here soon . . ."

"*Shhhh* . . ." he said, and turned her face toward his, tender. His steady green-flecked brown eyes fed her a steady flow of trust. She sensed how hard he was trying to be strong.

But she was scared, and he was scared for her, and there was no getting around that fact.

So when he kissed her, warm and full, it did almost everything a kiss should do.

The shadows shifted behind them, as the rude glare of headlights shone through the stained glass door. They could hear a car pull up, and they nervously patted themselves down, and wiped away lipstick traces. It was showtime.

"Just tell me it's gonna be all right," Esther said.

"It's gonna be all right, okay?"

She nodded, and he kissed her softly.

"I swear."

She trembled, and they nodded to each other as he stood, then helped her up, smiling as he stooped to pick up her glass and take his place at the bar.

Leaving Esther these precious last moments.

To rally herself, before the flood.

Chapter Three

The tidy little white sedan pulled timidly into the dirt parking lot, as if afraid to stop here on a night like this. It eased to a halt beside Esther's SUV, but did not cut the engine. Gospel music played softly inside, as if to dispel the gloom. The headlights glared, kicking long shadows through the yard.

Emmy Patton sat at the far corner of the passenger seat, nearly pressed against the door. She avoided her gaze in the rearview mirror. She had no use for makeup. She was not proud—and frankly, pretty enough to get along without it—but she knew her face right now looked like a paper bag full of rain.

She'd held it in all day, through the endless police interview, the harassing calls from the IRS, and then the service. It fell to her to organize and preside over the outpouring of grief as Jake's congregation of the airwaves said good-bye.

It had seemed selfish to break down when so many lost souls needed guidance to make it through the day without getting roaring drunk and fighting in the chapel. It had seemed wrong, too, to cry in front of those people.

But she was only twenty-two, and this level of tragedy was new to her. She was a sheltered small-town girl from a nice Southern Baptist family, a straight "A" student with a major in business, and how she had wound up dealing with all this madness was almost beyond her imagining.

So if she cried now, who couldn't understand? Jesus did, certainly. But as for the rest, she felt judged for her feelings. As if it were wrong to believe so strongly, in someone or something.

And that didn't help, not at all.

So she sat there, traumatized, frozen in place, not even crying: just staring out through the windshield at the house, with fear brimming in her eyes.

"You don't have to do this, you know."

Mathias turned sideways in the driver's seat, pointedly averting his hangdog eyes, popping his knuckles and steepling his fine pianist's fingers on the steering wheel. He was a thin, gangly young man, slightly younger than her, also clean-cut, sheltered, and incredibly nervous.

Emmy said nothing, and neither did he. She knew he meant well, but she sure couldn't feel it.

She felt a bit of calm as she fixed her gaze on the stained glass window in the front door. It was beautiful, churchlike, beguiling, the pure liquid colors animated by the glow of dancing firelight, while the music bled from one syrupy proclamation of chaste Christian love into another.

It struck her funny, in a way she'd never let herself laugh at, how easily most of these born-again ballads would become standard semipornographic pop songs if you just changed Jesus to a girl's name. Like Rhonda.

Or Emmy, she added, chastening herself.

The fact was, everybody had weakness and wounds to overcome. That was just God's truth. The essence of sin was a falling-short of the glory of God, and all humankind was guilty.

But was it not a very special sort of sin to transpose your base sexual feelings onto the love of the Lord?

She didn't know the answer—was deeply struggling with how to ask the question—but she knew it was sinful to sit in judgment on the music on the radio. And promptly apologized, in her heart.

"Emmy," Mathias said, a little louder this time. "You know, we can just turn around." He shifted the car into reverse, let off the brake just a little.

The jerky motion shook her out of her reverie. She turned to him sharply.

"No!"

He stepped on the brake, shrunk back as if stung. She shook her head, and he put it back into park.

"The church is my responsibility now. You have to understand that. You have to respect my . . . my *responsibility*." Her voice went up half an octave at the end.

"I know. It's just that . . ."

"It's not just what we want, Mathias. You know that."

"I know, but . . ." *You've done enough for him today*, she knew he wanted to add, and it made her want to scream. Her hand reached for the volume knob, ready to turn it up and cover the sound.

Then she caught herself. Took the proverbial deep breath. And shot him the very best smile she could gather, uniting them around what mattered.

"We have to do what's right by the Lord," she said.

Mathias nodded in defeat, and turned the key.

The engine cut off, along with the music. The headlights shut off, plunging the yard into deeper darkness. The ticking of the engine was like jumping beans in a coffee can. Aside from the wind, it was the only sound.

They exited the car and started walking toward the door, Emmy pacing ahead with her lips pursed and eyes locked on the glimmering stained glass. She could feel Mathias behind her, with his arms half out, as if she might faint and need catching.

Indeed, she did feel faint, felt the world turn unreal.

The wind soughed and whistled through the eaves of the long, low house, bone-gray oak leaves swishing around her feet and the clankity, old-fashioned playground equipment.

She had a terrible, visceral sense, just then, of a deeper shadow in the dark. As if something unseen were swooping over them, watchful and malign.

Then the front door opened, and a woman in black appeared, genial and smiling.

"Hello. You must be Emmy."

"Mrs. Connaway."

"Call me Esther. Thank you so much for coming."

Mathias and Emmy entered stiffly. Esther closed the door, ushered them toward a small couch.

The living room was dimly lit and sparsely furnished, with pale yellow walls and age-stained lamp shades that muzzled the light. Uneasy shadows from the fireplace danced on the walls.

A handsome Latino in a *guayabera* shirt was tending the fire. He turned and smiled at them. Emmy nodded in his direction, then looked at Mathias. Adrift in his own anxiety, he quickly picked up on her unasked question. *Who in the world is that?*

"Please have a seat," Esther said. "Can we get you something to drink?"

"Nothing for me, thank you," Emmy said. Her eyes bounced around the unfamiliar room in search of an anchor.

That's when she noticed the pictures on the mantel above the fireplace.

"I'd like a ginger ale?" Mathias said, but she barely heard him. Her focus was locked on one picture in particular.

A framed wedding portrait.

Of Esther.

And Jake.

* * *

Dear God, Esther thought, as the tears welled up in the young girl's eyes. She felt it welling up inside herself, flinched against it . . .

. . . *and then the sobbing began*, Emmy balling up on the couch and wailing. Her young companion awkwardly tried to comfort her, but clearly did not know how.

Esther cast a *help me* glance at Eddie, then rapidly yanked it back.

The fire roared and leapt out of its bed, as if the wind gusting down the chimney had turned to kerosene.

Eddie sprang into action. "Okay! Ginger ale for you. Ms. Esther?"

"Please."

Eddie went to the kitchen to fetch the drinks.

Emmy was still sobbing. "I'M SO SORRY! I'm so sorry . . . I promised myself I wasn't going to do this . . ."

"It's okay . . ." Esther said.

"I can't believe he's actually dead!"

Esther was tearing up, as well. "I know . . ."

Suddenly, both of them were crying: Esther just standing there, trying gallantly to hold it in, Emmy doubled over and not even trying, both rendered equally ridiculous by grief.

Esther watched Eddie bring the young man his ginger ale, nobody speaking a word. Eddie clearly ached to hold Esther, but that was out of the question. Not in front of the others.

So he just gave her the drink.

As the wind whipped up outside.

And for a moment, the lights flickered and dimmed, as if the power might go out.

Chapter Four

Outside, a vast, dark cloud engulfed the moon, giving too much substance to the almost living shadows racing rampant across the desert plains. There were spirits in the air tonight, rising up and reaching out as if to swallow the world.

There were spirits in the house, as well, coursing invisibly through the forbidden regions, the locked rooms, the cold spots no fire could warm.

Throbbing, formless fury, but growing and regaining cast-off shapes as they fed on the residue of pain and poisoned memories stored up in those walls.

Feeling the walls, and the walls within walls. Feeling caged. But not for much longer.

They wrapped themselves around the knob of the locked door at the end of a long dark corridor, the stubborn steel turning to ice in their shadow hands, and managed to turn it, very slightly.

And that was great, but it was only the beginning.

They passed through the door and floated down the long corridor to the edge of the living room, crowded as near as they dared to the withering glare of the fireplace.

Close to the living voices that grew louder and more strident, as if they knew exactly what the shadows fed upon, and were resolved to give them a feast.

* * *

The bonding portion of tonight's encounter was clearly at an end. Now they were getting down to it, and the only warmth came from the roaring flames.

"But here's what you have to understand," Esther was saying. "Jake and I had an arrangement . . ."

". . . to keep the church separate from your daily lives," Emmy finished. "I understand that. That's why—"

Esther cut her short with a wave that almost slopped her drink. "The problem is—I'm sorry—but the fact is that he didn't."

"The church is a registered non-profit . . ."

"Yes, but he was dipping into assets that weren't covered by that at all. My personal assets—"

Emmy's turn to interrupt. "That's your own concern."

"Well, yes it is. But since he declared them 'church expenses' whether they actually were or not . . ."

"I don't believe that—"

"They are getting ready to take away my house." Esther's eyes flared as she said it. "Take away the house that I grew up in, and take everything I own, because of debts that Jake incurred. And what I need to know is, how much was he making? And where did all that money go?"

The fireplace popped—loud as a gunshot—and the wind swelled outside, as everyone jumped. Eddie returned to check the fire.

In the fireplace, the logs were already burned through, and reduced to embers, yet the fire burned as if fed by a gas line. Eddie pulled the screen back, quizzical. Added a few more logs, which ignited instantly, singing the hair on his hand and forearm to wispy curls of ash.

"All the money went straight back into the Church of Eternal Life," Emmy insisted.

"I only wish that were true."

"Emmy . . ." Mathias tried to intervene.

"Don't you believe in Jesus Christ?" Emmy demanded.

"Well, of course I do!"

"Then where is your faith in the Gospel, and in your own husband?"

Esther rolled her eyes.

"*Your own husband*," Emmy continued, "who devoted his life to his ministry? Do you have any idea how many lost, desperate souls depended on Jake for their faith?"

"That's exactly what I'm trying to find out!"

"That's because you *only care about the money!*" Now their voices were notching up in pitch as well as volume, each one's high points climbing to top the other. "You couldn't even be bothered to show up for the services today . . ."

"I think," Esther cut in tersely, "that I made my reasons clear enough . . ."

"Couldn't share in the grief and mourning . . ."

"I said my good-byes in private . . ."

"Couldn't bear to face his loving congregation . . ."

"Oh, please." Now Esther's voice took on a bitter condescension. "How many women were at the viewing today?"

Emmy blushed. "I don't see . . ."

"How many panties got stuffed in that coffin, in the course of the viewing?" Esther trembled as she spoke. "How many tearful ladies, dressed to the nines, came up to pay their respects, knelt down and dribbled tears? Dribbled tears"—she swigged on her drink—"as you say, on my husband?"

"I—"

"With all due respect to your feelings," Esther continued, "and the feelings of his 'congregation,' I think I've suffered enough. If any further explanations are due, then they are owed to me, and not the other way around."

*   *   *

The half-reborn spirits huddled in the chill darkness and observed, with great glee, the banked and blossoming human flames. The more brightly they blazed, the more profoundly they might flare up when extinguished. And thereby feed the deeper dark.

What fools! What food! And they hardly had to hide . . .

Between the wailing wind, the unheeded alarm of the fire, and the clamor of their own voices, the living would never hear the others coming.

The spirits laughed, also unheard, except by each other.

As they reveled in the gathering Change.

Chapter Five

The weathered wooden gate to Jake's shithole hacienda was propped open, so Jasper Ellis gratefully drove on through. It wouldn't be good to have his tricked-out extended-cab pickup truck parked on the street, where the cops might see it, and start to draw all the wrong conclusions.

The whole idea was to get in and get out, as quickly as possible.

And let their scarlet Mystery Woman have her say, if that was what she really wanted.

But it wasn't exactly like they were trying to sneak in. The music was cranked, just the way he liked it, and as usual, Christian's mix disk had cued up something uncannily appropriate: a superdramatic hair-metal version of the military burial anthem, "Taps."

"Bah-bah-BAH!" Christian howled from the passenger seat, singing along with the melody while frenetic fifth-generation Van Halen clones noodled bombastically in the gap. Christian sang with an eerie Bruce Dickinson/Iron Maiden falsetto that—at another time, in another world—might have made him a star.

Jasper laughed, took one hand off the wheel, and vigorously air-guitared like a guy who actually knew where the notes might land. "Bah-bah-BAH! Wah-wah-wah!" he warbled atonally, while Christian joined in, exhaling pot smoke like a musical chimney.

"JESUS CHRIST!" yelled a womanly voice from the back.

But it was too late—almost time for the crescendo— and at this point, there was no way they weren't going for broke.

So Jasper took the joint from Christian, toked hard as they rolled by the black metal backyard gate, the garage, and then the house itself, exhaling hugely as they rounded the corner to a bleak playground, where two other cars were already parked.

"BAH-BAH-BAAAAAAAAAAAH!!!" they howled in unison, with painful sustain, until even the Mystery Woman laughed . . .

"BAH! BAH! BAAAAAAAAAAAH!!!"

There was a great flurry of tom-toms and dope smoke, to go with the how-fast-can-you-riff arpeggiations and the warbling screeches of the clowns in the front seat.

Then an awesome silence fell, as Jasper slipped it into park, right behind the white sedan.

And they all sang, softly, "Bah-bah-baaaaah."

Jasper cut the engine.

From the backseat, the very soft sound of applause, and the voice, now sultry and cool.

"Thank you, boys, for cheering me up."

"Not a problem," said Jasper. Christian toked intently, but nodded his head.

"And I'm sure everyone within ten square miles is feeling much better now, too."

Jasper laughed, took the joint from Christian, hit it like Louis Armstrong's trumpet. Christian blew self-congratulatory smoke rings out the window.

"Hard to believe," she continued, "you guys are only, what, thirty-five years old?"

"So sad but oh so true," said Christian, grinning.

And it was, at least, oh so true. Despite his shaved head and close-cropped beard, his street-beaten boxer/hard-case look and just-got-out-of-prison suit, Jasper not only had the soul of a twelve-year-old, but could turn anyone who locked eyes with him into a twelve-year-old as well.

In that respect, he and Christian had a lot in common. It helped explain why they were still friends—since second grade—while so many others had drifted off into more predictable, less hilarious adulthoods.

Christian had the same unkempt scraggle of dark, shoulder-length hair that he'd decided on in junior high. He was by far the least fashion-obedient gay man Jasper had ever met, though his rakish goatee was always meticulously trimmed.

"You know what?" Jasper said, exhaling medical-grade Humboldt plumage. "Fuck sad. I'm proud to be socially retarded."

"I've already fucked sad," said the voice from the backseat. "Maybe now I can fuck happy for a change."

He couldn't see her face, as he turned around. If there were tears, the moonlight did not glint upon them. All he could see was her silhouette, the reddish tangle of luxuriant tresses that let her hide in plain sight.

But her voice sounded strong, and that was important. If she were weak, he would just back right out and sail. As it stood, the whole thing was her call.

Last call.

Either out, or in.

"Look," he said, "all we're sayin' is, fuck that guy. And fuck these people."

"I still don't see what you think you're gonna get from all this," Christian piped in.

"I guess you never heard of 'closure.'"

"Didn't Oprah invent that word?" Christian guessed.

Jasper laughed. "Yeah, yeah. I think it's a TV word for 'bullshit.'"

"She invited me here," said the voice from the backseat, "because she wants to know. I think she deserves that much."

"You don't owe her dick."

"Would you just let me out, please?"

Jasper hit the power locks so their passenger could open the heavy door and slide out.

And that was their cue, as well. Sighing, resigned, Jasper and Christian threw their doors open, and stepped out into the night.

The whole point of this exercise was to back her up, as they had been doing since the moment they met her. Stepping up, when no one else would, for a woman who deserved so much better than she'd gotten.

Walking her to the stained glass door.

And whatever lay beyond.

Chapter Six

When Esther's father died, the house had filled up for almost a week with old students and friends from the free school, and the activist days before that.

Mom had been rudderless and devastated, but every caller came to the door with wine or pot brownies or a casserole, and a story about Dad that she'd forgotten or never heard.

Many were misfits, hermits and drifters who hitchhiked from as far as Alaska. But one owned a software company, one was a nationally prominent gay rights activist, and another lived on an island in Micronesia, and had founded a free school there; and one of *her* students was the closest thing the tiny nation had to a president.

The wake had brought the best of Dad back to Mom, who had been worn half to death caring for him in his last days. It let her say good-bye, and prepare to face the future—until, of course, her body revealed its own plans, and she dropped dead of an aneurysm, six months later.

Now Jake was gone, and Esther had only just begun to come to terms with her own version of widowhood. But instead of nourishing her soul, every caller to this wake seemed to take a little more of it away.

Emmy and her squirming boyfriend were more than

bad enough. But this *woman*, this trollop on her porch, could diminish her, eclipse her, maybe even steal her grief. Esther knew that she would be helpless not to measure herself against this interloper, and have to decide whether Jake was more than one man, or if she was just less than a whole woman.

Esther took another swig of scotch, opened the door, and put on a brittle smile.

"Hello," she said. "You must be . . ."

"Evangeline," said the Mystery Woman, and stepped into the light.

Esther's breath sucked in, as did her tummy. Not just in surprise at her beauty—and a beauty, frayed more than flawed, she certainly was—but at what it said instantly about her.

Evangeline's flowing hair was a deep chestnut red that cascaded down, thick and luxuriant, over her bare shoulders. Her face was angular, like Esther's, but heart shaped. Bigger, achingly expressive eyes. Fuller lips. More pronounced cheekbones.

And wider curves: an hourglass figure in ways that made Esther feel almost boyish by comparison. She was what Jake would have called "bodacious"; and the red dress that clung to her plush breasts and generous hips made it plain that she had not come to mourn.

She was curvy in a way that men would judge a sign of ripeness, of readiness to rut and never stay for breakfast. The seedy carnality was only enhanced by the weary cunning that blazed in her emerald-amber eyes as she took Esther's measure and tossed out her hand, let it be caught.

God damn you, Esther thought.

And then said, "Thank you for coming."

"Please," Evangeline said. "Don't thank me."

Evangeline slid past her and hung her coat up in the closet with a blasé familiarity that made Esther's face flush. She started to shut the door, when a strapping bald stud shouldered into the gap, scoping Esther out with a wicked, disarming grin.

"Hey," he said, his voice a low rumble, like a big cat's purr. "Lookin' good. I'm Jasper."

They locked eyes for a second, shaking hands. He had caught her already flustered, and something about him crossed her wires. Wasn't he the boxing coach, from that second-rate gym across the street from Bally Total Fitness? The one that always checked her out in the parking lot, where he seemingly lived just to smoke and flirt?

Eddie must've noticed from across the room; she heard a serving tray dropped too hard on a table.

Jasper picked up on it and grinned, moved on.

"Pleased to meet you . . ." Esther said to his back as she pushed the door shut. God, she'd let him walk away thinking he'd made her wet. She knew that type well enough. She'd fallen for it once, and was still waiting to hit bottom. Only amateur vampires had to bite their victims.

She saw him throw another sly glance over his shoulder—he moved like a fighter, a confident predator—and it pissed her off to note that, yes, he did get to her a little.

A brisk rap on the door at her back made her jump. She opened it and another stranger sidled in. Though his hair was an artfully tousled haystack and his suit was decades behind Jasper's, something told her that if Jasper was her new pimp, this one was her hairdresser.

"Hi," this one said. "I may be a Christian in name only, but this stained glass is gorgeous. Is it from an old church?"

"Thank you. Yes. We just had it put in . . ." Her voice hitched, choking on a nugget of unexpected grief.

Oh no, not again . . . Esther turned away for something to busy herself, realizing she looked lost in her own home.

Christian closed the door behind him and patted her arm with unexpected kindness. "Don't worry. We'll make this quick."

Emmy and Mathias, for their part, remained cloistered on the couch, looking totally bushwacked.

"Who *are* these people?" Emmy demanded.

"Awww," Evangeline cooed. Her sarcasm was caustic, but she seemed genuinely surprised. "You must be Jake's little Bible girl. Wow."

"She's a prostitute," Mathias muttered.

Christian rounded on him and snapped, "Oh, are you speaking from experience?"

Suddenly finding himself in a fight at the grown-up table, Mathias blanched whiter than his shirt. "I—"

It was turning into a brawl, and drinks hadn't even been served yet. Esther crossed the room to buffer Emmy. "I'm sorry, but you need to know how bad things are."

Behind her, Evangeline said, "And so do you."

Chapter Seven

The fire was burning hotter than ever, the new logs already reduced to livid pink coals. Esther turned away from it, but her hands almost immediately became chilled, as if a fugitive draft sucked the heat into the shadows, sucked the fire, the life, out of the house.

With everyone packed into the small living room, Esther shot a warning gaze at Eddie, who nodded and took up a tray and towel, bowing like a waiter. "Eddie will bring out the snacks in a minute," she said. "Can he get you anything?"

Jasper saluted Eddie from the loveseat. "Yeah, yeah. Let me have what the lady is having."

Christian deadpanned, "Just put it in a bucket, and let's pass it around!"

Evangeline didn't order. Esther caught her staring at the wedding photo, her back to the room. She was not crying, but Esther recognized—in the set of her shoulders, the tired defiance, the tension she'd been holding in—a mirror image of herself.

Good. At least someone around here knew how she felt.

Emmy's hands fluttered like hummingbirds as she watched from the couch. It wouldn't surprise Esther if she started screaming, "Sacrilege!" or "Blasphemer!" or something, she was so worked up in a righteous tizzy.

Esther had to keep the peace, but she felt a scream building, and knew if she set her glass down, it would crack. She was Jake's wife in the eyes of God and the law, and now his widow. Why was she trapped between these women with no claim on Jake, these strangers who had divided him up between themselves, and left her only his debts and his name, like a stain on her life?

Esther prodded, "And what will you have?"

Evangeline started. "Just water. Thanks."

Esther took another tug on her scotch, swirling the dregs and melting ice. "Really."

An octave deeper than was safe for a man of his size, Mathias intoned, "I don't think you can be a decent Christian and a drunk."

Esther laughed. "Oh, honey. Everybody at the Last Supper was sloshed."

"Including poor old Jesus," Christian joined in. "What do you think that whole water-into-wine thing was about?"

Emmy glowered. "I don't think that's funny at all . . ."

"Interesting you should say that," Jasper threw in, "cuz I've been thinking a lot about that lately. When Jesus went out in the garden and did that whole 'Father, why hast thou forsaken me' thing? Flat out, that boy was *hammered*."

"I can't believe you're saying this . . ."

"No. Think about it," Jasper went on, casually as if discussing sports trivia. "He knew he was about to die. And not just a regular death, but a horrible, torturous, agonizing death."

"Yes, but—"

"You don't think he was terrified?"

"He was the Son of God!"

"Yeah, yeah. But he was also just a man, right? That

was the whole point. He came down to earth, as one of us. And suffered like us. So he could show us how to live, even with all this pain and misery."

"Well, yes! But—"

"Lady, I'm just sayin': if he wasn't just a man, with the same fears that I have, then his sacrifice doesn't mean shit to me. He might as well be Superman."

Esther started laughing, stunned at her own amusement. Whatever or whoever Jasper was, she was suddenly glad he was here. "So you're saying . . ."

"I'm just sayin' that boy was drunk as a skunk. And I don't blame him a bit. Thanks, man."

Eddie handed him a scotch, then gestured to Christian. "One for you."

Christian took it with a nod and smile of thanks, then turned to Jasper.

"Let's go outside and have a smoke. Let them get down to business."

"Sounds like a plan. Excuse us, ladies."

Esther watched the men go out. Evangeline clearly balked just short of following them, but simply stood beside the fire and wet her lips with the water Eddie brought her.

Emmy and Matthias traded hissing whispers with their heads together like a lawyer and client kibbutzing during a trial. Matthias covered his mouth with one hand as if to block anyone reading his lips, but the frenetic chopping motion of his other hand made it clear what he was urging Emmy to do.

Emmy seemed sincerely clueless about the church's real holdings, and worse, she sincerely believed that there *was* a church. Esther had let Jake follow his vocation, do his own thing—*Know Your Self*, *Grow Your Self*, thanks, Mom and Dad—and she never intruded, because he was so very good at making you want to believe him.

The whole thing was little more than a scam, she accepted that; but with Emmy's twisted faith for a foundation, it had almost become a cult.

Esther studied Evangeline as she looked into the fire, lost in her own painful thoughts. The single-malt heat of her blood urged her to do her duty as a widow and drag this whore out of her house by her red hair, but she was sick to death of being the only one who stuck to the script.

She knew Jake had other friends, other associates, of whom she could only remember a name or a face or two. None of them had contacted her after Jake died, but she was aware of people watching her, of being followed. If anyone knew the truth about Jake and would share it with her, it was this woman, who seemed to silently curse her water as she sipped it.

Whatever the awful truth was, she needed to know, and now, before she caved in to denial and started to make a saint of him, like that poor twit Emmy. Evangeline had been to the bottom and clawed her way back, it was plain to see.

Show me the way, Esther pleaded. *Show me the way out of love with that bastard—*

Chapter Eight

The backyard was nearly as expansive as the front, cut off by the garage and the black metal fence down at the vanishing point, where the fallow pastures and trails of the back nine acres gradually gave way to the open desert.

It was clear, from back here, that this place really was the legendary hippie school Jasper made fun of, all the way through his own childhood hell. It was long enough to house half a dozen classrooms, easy, and still give the family some breathing space.

Jasper could imagine kids aged six to twelve, convening on this lawn to sit in the lotus position with their mandala coloring books and infinite assortments of magic crayons, in order to better understand themselves as rainbow warriors in a world that would thoroughly kick their pacifist asses the second they stepped outside.

And to think that the former Mrs. Connaway actually *grew up* in this place. And then wound up with Jake. Talk about the return of the repressed. It blew his mind how some people could be born into total freedom, and spend their whole lives looking for a cage.

But at least the swimming pool was nice; or it would

have been, if it weren't green with scum. Gone to shit. Like the lawn. Like the playground equipment. He wondered what kept Eddie so busy that he'd let the place go to hell.

They stood in the strange, dark yard and tried to pretend they felt at ease.

While the ill wind blew, and the shadows danced.

Jasper lit a cigarette, surveyed the empty property. Christian pulled out another joint.

"Dude," Jasper said. "This is just ugly, here."

"What did you expect? The whole place reeks of Jake. Gimme your lighter."

Jasper nodded, handed it over. Christian lit the joint. It took a couple of tries.

"I just hope this shit works out."

Christian held up the wait-a-second finger, inhaled hard, and croaked, "Our girl? She's rough and ready."

"Oh, yeah, no doubt. She could skin those people alive. It's her brokenness I'm concerned about."

"Okay. So it's not what they might do to her," Christian said, passing the joint, "but what she might do to herself."

"Exactly." Inhaling large, and thinking . . .

When he first met Evangeline two years ago, it felt like they'd almost instantly broken through to something real. There was pain and a deeply broken foundation that put her out there where bodies collided without really touching, but Jasper wanted her in spite of her damage, not because of it.

It looked, for about a week, like it might even work.

He wanted to tell her things he never told anybody; but when she did the same, up jumped the devil.

And his name was Jake.

The things that fucker had made her do, the damage

he'd inflicted on her just because he could . . . Jasper had seen love twist people into some awful shapes before, but when he knew all there was to know about Evangeline, he just could not accept it.

Because no matter how much he cared for her, and no matter how hard she tried to build a new life, she was not done with it. With him.

So long as Jake was alive, he held her in thrall.

Jasper could not resist a damsel in distress, but without Christian, he would have walked from Evangeline. Christian took her into his sewing circle and offered her a life outside of Jake. One that built up from the inside, with no sexual pressure involved.

Somehow, she and Jasper had gradually turned it from lovers to friends to more than friends: more like older brother and younger sister, with an undercurrent of perpetual, only slightly incestuous sizzle.

If that was wrong, fuck it: they weren't actually siblings; and when you got right down to it, real honest-to-God human feelings were always deeper and weirder than the puny little labels they were dealt.

So they stuck with each other, stood up for each other, progressively grew even closer than before.

And then—in one of those sudden reversals of fate that made you wonder if maybe Somebody Up There wasn't listening—the world had finally given Jake Connaway as good as he'd given.

What that would mean, in the long run, no one could say. But one thing was for certain.

If Evangeline needed backup, her boys were there.

Brother Jasper. Sister Christian.

Brothers and sisters, to the end . . .

A sudden, surprising burst of thunder rocked Jasper from his reverie. He followed Christian's gaze to the cold moon above, watched vapor shadows race overhead like cracks in the sky, felt a chill run through him that ran deeper than the autumn night.

From inside, they could hear the strident sound of women's voices. But it was muted by the door, the receding rumble, and the rising howl of the wind.

Something unaccountably sank in the pit of his stomach, and made the shot of booze in his belly freeze into black ice.

From the look on Christian's face, he was feeling it, too. "Oh, man," said his friend, with a kind of awe. "There is something going on here—"

"Yeah, yeah—"

"You know? And I'm not just talking about this place. This is way the fuck bigger than Jake. It's like—"

"Like a hurricane's coming."

They looked at each other, with mounting apprehension. The wind was dry and charged with positive ions, a Santa Ana, with not enough moisture in a thousand miles of sky to make a raindrop.

Then what were those ragged, black clouds racing across the moon?

"Oh, man, we're not on hurricane watch, are we?"

"Far as I heard, they weren't even expecting this storm, or whatever the fuck it is."

"Well, I don't know, then," Christian said. "But I'll tell you what. There is something really wrong with tonight."

Christian was dragging him down into worry, and Jasper didn't work that way. "Something wrong with the weed, maybe. Relax."

"I didn't figure you much for Bible study."

"I'm a complicated guy," Jasper said, stifling a giggle. They had shared more than a hundred deep conversations about religion, and fixed all its insoluble problems and forgotten them, more times than either could count. "I'm not saying I know if I believe all that shit in the book, but I feel something out there . . ."

"Nothing wrong with that. Nobody knows what's out there, but that's no reason to go making crazy shit up."

"Crazy like Adam and Eve riding dinosaurs to church? Or crazy like gays are Satan's pep squad?"

"The whole banquet of bullshit. But what with the mood and the man of the hour and all, I was thinking more about the Rapture. End of the world. Armageddon."

"Christian!" Jasper blew out pot smoke in an explosion of mock shock. "A confirmed atheist, and a fudge-punching atheist to boot." He shook his head, took another hit. "I feel your pain, man."

"Shut up, I didn't mean it like that . . ."

"No, sincerely . . . I know what you mean. Everybody has questions. Religion has answers. Crazy answers are better than no answers at all. At least they think they know what's coming, and how to prepare for it."

"You think praying and pledging all your extra money to a TV preacher is the right way to prepare for the end?"

"Hell no! But it makes them feel better. And what can you do, if the end is coming?"

"Roll a fatty, hug your loved ones, and kiss your ass good-bye."

"Exactly. Religion doesn't make them crazy. Being human does. It's human nature to think an end is coming, because we all have to die alone. But the world goes on, and knowing that kind of freaks us out even more than knowing we're going to die.

"Everybody freaks out about the end. Nuclear war. Y2K. Global warming. Invaders from Mars. It's natural to expect the end, and it's human to hope somebody out there has a good reason for ending it. What you're feeling is natural. But what's happening . . ."

Christian now recognized the creeping tone of gloom in his friend's voice. "So you think the world ends not with a bang, but with a weak-ass party?"

Jasper smiled at his friend's sardonic tone, but his eyes remained pinned on the horizon, a thousand miles away.

"No, not the end," he said. "But maybe the beginning of something we're not ready for, at all."

Part II
Mopping Up The Hard
Parts With Gray

Chapter Nine

Gray was so grateful not to have to drive.

The sinister white Cadillac cruised the desert high-way like a shark on a blood trail. Lightning flashed as it rounded the bend and swerved onto the off-ramp, but only sped up as it left the highway for the two-lane road, wending its way toward home.

In the passenger seat, Gray pulled out a smoke. He was a gaunt, jaundiced hard-ass in a rumpled black suit, with hair the color of ashes. Not counting occasional blackouts, he hadn't slept in almost sixty-four hours, but his hands were steady.

He didn't ever want to sleep again.

His head throbbed like impacted wisdom teeth, and his ears still rang. The stink of cordite and formalde-hyde was like plugs of charred steel wool in his nostrils. But he didn't have to watch the road, or his mouth, ex-cept to put the bottle in it, and then the cigarette, chas-ing each other.

And in between, he talked.

Meanwhile, the driver reached up and thumbed the dome light on, then checked out the pair of Polaroids in his hand.

The images were crude, overexposed, and tinted pea soup green from the mysterious process that made the prints expose themselves. Crude and harder to find every year, but if you didn't fuck around with computers and didn't want some nosy fucker at the photo lab sticking his nose in your business, it was still the only choice for the serious documentary photographer.

The first was a casual portrait of Frankie, eyes crossed and corkscrewed up to take in the hole in his forehead. That his lower jaw, his scalp and most of his face were scraped off long before the coup de grace was essential to really getting what the artist intended, with this particular masterpiece.

"Nice," said the driver.

It took a bit of squinting and a lot of faith to accept that the second was of Sugar: just as dead, but chopped and smashed like the dregs of a piñata.

"Wow," said the driver, genuinely touched. "Very nice."

"Thanks," said Gray. "I made 'em myself."

Gray never liked to brag, but he truly relished talking about what he did to Frankie and Sugar. When he confessed the whole soup-to-poop affair, he could relive it from without, stand back and admire the balls and the discipline he'd shown. Oh, if only there were a hundred of him—

The driver did not ask any questions at first, just soaked it up and smiled.

Nobody else understood or accepted the real Gray.

When Jake's corpse turned up in the desert, Gray was half dead himself, in the bag after a binge. But he reined in his hangover and went to work. The fuckwit sheriff ran the case with bloodhound diligence, but raced off right away on the wrong trail. Esther told them what she'd been told, that he was in retreat at a cabin in Apple

Valley, so they went up there to shake down the meth kitchens and burglars.

Only Gray understood and accepted the real Jake.

So only he knew where to look.

At a shitbox dive bar in San Bernardino, he found a barfly who knew the skank who took Jake home, and liked her well enough to eat only soup for the rest of his life. Why did these losers always play tough until things got permanent?

Gray found Sugar's condo tossed and empty. Blood seeping up through three layers of hastily dumped throw rugs and trash bags in the family room, the TV still on and tuned to the public access channel.

A short paper chase yielded a multitude of angles. Frankie and Sugar fought a lot. Frankie was a tweaker, a drunk, and an impulsive idiot. Gray figured he came in and stabbed Jake in the back in a white heat, because he'd never have the stones to kill in cold blood.

The state of the place told Gray how he clobbered Sugar, then took the body out to the desert in a drop cloth from the attached garage. Maybe he took Sugar with him, and maybe he left her here.

He picked up the phone and hit redial. The display showed a Riverside number in speed-dial memory—MOM. A bleary, cracked hag's voice came on the line cursing. "She don't want to speak to you, you shitbird! You go see the police and turn yourself in, if you're any kind of man . . ."

Gray stole a Ford Escort off the street and was in Riverside in half an hour.

In a rickety single-wide trailer in the Viking's Rest Motor Court, Sugar and her mother, Margie, gargled vodka and fought over the remote until midnight. Gray smoked cigarettes and played angles in his head until the lights went out in the neighbors' trailers.

When the blaring TV from Margie's trailer was the

only sound in the sultry night, he cracked a couple amyl nitrate vials under his nose to get into character, and came calling.

The screen door was locked, but he slashed it with his penknife.

Margie was passed out in the back bedroom, snoring to drown out *Celebrity Rehab*. Sugar drowsed on the couch, drooling from her fat, broken lips and swelled-shut eye.

Gray took Margie first, quietly. Pillow over the face to muffle three sharp knocks on the noggin with the butt of his pistol, to streamline the smothering.

Movies were full of shit. People struggled a lot harder in real life, when you tried to take their lives; and in Gray's vast experience, the less they had to live for, the harder they usually fought.

He was not big enough to contain the rush it gave him, but this was just housekeeping. Sugar was only the bait in the trap. He didn't say how much he ached to undo the beauty that killed his friend. He didn't have to.

Frankie had tuned her up pretty good, so Gray had to push the envelope to get his point across. It was not the first time he'd enjoyed sloppy seconds off Jake, but the first time he'd closed the deal with a carving knife and a curling iron.

The driver let him spare no details here, until Gray squirmed. "How was she? Did she get wet when you hurt her?"

The whore had tried to lure him in, begging him to take her even as he made cube steak of her face, tried to turn it into something she could control. But he couldn't be bought off. Fucking would be a sorry substitute for what he had planned.

When he was satisfied, perverse instinct told him to just walk away, leaving the mess for the world to stumble on, and wonder at what monsters walked among them.

But he wasn't stupid, like Frankie. He knew that you could take your pleasures any way you liked, so long as you took care to cover how it looked.

He had learned this from Jake, who was truly all things to all men.

As wild as he was with Sugar, he was careful not to break any bones. He left a cigarette burning in her outstretched hand, over a puddle of spilled kerosene from a hurricane lantern, and kicked over a couple of candles for coverage. The mellow yellow glow of the spreading flames was just bright enough to compete with the blue bug-zapper light of the TV when Gray got back in his car.

At a rest stop, he changed the license plates on the Escort and cut the old plate into confetti with a pair of tin snips. Up to a point, getting into the mind of one's prey was a sound tactic, but Gray hated playing with his food. To understand Frankie, you only had to know the ways of a cockroach. Every impulse was equally important to his tiny insect brain. To make him stay put, you just had to turn on the lights.

He texted Frankie on Sugar's cell phone. In the disgusting babytalk of her previously sent messages—*So sorry baby—U know 1 luv U!1!*—he warned Frankie that the law was out for him, that they were looking for him everywhere, just keeping it off the news to spare Jake's good name. *CTN—Mom spyz—U bustd my teef u asshol!!! Sit tite Baby—Where R U?*

The lovelorn dipshit tried to call sixteen times, but finally broke down and told her voice mail where he was hiding.

Sugarz com1n6 4 U

It was not just dedication to his fallen friend that made Gray pop eight methedrine with cold coffee and get back on the southbound 15, without an hour's sleep.

Gray always believed that you put a bad day to bed before you went down yourself, and very high on Gray's shit list was the republic of Mexico, and everything in it.

(An aside: it would be far easier to ask Gray to make a list of his friends, which he could fit on his thumbnail for easy consultation. The other list, of everything he hated, was life-size, and he lived in it. This was not just bearable, but almost sweet, whenever he could cross an item or two off.)

Frankie was holed up in a motor lodge in Calexico, wrapped up in rancid sheets with a saggy Mexican whore who didn't wake up when Gray dragged her paramour out of the room by his peroxide locks and dumped him in the trunk of his own car, just before dawn.

So much for true love. Frankie seemed to have overcome his heartbreak just in time to soak up the new one Gray had planned for him, out in the desert.

This last part went on until well after lunchtime, but the driver had only one question.

So much for Frankie.

Only when he ran out of words, and the bile they floated on, did Gray take note of his surroundings. The engine flat-out roared like on a dead straightaway, but they were winding up the switchback road that went up the canyon wall. A terraced wedding cake of a mountain, with ledges just large enough for folks in fancy Spanish-tiled houses to look down on their lesser neighbors.

As they neared their destination, a bolt of pleasure hit him harder than the rotgut in his belly, and sparked warm but shivery jolts of anticipation throughout his exhausted body.

To think he would have left all this behind. Life was sweet, and about to get a lot sweeter.

The shit list he lived in was about to get a lot shorter.

Part III
Letting It All Hang Out

Chapter Ten

It was Evangeline's turn up at bat; and no matter what, she was not going to break down, nor was she going to take a drink. Not now, when she was almost free.

And certainly not here, in front of these people.

Just let me get through this, she prayed, but not to God. No God who couldn't have spared a lightning bolt for Jake Connaway twenty years ago was worth praying to.

All eyes on her, burning as cold as the fire was hot. Fuck. She should have followed Jasper and Christian out for a smoke.

"So let me get this straight," she said. "You want me to spill the beans on Jake." Esther nodded like her neck needed oiling. She wasn't even halfway out of Jake's shadow, even now. "Okay. So what do you want to know?"

"I'm not sure I want to hear anything you have to say." Emmy just sat, pointed at her, not seeing.

A warming glow of livid bitterness, like a belt of good brandy, kindled in Evangeline's gut. Fine. Maybe this wouldn't feel like work, after all.

"I met him when he was still on his first marriage," she said. "He was in a band then, spending all her money on guitars and blow. Until he found Jesus"—she pointed a nod at Emmy—"and realized he could make more money off of him."

Bible Girl started to honk out loud, but Evangeline wasn't having it.

"Jake's been doing me for the last fifteen years, all right? Paying me to do it for the last ten, when he wasn't pimping me out to others. Man's the sickest mother-fucker I've ever met."

"Omigod . . ." Esther's voice was like a tire deflating.

"I went from a nice little high school junior to a junkie, to a hooker, to jail, to rehab . . ."

"I told you!" Mathias piped in.

". . . to a nice little job as a secretary." Faux wistful, as she said it. "To a junkie. To a hooker. All thanks to Saint Jake. And believe me, you don't have to take my word for it."

Emmy tried once again to interrupt, but this time no sound would come out.

"There are so many witnesses to his crimes—*so many people* whose lives he screwed up—that my little story's like a drop in the bucket. But you know why nobody talks? Because either a) they *believed* in him"—she winked at Emmy, because she just couldn't help it—"and/or b) he had something on their asses. A little incriminating evidence. Or maybe a lot."

Everyone's mouths were hanging open, though Esther quickly poured some more scotch into hers. Evangeline understood completely, but that did nothing to subvert her mounting rage. She focused on the ladies, staring hard from one to the other.

"You look all shocked. But I think you know more than you're letting on. Both of you. And that's what pisses me off."

Eddie looked at Esther. Mathias looked at Emmy. Both women looked stricken, and neither could conceal it from their men. Or each other. Or themselves.

"Emmy?" Mathias chafed her arm, but he might as well have been combing spaghetti. Emmy looked, for all the world, as if she'd gone into an ecstasy of prayer; but Evangeline knew what was playing in the Little Chapel of Emmy's Head . . .

. . . and Emmy couldn't help it, and more than she could stop her face from turning red as the burning embers. Her shame, and the sense-memory of it, was too close to the surface.

She closed her eyes, and Jake was there: standing massively upright as she knelt before him in the grass by the rickety jungle gym right outside this very front door, less than two weeks ago today . . .

. . . and his eyes never left hers for a moment, not even as his hands went down to undo his belt buckle: a jagged metal lightning bolt with the letters "JC" emblazoned across it . . .

. . . and when his pants slid down to his knees, then ankles, she had tried to close her eyes, but he wouldn't have it . . .

. . . and then she knew, for the first time, what Eve's apple of temptation truly looked like, in the flesh . . .

. . . and he said to her, "This is what a man looks like. And this is what a true man wants. If you want to be with him, you will want that, too. You will come to need it. To recognize it as most holy communion. To recognize it as prayer . . ."

. . . and when she started to cry, he reached down to stroke her hair, ever so subtly pulling her closer, so that she and the apple at the end of his staff were almost mouth to mouth . . .

. . . and that was when he said, "You know I love you . . ."

. . . and she did not bite, but kissed instead . . .

Less than fifteen seconds had elapsed in real time, since Evangeline dropped the bomb. But as Emmy snapped back, all eyes were upon her.

Including Mathias, who looked stunned to the core.

"I knew it . . ." muttered Esther.

"I—I . . . !" Emmy yelped in protestation, then froze.

"Oh, you are so in love with him." Evangeline rolled her eyes, but it was less judgmental than knowing.

"He told me, over and over," Esther murmured. " 'I'm not nailing that little girl. It's all in your head . . . ' "

Emmy turned beseechingly to Mathias. "I never went to bed with him! I swear, I never did . . ."

The whore laughed. "If I know Jake, he had you wigglin' like a fish . . ."

"I'M STILL A VIRGIN . . . !"

PA-POW! A knot in the blazing fireplace exploded. Everyone jumped, but none more than Emmy, who snapped in that moment and broke down, sobbing. She could feel Mathias shrink away from her on the couch, as if something unclean was seeping out of her.

And it was. Dear God, it was. She could feel her sweat burning and cold all at once, drenching her as her walls tumbled down. She had been so strong all day, had come here ready to be *so strong* . . .

. . . but all it took was one well-placed kick to pop her like a ketchup packet, letting everything out for all to see. So weak. So vain. So exposed and ashamed.

Not just in front of them.

But in the eyes of the Lord.

"So," Evangeline said, "what else do you want to know?"

Chapter Eleven

The demons hung above for the moment, eating it up, enjoying all the people from an angle askew. Watching the shadows dance, as the house lights faded once again, then reared back up. Wind roaring.

And the fireplace roared as well, as Eddie knelt before it, pulled back the screen, and thought *this can't be right*.

The typically slow-burning dogwood and yellow birch was going up like sugar pine, thick quartered logs that should burn for an hour reduced to cinders and ash in fifteen minutes.

It didn't make sense. The wood was dry, but not *that* dry. Not like somebody poured gasoline on it. He piled the last couple pieces on, and watched them ignite the second they hit.

"I have to chop more wood," he said.

Jasper's cell phone rang. He passed the ebbing joint back to Christian, reached into his jacket. "Excuse me for a second."

Christian nodded. "Time to check in on the ladies."

"Exactly." Then into the cell phone, without losing a beat, "Lisa. Hey, baby. How you doin'? Yeah, yeah. We're almost done . . ."

Christian moved to the glass back door, which opened just before he got to it. Eddie nodded at him, slipped past, headed off behind the front of the house. Christian entered, pulled the door shut behind him.

The cold was bracing as Eddie rounded the corner of the house in his shirtsleeves. It was a nice little shock to his system after the heat of the fire. And the sound of the wind was a merciful balm from the emotional war zone inside.

In the wide walkway between the house and the property wall, the moonlight barely penetrated, leaving darkness so thick you could cut it with an ax.

Fortunately, one was waiting for him.

Right next to the woodpile, and the chopping block.

Eddie flipped the switch to the overhead light, yanking back the shadows. It was a hanging lamp, and it swung on its chain in the wind, casting its light beam back and forth in long, unnerving semicircles.

In the background, he could hear the voice of Jasper, smooth and low. "You're hilarious. No . . . no. I can't wait to get my hands on you, too . . ."

Eddie put a log on the block, picked up the ax. The women were still arguing inside, but he couldn't quite hear what they said.

"Yeah, yeah. Exactly." Jasper's voice, louder. "You get the fucking joke, honey. That's all I ask."

Eddie looked over, saw Jasper round the corner, having wandered back to see what was up. Jasper waved with his cigarette-and-scotch hand.

Eddie brought down the ax.

Chapter Twelve

It didn't take long for Esther to bring things back around to money. Now Evangeline was contemplative, looking back over the years.

"Well," she said, "there was a boat I know he totaled. Every couple of weeks, he went to the casinos, gambled, had strings of call girls. And I think he had a Hummer for a couple of weeks that ended up at the bottom of a ditch."

"Oh—I did see that Hummer." Esther nodded to herself, as much from alcohol as memory. "He told me it was a congregant's. Never mind that not once did people congregate here, but . . ."

"He told me he would show me the inner sanctum . . ." Emmy said quietly.

Christian laughed out loud. He couldn't help it. Evangeline bit back her own laugh, and shushed him loudly.

Emmy, for her part, was a little too stunned to do anything but flinch as she continued. "Heaven's Glory. A magnificent temple he was building . . . when I was ready to finally be saved . . ."

"Oh, sweetheart. No, no, no," Esther admonished, slightly slurring the words. "No magnificent temple. And no life everlasting. At least not for him."

"Amen to that," said Evangeline.

"That's why, if I can just get the two of you to help me . . ." Esther continued, gaze swimming between the two of them with drunk, conspiratorial fervor.

"Then what?" Evangeline, straight to the point. "What else do you want from me?"

"An affidavit—"

Evangeline's turn to laugh. "You want me to go to court?"

"And testify against him. Yes."

"And I would do that why?"

Esther looked at her like she was supposed to be smarter than that. "Revenge?"

"Fuck revenge," Evangeline sneered back. "He's already dead. You honestly think he gives a shit?"

"Okay, then. Justice."

"Yeah, like that's gonna happen . . ."

"It could, though!" Esther took a staggering step forward. "It could, if people would just tell the truth!"

"Let me tell you something about telling the truth," Evangeline said. "Most people tend to frown upon it. That's why it hardly ever gets told."

"But—"

"Let me put it this way: I don't have an album's worth of my original songs up on MySpace, okay? This is not a career move for me. The only thing that happens is, I'm Whore Of The Week on national TV, and my life gets more fucked up than it already is."

Esther jittered in her heels. "So you're saying no?"

"I'm saying fuck no."

"What if I gave you money . . . ?"

"Yeah, *that'd* look great in court!" Evangeline barked out a laugh. "Have you even thought this shit through? 'Widow Pays Prostitute to Testify Against Dead Husband.' I mean, Jesus Christ almighty!"

Esther stared at her empty glass.

"And what about her?" Pointing at Emmy. "You gonna drag her ass up on *Judge Judy*, or *Dr. Phil*? 'I Was a Philandering Slut For Jesus'? You honestly think that's a plan?"

Emmy reacted as if physically slapped. "I think it's time to go . . ."

Chapter Thirteen

Jasper wrapped up his chat with tonight's little hookup—
the lovely Lisa—just as Mrs. Connaway's faithful servant
finished scooping up the firewood.

This Eddie guy was an interesting piece of work.
Very smart, in that he said very little. One poker-faced,
inscrutable motherfucker.

The only gaping hole in the charade was the fact that
he was here at all. Which was, clearly, because he loved
that woman. And she loved him, too, though maybe not
in quite the same way.

In other words, he and Eddie had an awful lot in
common.

So Jasper felt kind of bad about his natural flirtation,
the fact that Eddie had instantly pegged him as a scum-
bag. It was not a label he carried lightly—like Eddie, he
cared far more than he was liable to admit—so he hung
by the light switch, flashed a grin, and said, "Hey, man.
You need a hand with that?"

Eddie shook his head, said nothing, stepped forward.
Jasper nodded, waited for Eddie to pass him before
flicking off the overhead light and following.

Then they were walking semiuncomfortably together, and that shit had to end. So Jasper muscled it up

and said, "Hey, Eddie. Listen. Just so you know, I'm not here to fuck up your life. Okay?"

Eddie kept walking, said nothing.

"I'm just here for my friend, cuz she was scared to come alone. And as soon as they're done, you'll never see my ass again. Or any of us. We don't want anything from her."

Eddie nodded, said nothing, kept going. So Jasper stepped ahead of him quickly, up to the back door, put his hand on the handle, turned, and looked Eddie straight in the eye.

"All I'm sayin' is, guy to guy: you're a thousand times better man than Jake. Okay?"

Eddie said nothing; but as they looked into each other, their eyes said it all.

They were—at least for the moment—cool.

The women were really going at it in there. Jasper smiled and opened the door, stood back and made way for the Firewood Express. Eddie stepped through. Jasper followed into the fray.

Neither of them saw the headlights that poured in through the driveway, made their way across the back of the house.

The cold yellow glow of the harvest moon seemed to eat up the stars as it crept up over the horizon. To the north, the deeper black of massing thunderheads piled up like new mountains, marching on forking snake tongues of dry lightning.

The flood of moonlight muted the blazing Cadillac high beams that painted the yard. Then the moon, gobbled up by outrider clouds, seemed to avert its gaze.

The Caddy's headlights cut out along with the rumbling engine, entombing the yard in perfect darkness.

"This is it," said the driver. "You comin' or what?"

"In my pants. Just gimme a second." Gray thumbed the wheel on the tarnished brass Zippo and lit his smoke, exhaled with genuine pleasure, and opened the passenger door.

Now Emmy was standing, and the women had triangulated: face-to-face, emotions running high. Eddie scooted quickly to the fireplace, set down his armload. The rest of the men wisely hung back and watched. Even Mathias, who blurted out, "Emmy?" while remaining glued to the couch.

"I don't think I can be here anymore," Emmy continued, turning toward the door.

"Good for you." Evangeline stepped aside. "Get out, while you still have something to save."

"NO!" Esther shouted, stepping up in Emmy's face. "Emmy, please! Talk to me! I could lose this house!"

"Honestly?" Evangeline said. "No offense, but I hope they burn it to the ground—"

All at once, the lights flickered, then went out entirely. Yelps of surprise in the dark.

Then everyone stopped to stare at the only light in the room . . .

The fireplace.

Which was roaring like a doorway to hell . . .

Gray jogged across the yard to pull the gate into the yard shut, buttoning up the house. He could only just make out the nearest neighbor's split-level ranch house, a hundred yards back from the road, all lights out but the fitful blinking of a TV in an upstairs bedroom.

Lightning stabbed at the land, some miles off to the northeast. He heard the thunder, an arid, angry detonation, only five seconds behind the flash. It reminded Gray of a police helicopter's searchlight.

The air tingled with charged ions, but there was no smell of water: just angry, electric air, and the relentless lightning strikes, drawing closer.

Like something upstairs was looking for someone down here.

Fuck, his brain must be broken. Gray ran to catch up with his companion, who had crossed the yard and clomped up the stone walkway that girded the house with long, elastic strides . . .

Inside, the lights flickered back on, strobing unnervingly all the way down the hall to the back. For the first time, Emmy found herself staring down its length. It looked, suddenly, like a low-rent version of the Haunted Mansion at Disneyland: up until tonight, the scariest place she'd ever been.

Mathias stood at last, and she clung to him, half dragged him toward the door.

Then the phone rang, and she actually screamed.

"JESUS CHRIST! Just wait, please!" Esther grabbed the phone. "Hello . . . ? Yes. Yes, it is, Officer. Thank you. But this isn't a good . . . what?"

Emmy opened the front door, but didn't quite exit. Watching Esther's whole body tense.

"I don't . . . oh my God . . ."

"What?" Evangeline's shoulders hunched up defensively, and Emmy noted with awe that she was terrified, too.

"Oh, Jesus, God . . ." Esther moaned into the phone, her narrow eyes widened as far as they would go.

Emmy backed out of the doorway, onto the front step, into the strobing porch light . . .

. . . *and there was a man striding toward her in the darkness. Her own eyes widened to accommodate the sight. The flickering lightning lit him from behind, so that she could only see his shape.*

But the silhouette was huge, and impossibly familiar . . .

. . . *and as the first rays of the porch light hit him, she knew for a fact who it was . . .*

Chapter Fourteen

Esther hung up the phone, let it dangle from her hand. All eyes were upon her as she struggled toward speech, unable to believe it herself.

"There's been a . . ." she stammered. "They said it was a massacre, at the chapel."

"No . . ." Evangeline moaned, letting the word stretch out.

"And Jake's coffin—the—"

"Omigod . . ."

"The body is missing—"

BLAM! Emmy raced into the room, slamming the front door behind her. She fumbled with the lock, flush with panic.

It went *click*.

And as she turned to face the rest of them, a huge black silhouette filled the stained glass window behind her.

For a moment, time itself went paralytic. No motion in the room. No sound. A universe in stasis, locked between off and on.

Jasper felt the paralysis in his bones, for that long frozen moment. It was a feeling that he recognized, very clearly, as terror: the kind you normally only had in dreams.

Then the moment unfroze.

And things started happening very fast.

BAM! BAM! BAM! A fist slammed against the wooden door, so hard that the stained glass began to shatter.

Everyone screamed, including Jasper, his adrenaline jacking up into the red zone.

BAM! BAM! BAM! As the wood began to splinter as well.

"Who IS it?" Esther yelped, cringing back.

"It's not him. It can't be him—" Emmy muttered mechanically.

BAM! BAM! BAM! Then the doorknob started to furiously jiggle, at speed-freak speed.

"God damn you!" Evangeline shrieked.

And that was enough of that shit. That was all that he could stand. Her scream broke the spell, popped him out of inertia.

It was time to beat the fuck out of someone.

Jasper stepped forward, nudged the Bible babies out of the way. Behind him, he heard Eddie run to Esther, heard her moan as he held her close. He shot a quick glance at his friends behind him. Saw Christian come up beside Evangeline, the both of them wide-eyed, still blank with fear. He flashed them his very best wink and grin.

Then he turned around, just in time to watch the door blow off its hinges like a church exploding, stained glass flying everywhere . . .

. . . *and Jake stepped into the room, as the door hit the floor: flesh mottled with death, funeral makeup still on, eyes blazing like bloodred coals . . .*

From Jake's point of view, the moment was priceless. So many gaping faces to enjoy. So much awe in his presence.

He couldn't have asked for a better resurrection crowd.

It was kind of surprising to see Jasper Ellis there, dancing back from the door as it skidded toward him. But as tonight had clearly demonstrated, there was a first time for everything.

And then there were his E-Girls: the Big Three, together again for the first time ever. At least insofar as he knew.

He'd expected Esther to be draped around Eddie, although he'd half hoped he might catch them in bed.

But seeing them all together now—screaming and shrinking back, mostly in pairs—made him feel like he'd died and gone to, well, *here*.

Which, at the moment, felt an awful lot like heaven.

That was when he started to laugh, and once he started, it was impossible to stop. He looked at them, each of them, deep in the eye. And the deeper he looked, the funnier it got.

And just when it couldn't get any funnier, Jasper made his move.

Jasper wasn't an idiot. What he wanted, more than anything, was to run.

But here he was, the first line of defense, and he had no fucking choice. Surrounded by screams, he turned his own into a roar of rage.

Then he winged his glass of scotch straight at Jake's head, an overhand pitch that missed by an inch, but made Jake flinch, and that was a start.

Bible Boy's ginger ale was still on the coffee table. He thought about throwing it, went *fuck that*, then just grabbed the coffee table and threw it, instead.

"COME ON!" he bellowed, marshaling the troops, as Jake backed up, raised his arms defensively. The table fell short, but the opening was there.

Jasper charged, headfirst.

The goal was to knock his ass down. If he got him down, he could pound his face in, grab his skull and smash it flat on the pavement.

Once down, the others might join in, if Jasper needed help pinning the fucker. They could kick him, pound him, take him apart, do whatever it took to make this stop.

He thought all this in the milliseconds before the crown of his head collided with Jake's belly: making Jake whoof and half double up, pile-driving him back toward the door.

Jasper's legs pushed forward with all their might, while his hands went down to grab Jake behind the knees, prepare to buckle them out.

Then Jake threw an uppercut that punched him in the chest.

Punched straight through his chest.

And out the other side.

It all happened so fast that he could feel his own lung flapping out the back of his jacket, almost before the blow to his chest fully registered. He screamed, and it came out in liquid form: a gush of blood from the mouth that doused Jake's crotch and pants legs, like a period gone horribly wrong.

He felt himself hoisted upward, on the pivot of the arm that impaled him. His eyes shuddered into focus just in time to meet Jake's gaze.

Jake looked almost as surprised as he did, although a whole lot happier about it. His death, after all, was over.

But Jasper's had just begun.

The rest of Esther's little garden party stampeded out the back door in a tangle-legged knot. But they all screeched to a halt when a crack of thunder split the night and a dazzling flash blinded them.

Or maybe it was Gray's gun, going off one second later. Like an echo, doing much the same thing.

Evangeline skidded out of her high heels and almost deep throated the hot barrel of Gray's .45. She recoiled and took a startled step back into the herd.

"You wanna get back in the house now," he informed them, smoke curling from the Camel caught between his grinning lips. "Jake won't like it if I blow your tits off. But I'm sure he'll understand."

He stepped forward, herding them, and they went back easy. Just the way that God intended. There were six of them, but he'd popped a fresh clip in, so bullets were definitely not an issue.

And the people who knew him clearly knew that he meant business. And the people who didn't had gotten the hint.

"*Cocksucker,*" Evangeline hissed: almost a whimper, almost a curse.

"Uh-huh. Do tell."

"You killed those people tonight . . ."

"Maybe one or two. Let's just say I'm already warmed up. And you know what else? I don't think they're gonna be coming back anytime soon. Now get back in the fucking house. Ladies first."

Jake was still up to his elbow in Jasper, who was horribly *still alive:* fighting with the last of his strength, using those final moments to try and claw out Jake's throat.

For Jake, the struggle turned suddenly desperate. He had his free hand wedged under Jasper's chin, forcing the head back as far as it would go, as he tried to yank his arm free: a frantic pushme-pullyou that strained his spine almost as much as Jasper's. Even dying, the son of a bitch was strong.

But Jasper was going away now: limbs flailing on

automatic, mind barely aware. The darkness was calling, in a howl like the wind, urging him to let go.

Which he finally did, as Jake yanked free.

What hit the floor was just a human-shaped lump of empty meat.

Jake teetered slightly in the strobing lights, took a moment to revel in the kill. If his heart still pumped, it would be pounding right now. And the fireplace roared, as if in thunderous applause.

That's when the others were herded back in.

Emmy was first.

This was gonna be fun.

Chapter Fifteen

The blood-drenched monstrosity standing before her could not be the man she loved. It was a dream, or a punishment from God, or a demon made flesh. But not Jake. Not Jake.

Then it smiled at her, and Emmy knew that smile. It was the one he used to charm, to smooth over the rough spots. It was the one that she had fallen in love with.

And the voice, as it spoke, was his, too.

"Look at you. My little Bible baby." He stretched out the last words affectionately, just as he reached out with gore-matted arms. "Don't be scared. It's all right. Come to me."

Emmy shook her head, but her legs started walking toward him, knees almost buckling with the effort.

"That's right. There's my girl . . ."

As if in a dream, she took another helpless step. The smell got to her, the closer she came. Emmy held her breath and forced herself closer, tears streaming all the way down her chin.

"My faithful puppy . . ."

Then he closed the distance, grabbing Emmy in a huge embrace, squeezing so hard that she wheezed and turned nearly as red as the blood on his hand, now painting her face and hair.

"And have I got a bone for you," he half crooned in her ear.

Dear God, he was hard as a rock.

Then he pushed her back to arm's length, held her taut by the shoulders.

"But first, I gotta gives kisses to the missus!"

The next thing Emmy knew, she was thrown to the floor so hard that she bounced off the tiles, barely managing to get her hands up in time to keep her nose from shattering.

The pain was as harsh and jarring as the shock. But then Esther screamed, and Emmy rolled over, just in time to watch the Jake-thing sweep his shrieking wife up in an almost-dancerly embrace: a violent tango move that bent her backward at the waist as he loomed and leered above her.

Jake opened his mouth, and his black tongue came out. Black as his eyes, in that flickering moment.

Then he pasted her with a kiss, burying that tongue in her screaming mouth.

A moment later, Esther hit the ground, vomiting crackers and scotch and a bile not entirely her own.

That left Evangeline as the last woman standing; and Emmy watched as she stood there, rigid and quaking and shaking her head, as if *refusing to believe in him* would somehow make him go away.

"Aw, check you out," Jake cooed. "Aren't you a sight." Almost sympathetic, as he moved in slowly.

"WHY AREN'T YOU DEAD?" she shrieked at him.

Coming closer. "Now what did I always tell you?"

"NO!"

Closer. "There's not a power in heaven or earth could keep me away from you, baby . . ."

"NO . . . !!!"

Evangeline launched herself at him, swinging wildly with her fists. He laughed and fended her off. He was bigger and stronger, but she was ferocious.

"DAMN! Look at you go!" To the men, he added, "See why I could never resist this one? I'm tellin' ya, she's one wild little ride . . . !"

Then Evangeline punched him right in the face; and Emmy felt a sudden, strange flush of exhilaration.

It flashed at the moment his laughter dried up.

And died the second he slapped Evangeline so hard that the woman's eyes went blank, and she dropped to her knees.

"NOT IN THE FACE, YOU FUCKING WHORE!" he howled. "What did I always TELL Y—!"

There was a whir of motion from Emmy's left, so fast she barely had time to clock it. She hadn't seen Christian move to the fireplace, pick up the fireplace poker.

But suddenly, there he was, coming up beside Jake and swinging.

Jake whirled, a blur with an arm at the end that caught the poker and wrenched it sideways, Christian screaming as his wrist loudly snapped.

Then Jake kicked him in the belly and he doubled over, dropping to his knees with the others.

"ANYBODY ELSE?" Jake bellowed.

But the only ones left were Mathias, and Eddie, and the man with the gun. None of them moving an inch.

Jake cackled, shaking his head. "WOO-HOO! You wanna talk about little bitches! I gotta admit, though, Esther. You sure know how to throw a party."

Then he turned to the man with the gun and said, "Gray! Check it out, man! You catchin' all this?"

"Yeah, you bet," the gunman said. "It's like date night at a battered women's shelter. Can we just do this, now?"

"Oh, come on! I'm back, baby! I'M BACK FROM

THE DEAD! You know anybody else since Jesus who was able to pull that trick?"

"Look, I'm not trying to piss on your parade . . ."

"Then don't . . . !"

"I just happened to notice that your front door blew up, and there's blood all over the fucking place . . ."

Jake's dead eyes blazed. "Well, excuse *me* for livin'!"

"And last time I heard, you had things to do, before the cops show up. Which you know they're gonna do."

Jake paused, thinking. The fire in his eyes went down.

"That's right."

"Important things."

"All right. You're right . . ."

"So . . ."

"You made your point. Shut up."

Then he turned to the others, in evangelical mode, Emmy wincing as his gaze swept lingeringly past her own.

"And as for you—my dearly beloved brothers and sisters, who are gathered here together cuz you love me *so much*—don't think I can't see what you're doing here. A little gathering in secret. Talking shit behind my back."

Thunder boomed. Lights flickered like lightning.

"You better hope to God you didn't touch my part of the house."

Esther looked up from the puke on the floor before her, panic in her eyes. "We didn't go in there, Jake! I promise!"

"Not the whole time I was gone."

"I swear . . . !"

"I can fix the door," interrupted a voice.

Emmy turned—*everyone* turned—to look at Eddie.

Esther's handyman, or whatever he was, stood straight and stared Jake in the eye. He was trembling, yes, but there was something solid underneath the terror that kept his voice astoundingly steady.

"When we put in the stained glass, I took the old one out back. It's still good. The hinges fit."

"I bet they do," Jake fired back. "And I like how you fucking change the subject. You been back in the deep end, where you don't belong?"

"Just leave her alone, and I'll take care of it."

Jake laughed. "'Just leave her alone.' You all know that he's bangin' her, right? Just so nobody thinks they've got the moral high ground, here . . ."

"Jake, please!" Esther moaned.

"Shut up. *God*, you stink." Jake sneered at Esther, poked a thumb toward Evangeline. "You're as much of a whore as she is. At least she gets paid. You have to pay *me* to fuck you anymore."

Then he turned at last to Emmy, and she felt herself not just shrink, but *diminish* beneath his nightmare gaze.

"As for you . . ." he said, "well, you're gettin' there. I like that you come when you're called. But you've still got a lot to learn. You've all got a lot to learn tonight."

When the thunder boomed outside, it was as if God agreed entirely. Jake noted it, too, and it made him smile.

The world as they knew it was over and done.

And final Judgment was at hand.

Part IV
Gospel Of The
Resurrection, From
The Book Of Gray
(45 Minutes Ago)

Chapter Sixteen

If he lived to be a hundred, Gray would never forget a moment of it. He'd been hit with a Bible more times than he'd opened and read one; but he knew the story of Saul, who was struck from his horse by a vision that transformed him into the apostle Paul, on the road to Damascus.

Gray had seen the same thing happen to epileptic feebs and schizophrenics. And he wasn't a born-again Jesus freak. In fact, he wasn't transformed at all, so much as he was confirmed.

What happened at the chapel did not reassure Gray that there was a God. Such a revelation would have truly fucked up his day. After today, he knew that whatever absolute power looked down from heaven was not down with the hypocrite Bible-thumpers or the kiddie-rapers or the ragheads, but on *their* side . . .

Gray was free to be the same as he ever was.

But the world, itself, was brand-new.

A miracle, but how different it all looked, only a few hours ago.

He'd gone back home after burying Frankie in Death Valley, and drank Everclear until he tried to stab some bitch on his TV. Even so, he could not sleep until he'd paid his final respects.

Sitting in a pew in the back of the chapel throughout that murderous service—while the mealymouthed Unitarian minister babbled at the lectern—Gray had put aside his plans for the future and his regrets for the past, and just let himself simmer. If he was any less strung out and hungover, he might have broken down and cried.

He moved only to duck outside for a smoke, and to discreetly heave bile into the hymnal holder in the back of the pew before him. Gratified to discover he was not the first.

The rage oozed out of him like toxic waste, without depleting the bottomless reserves of it stored up in his soul. The hardwood pew should blacken and smolder under him. The spent human trash in the rows before him should clutch at their throats and choke to death on the fumes coming off him.

But Jake's wasted TV flock just kept sobbing and nipping from their flasks, wallowing in their shallow, secondhand sadness like junkies drowning in two inches of bathwater.

How he longed to teach them what real grief felt like. He was not about to debase himself by wishing or praying for anything, but he would gladly stuff the world into that fucking box, to have his friend out of it.

He had met Jake Connaway ten years ago in L.A., right before they both got kicked out. Gray was delivering coke for some people who were probably still looking for him, and Jake was fronting a shitty metal band and living in some has-been soap opera star's guest house, until she caught on he was fucking her daughter on the side, not to mention half the sluts on the Strip.

Gray had reached the end of his rope, and was danger-close to exploding. L.A. was a sea of people; somebody witnessed every goddamned move you made. Drugs and alcohol never quite did for him whatever they did for other people, and sex was just how nature tricked idiots into making more idiots.

His only real pleasure was in observing the pleasures of others, and the depths of degradation he could lead them to in pursuit of said pleasures.

But if Gray was an explorer of shame, Jake was an artist.

As hopeless as Jake's band was—and they made David Koresh's band look like Van Halen—it was a license to hunt poon, and Jake seemed to be the happiest man in Hollywood. They paid for his coke. They went down on his friends and "business associates" for the price of a smile. They ripped each other's hair out in hilarious catfights, but never came after Jake.

Gray could make a dumb slut suck him off for a gram of blow, then watch the fun as she snorted pure scouring powder; but Jake could make them believe in him so strongly that they'd tell him it was the best blow they'd ever had, and keep coming back for more.

With Jake around, the fun never stopped.

Jake and Gray burned through their L.A. connections about the same time that Jake realized his supernatural charisma could serve a higher calling. The church was a perfect front for all kinds of fun and games, but it never grew into the massive sucker-fleecing operation it could have been. As always, Jake rarely saw past his own dick, but he almost seemed to be buying his own line of bullshit lately. He talked a lot about death and resurrection in the small hours, when there were no suckers around. He asked questions nobody could answer.

Gray guessed he had all his answers now.

* * *

Eventually, the po-faced cow who ran Jake's church took up the mic and bleated for the congregation to cough up some coin to keep the church alive.

Check, please, Gray thought, biting back acid. *Amen to all this horseshit.*

The faithful stirred and meekly cleared the chapel, cried-out and eager for the next spiritual fix, or at least happy hour at the nearest honky-tonk. The church-chick had a good bodice-ripping cry on the coffin before some sunken-chested waif in a cheap suit led her away.

When the minister and a pair of deacons hovered in the wings to take the coffin away, Gray pulled himself out of the pew and shuffled up the aisle, feeling like he was about to stop a wedding. His empty stomach convulsed.

Someone laughed in the back of the chapel. An old man in grass-stained overalls swept the bottles and cans out of the pews.

It didn't hit home, of course, until he looked inside the box. Gray had seen plenty of dead people, and felt the whole range of emotions such sights could inspire. But Jake in the box looked like he'd never been alive at all. This was a puppet, with a face as cold and shiny as Lincoln's face on a penny, and just as likely to breathe or blink.

It looked like they stuffed cotton under his skin; the angles were all subtly wrong, teasing Gray with the pos-sibility that this wasn't Jake Connaway at all, but a bad imposter.

But there was no refuge in lies. He'd known it was Jake, and how he'd met his end, as soon as he heard the news. It was as traditional a fate for small-time ministers as rock stars choking on puke: to be found with their pants around their knees, and a cuckold's knife in their back. *How many times did I tell him not to go out alone?* Gray needled himself. *How many fucking times did I warn him?*

An arrangement of roses festooned the top of the coffin, and wreaths and bouquets crowded close around the coffin. Someone must've thought it looked pretty, but it was only further testimony to Jake's passage. He had nasty pollen allergies, and hated flowers almost as much as Gray did. The flowers were like a mirror held to his unbreathing lips, to prove that he was never getting up.

Gray looked down at Jake's hands folded neatly across his chest, noting with grim amusement how many pairs of panties were stuffed into them, like a rank bouquet of wilted lilies.

The three men milling around at the edge of the dais inched closer with the trolley on which they planned to carry Jake to the fire. Gray lit a cigarette and blew a fuck-off cloud of smoke in their direction. They didn't take the hint and leave, but got deeply involved in studying each other's cheap patent-leather wingtips.

Gray took out a pair of Polaroids and slid them into Jake's breast pocket. His mouth was sour and dry, his voice a croak, when he leaned over and whispered, "They paid all they had . . . but it wasn't enough, was it?"

The coffin lining was quilted, silky mother-of-pearl, like the plush lining of a fruity European pistol case. They would probably dump him into a cheap plywood box before they slid him into the crematorium.

It's what he wanted, true enough. Jake didn't want to be cut up, and he hated being locked in the dark.

In another minute, Gray was going to start crying like a slit throat. He felt dizzy. He clung to the coffin, willing the grief to go down the memory hole, or to change into something else.

This was all wrong.

This didn't happen to people like Jake. They didn't slip in the shower, or choke on fish bones, or get stabbed in the back by strangers. The world was made for men like Jake to fleece, fuck, and forget; and when the end came, it would be something glorious, not a cheap death in a slut's bed.

Wrong, all of it. Far too much wrong for just Frankie and Sugar to soak up. A world without Jake in it was just wrong, all the way around—

"Pardon us, sir," the minister mumbled, a sorry smile and runny cunts for eyes, "but we must move on . . ."

Gray raised his fist and almost knocked the cock-sucker's teeth out his ass, but he pounded on the coffin instead. The heavy, hollow slave-drum sound reverberated through the chapel.

A burly, booze-breathed deacon reached out to take Gray's arm. "Hey, buddy, take a couple days off . . ."

Gray turned to look at them. His jacket sagged open. The mouthy shitbird saw inside it and went white. "Hey, we don't want any trouble—"

Gray said, "But *I* do."

What should have happened next would probably not have amounted to much. Gray was certainly distraught, but never stupid.

What Gray aimed to do was walk away, down the aisle and out to his car—already packed—and get on the blue road to Vegas, where he would go on a bender until he felt ready to face facts and start over.

The deacons would have fed Jake to the flames, blasted the display coffin with Lysol, and gone home to their loved ones and tonight's NFL game. And that would have been that.

Nothing was going to happen . . . but God, or the Devil or Darwin, or the blind idiot god of chaos at the center of the whole, meaningless mess, looked down on that chapel, and made a miracle.

They all jumped back when the lower panel of the coffin lid flipped wide open, cracking the drunken deacon in the forehead like a fatally good idea. Roses and

G-strings flew. Jake's legs kicked spastically out at the backpedaling deacons.

Gray was just as startled as the other douche bags when Jake's legs went crazy, but he chalked it up to rigor mortis, gas shifting in the corpse, an electrical short . . .

Anything but what happened next.

Chapter Seventeen

Jake Connaway wept.

Burning all over, buried in darkness, somehow he still had some vague notion of where he must be when he heard voices over the thudding of his feet. Far off and muffled, but he recognized one of them.

He opened his eyes, but saw nothing. He tried to speak, but his lips were stitched shut. Dry as a spinster's snatch, his tongue probed the foreign object transfixing his mouth.

Nylon thread lanced his lower lips at either corner, and fastened them to a hook through his upper lip, where the tender flesh met the gums of his teeth.

His eyes burned like onions in his face, like something was in them. He rubbed them with his fists and pried out the tiny studded rubber cups jammed under his eyelids. Watery light flooded in, but he could only make out blurry, shaggy shapes stumbling back from his bed—no, his box.

All at once, it dawned on Jake that this was not a hospital.

Flexing his jaws, he tore stray threads out of his lips, but his first words came out as a muffled growl. His fingers found wads of cotton packed into his mouth.

Pulling it out was like unclogging a blocked toilet. It just kept coming and coming, but finally, the tail end of it, stained with yellow and maroon drainage, slithered out of him.

Jake sat up in the coffin and howled a blood-curdling shriek that went on and on like an air raid siren, then broke up into gales of rusty laughter.

He threw his arms up like a champion boxer, or a stage magician bathing in applause for the most amazing motherfucker of a trick ever performed. "TA-DAA!"

"Sweet Jesus on the cross!" cried the minister.

The deacons backed off the dais as if it were electrified. The drunk one tripped and fell into the first row of pews, stunned by the blow from the coffin lid. The minister sank to his knees at the foot of the coffin, overcome by this proof of God's grace at the worst possible time. The old janitor dropped the broom and turned to run.

"Fuck yeah!" Gray whooped, but buttoned up in a split second, hand on his shoulder rig. "Nobody move!"

Nobody listens at times like this. For his part, Gray was glad they didn't. A big, rancid grin split his face.

The gun leapt up level with his eye and barked twice. The janitor jogged up the aisle like his hip joints were full of gravel. The bullets took him in the neck and the base of his curved, question-mark spine. He belly flopped in the aisle like trying to ride a Slip 'N Slide, and lay still.

The drunken deacon seemed unable to figure out how to get up and run, but he slid down the long pew with his arms up to catch any bullets aimed at his face or heart. His grubby palm stopped the first shot, but it punched through and smashed out his teeth.

Gray shot him twice more, in the right eye and the throat, whipping his ruined head back over the splintered pew and slinging gray matter into the cheap seats.

The other deacon flipped the coffin trolley at Gray and ran squealing for the outside aisle, bent low at the waist.

"STOP, MOTHERFUCKER!" Gray didn't expect the idiot to stop, but he did expect him to panic, and the idiot didn't disappoint.

The screeching deacon reached the back door, but pushed on it, despite the big brass handle and the sparkly decal above it that said PULL. When he did pull the door, he hit his own foot and kicked the door shut, so he was still very much in play when Gray came down the center aisle and put one through the side of his neck from thirty yards. Arterial blood splashed up the chapel wall as the deacon sank to the floor.

A sharp, dry little laugh erupted out of Gray's pounding chest like driftwood cracking. He slapped himself, but found he couldn't stop. He had the giggles, and bad.

He turned back to the dais, but found the minister gone. Checking the slide on his automatic, he stalked up the outside aisle, until he stood over the crawling creep.

"You talked a lot of shit about the afterlife, fat boy."

At his feet, the minister blubbered prayers into the pool of tears and snot on the well-waxed marble floor.

"You don't *really* believe all that shit, do you?"

Maybe his head shook like it was going to screw right off. Maybe he was just having a heart attack. God let people off that easy, but not Gray.

"You want to know what I think?" Gray knelt and stroked the minister's hair with the barrel of his gun. "I think *this* is hell."

The minister jumped at the kiss of red-hot metal on his flabby neck, but offered no rebuttal.

"So you've gotta wonder . . . where are you going now?"

A hand fell on Gray's shoulder, heavy enough to trap his arm. Gray whirled and threw a wild punch, but Jake stopped it cold.

Smiling down at his friend, his red-rimmed eyes and mouth weeping amber fluid, Jake spat out a wad of cotton and croaked, "Bring him here, would'ja? Alive, if possible."

Gray took a step back as, once more, reality cockpunched him and stood back to watch the fun. This body, this thing he'd wished to see walk more than anything . . . it walked, it talked, but was it really . . .

"*Jake . . . ?*"

Jake's huge, slightly greenish hand slapped Gray on the back and gave his arm a playful squeeze that would leave a bruise on the bone. "Good to see you, too, man. Now get that prick for me."

Grinning, Gray caught the bawling minister by his sweaty collar and dragged him back to curl up on the toes of Jake's size-thirteen patent-leather wingtips.

Jake hung his head and let the spirit come into him, as he did whenever he was about to launch into a sermon.

"You really did spout off an awful lot about heaven and hell, back there," Jake husked. Short of breath, as if he'd lost the trick of breathing, and had to remember to draw in air to speak.

Working out a post–rigor mortis kink in his neck, Jake bowed down over the quivering minister. Smiling.

"I forgive you for that, but I'm here to school you. I could tell you what I saw on the other side, but you don't have to take it on faith anymore."

Jake lifted the minister up by his lapels until his toes barely scraped the floor.

"I came back to *show* you."

He set the minister on his feet and placed both hands on top of his bald head, as if to confer a blessing. The minister seemed to hang from Jake's hands, animated by them alone as they stroked the slack contours of his face and came to rest at the corners of his half-open mouth.

The minister gave no resistance as Jake slid his thumbs into it, but he tried to pray. "J-J-J-Jesus . . ."

"No. It's Jake."

His thumbs slid up to the webbing of his palms in the minister's cheeks. Whispering, "*Shhhh,*" he took hold of those chubby cheeks and, as easily as you'd take the wrapping off a birthday present, ripped his face off in two runny handfuls.

"*Hallelujah!*" Jake cackled, flinging the scraps of face at the cross behind his coffin. "Let us pray."

And they did.

Chapter Eighteen

Admiring himself in the full-length mirror in the work-room of the funeral home, Jake tried to keep his run-away emotions in check. His unbridled joy at the sight of his body was tainted; but all things considered, it was not so bad.

He tore off the suit, slitted up the back like a doll's clothes, and ripped away the heavy plastic body-condom wrapped around him to keep drainage from staining the fancy display coffin. But his laughter died in his throat when the harsh embalming-room light revealed his naked body.

His skin was a mottled yellow-gray where it stretched taut over muscle and bone, but sagged alarmingly at his abdomen, where the puckered lips of the autopsy inci-sion terminated at his groin.

His spine felt cramped. The stab wounds in his back and belly were not healed, but sealed with superglue.

Probing his head under the stiff, sticky mass of his hair, he found sutures in his scalp, a semicircle over deep grooves in his skull, where they cut his skull open with a circular saw and took out his brain. Maybe they dumped it back in, or sent it to a university for med students to jab with scalpels, but his thoughts of outrage and revenge had to be coming from somewhere . . .

His heart was not beating. His belly was emptied of organs, and filled with packing material, scarecrow stuff. Whatever was in his veins, it wasn't blood. He felt a mild burning sensation, inside and out. Formaldehyde.

Rude holes had been bored into the base of his neck, upper arms and thighs, and a sliced and dilated segment of artery or vein peeked out of each, like the puckered neck of a deflated balloon, stretched out and bloated from where they pumped the shit into him.

To his delight, some things worked as good as ever. The shriveled club of his cock responded eagerly to his chafing hand, swelling to jut out like a riot baton, though the fumes from the amber droplets that oozed from his urethra made his eyes sting.

No, this wasn't so bad. He'd never eat again, but he'd never need to shit or piss, or get sick or hungry or tired. He was remade better than before, reborn to spread the word and sow his seed, and woe to the sinners who defiled him as he slept.

He was not alive, but so far from dead. He felt the formaldehyde in his veins like pure grain alcohol, bathing him in that golden glow of invincibility that only a good, stiff drink can provide.

He felt good, but he could not forget, let alone forgive, what they had done to him.

They cut him up and filled him with weed killer to cover the stink, and they would have burned him if he hadn't put his foot down. Dumped his ashes and gotten on with their lives, as if he had never been.

"Over my dead body," he croaked, and made himself laugh again.

He noticed Gray in the mirror, hanging in the doorway with his eyes riveted to Jake. He held out another of

Jake's suits on a hanger. "She dumped a bunch of them here."

Jake turned and strode across the tiled floor to take the suit.

"Where you want to go now?" Gray asked.

Jake caught him watching as he stepped into his slacks. Bitch couldn't be bothered to send him into the fire with a decent pair of boxers.

But that could be easily remedied.

"Take me home," he said.

Part V
Putting The Haunt Back
In Haunted House

Chapter Nineteen

The way they dragged their feet as their sorry procession came down the hall, you'd think the party was over. But even if everything Esther thought she knew about her husband was turned on its ear tonight, she was no idiot.

What she feared about him had been proven, and she knew that whatever force had raised him up, it was not concerned with any justice but Jake's.

And nobody knew how to punish like Jake Connaway.

Jake led them at a lanky, halting pace, keys jingling in his hand like they would open a honeymoon suite. Esther and Evangeline came close behind him, in shell-shocked lockstep, like the brides at a polygamist wedding. Emmy and Mathias followed closely, clinging to each other like Hansel and Gretel, lost in the Black Forest.

"My wife's the kind of person that likes to keep up appearances." Jake chuckled, percolating phlegm deep in his chest. "Doesn't do such a great job of it, these days. But it's what she likes to do . . ."

Eddie and Christian dragged Jasper's dead body behind them, which left a wide trail of blood, like a carpet of crushed roses, in its wake.

Gray came last, kicking at Jasper's heels and wistfully twitching his trigger finger.

It was a slow death march down the corridor, but Jake the jocular host had forgiven them for leaving him behind, and didn't rush the tour. Nobody else dared to speak.

Jake paused before a door at the end of the hall. Making a little show of finding the right key, he unlocked it, turned and favored them with a sly grin. Hard to tell if he was breathing, but the formaldehyde fumes were a miasma around his head.

"So that was her nice little side of the house." He tipped them a wink. "But this is mine."

Jake threw open the door, or maybe the cold wind sucked it out of his hand, pulling the heat and light of the house into the empty darkness. Silly, but that was what it felt like: not just cold, but a perfect vacuum.

The knob hit the wall hard enough to punch a hole in the Sheetrock.

Once, this half of the rambling ranch house had been the free school. The hall opened into a communal classroom space, with satellite rooms and another hall branching off it. Once, the walls had been plastered with hippie artworks like God's eyes and macramé tapestries, and children's finger paintings of Jerry Garcia and the Dalai Lama.

All of it so long gone, now, it was retroactively undone. This place could never have heard children laughing.

Darker and bleaker in here, even when Jake pawed the light switch, but the room almost glowed with the reflection of his savage intensity. The décor was stark and modern, smoked glass and chrome, and a convincing cast of office furniture, like a diorama of the habitat of the Successful American White Male. Esther hadn't found any genuine records of her husband's "business" here.

The art was apocalyptic with a dusting of religious imagery to sweeten the raw carnality, and set the right context for Jake's favorite artwork: the many, many mirrors.

Jake prowled the room, taking in the hidden details in sweeping, jerky arcs like a falcon, and finally nodded, smirking at Esther as if to say, *Nice try, bitch*.

The computer was on and running a screensaver, and the file cabinets were rifled. A few of the open ones were filled with sealed reams of blank Hammermill typing paper, for heft.

Esther flicked her tired eyes at the faces of the other women whenever she could avoid locking eyes with Jake, looking for traces of things better left unsaid. She'd barely ever gone into this room once Jake settled in and laid down the law, and never any farther into his domain, unless he carried her—practically hooded like a kidnap victim—to his bed.

Emmy looked more lost than ever, and seemed to want to wilt into Mathias's arms, if only he could hold her up.

Evangeline was cagey, looking from the empty cradle of the cordless phone to the chairs and tables, all the while seeming to chew her lip and try not to swoon.

Jake looked around at each of his mourners, as well, seeming to swell up with the old time evangelical spirit, his eyes to gleam brighter, as if he sucked something vital out of each of them.

"You wanted to know, so now you will. And then everybody will. Now get your asses in here."

They didn't hesitate, but every step Esther and Evangeline took was half the length of the one before, like that silly old paradox, so they might never make it at all.

Both kept their eyes on the floor and their hands crushing each other at their waists. The sight of it made whatever Jake was using for blood these days flush his pale face. If only he could have had them both . . . but tonight, he could have much more. All of it.

Gray herded them in with judicious pokes at Eddie and Christian and kicks at Jasper's corpse. The picture window in the dead man's back slurped and dropped a flapping lobe of lung, shredded by shattered ribs, dragging behind Jasper like a loose shirttail.

Christian, towing his best friend by one hand and trying to see only the floor in front of him, bit back a searing heave of undiluted alcohol puke. If he so much as dripped on the rug, he sensed that Jake would put his fist through his face, never mind what the wreck of Jasper's torso was doing to the ghastly deep-pile shag.

He wiped his mouth with the velvet sleeve of his wounded arm, and kept his mouth shut.

They followed Jake through the office down the far corridor. They could see a picture of Jake on the wall at the end, but it seemed impossibly far away. The light sconces flickered and cast long shadows, added years to sunken faces. But it all seemed horribly by design—as if the place sucked the life out of everyone it touched, just like its master.

Jake led them, shivering, to another odd dead end. Straight ahead stood a pair of doors, both padlocked, flanked by another pair, both standing open. To the right was his bedroom. The bathroom was to the left.

Jake's expansive gestures seemed like an attempt to hold up his surging ego, or just to contain it. Jerky with rogue impulses chasing across his face and down his massive limbs, he had some trouble snapping the key into the lock of the closed left-hand door. *Honeymoon jitters, heh heh . . .*

Gray pressed closer, crowding them into a tangle of limbs so they'd trip each other up if anyone tried to bolt.

"This," Jake said, "is where the magic happens. This

is the Church Of Eternal Life. And don't you fucking forget it."

The door squealed when Jake threw it open.

The whole back end of the house was Jake's studio: a DIY video production facility, with computers, monitors, lights, mics, cameras, a green screen that covered one whole wall, shelves containing hundreds of archived VHS tapes and DVDs, a rollaway pulpit with a sampling keyboard hidden behind it, and a rough-hewn wooden cross on wheels, big enough to crucify Hulk Hogan.

To the untrained eye, the setup would look pathetic: the lowest rung of religious entertainment, ground out by a solitary crank too unstable to face—or too cheap to pay—a studio crew, let alone a live audience.

But as they entered the room, wary of traps, the selfish ingenuity of it soaked in. Jake would sometimes use burnouts from his church to come and do the grunt work, but the beauty of the setup was that he didn't need anyone to tape his show.

The cameras were trained on the green screen in an adoring semicircle, and a live editor control board had been set up on the floor beside Jake's duct-taped mark on the floor (a cross, naturally). It looked like a guitarist's effects pedal rig, but with it, Jake could direct the show as he performed, cutting it live with his toes.

Clearly, all those years of playing in crappy, overblown rock bands had finally paid off.

Jake did not enter, but ushered Mathias and the women inside. They took it all in, becoming more frightened than ever, pressed in a row against the heavy, movie palace drapes that covered the wall nearest the door.

They could feel this was the worst room in the house.

In the hallway, Jake watched the men drag Jasper's body toward him. Gray cocked his head like a dog hearing a whistle. Jake tossed him the key ring and waved at the bathroom.

"Okay, you," he sneered. "Tinkerbell." Pointing at Christian. "Drag the body in there. Pool boy, you back off."

Christian and Eddie looked at each other. If anything passed between them, an invitation to do something stupid, it didn't get far.

Gray raised the gun and looked like *he* was the one holding *it* back, when it couldn't wait to introduce their faces to the wondrous innovation of lead-projectile dentistry.

His smile almost bit Eddie's nose off. "I don't ask twice."

Eddie backed off. Christian dragged Jasper one-handed into the bathroom. Gray took out his keys and locked the door behind them.

Chapter Twenty

Christian let go of his dead friend's wrist and looked hopelessly around the flickering bathroom, nursing his fucked-up hand, which was painfully twitching in time with his galloping heartbeat.

He never—almost never, anyway—cried in front of Jasper. And he sure as hell wasn't going to cry *on* him, if it wasn't going to fix anything.

He was doing fine, running water in the sink to sluice off the blood and trying to make sense of his right fist, which felt like a beanbag filled with hamburger and smashed breadsticks; if not for the jolt of transcendent agony when he prodded or tried to move it, he would not believe it was a real hand at all, but a cheap prosthetic from a joke shop.

All right, fuck it, he'd cry.

The door was a stout one, the walls solid enough that nothing the Wrong Reverend Connaway did in here would upset the help. You'd never have to turn on the sink to cover the sound of your clinkers hitting the bowl in here, for sure.

Alive, alone with his best friend's corpse, Christian let himself come a little unzipped. He cried, but he'd be damned if he'd kneel down and pray.

Christian didn't need to believe in God. He wasn't one of those burned-out Bible-humpers or recovering Catholics who, deep down, were really just *mad* at God, and trying to get his attention by ignoring him.

For Christian, this life—such as it was—was still chock-full of miracles, both authorless and by human hands. In those moments when, for instance, he sank a triple-bank shot and shut down a pool shark with the whole bar watching and three pitchers under his belt—or when he rode behind a motorcycle with a guy, and pressed against his back until he felt his heartbeat, and breathed in the emerging scent of his skin and hair, and knew that tomorrow he'd be making his infamous Clamato omelets for two—he knew there was no other life behind this one, and he wouldn't have it any other way.

And when the realization was driven home by a death in his circle of friends or even on the side of the highway, he did not get sucked down into despair, or entertain thoughts of committing to putting only one Jewish carpenter's body and blood in his mouth for the rest of his life.

Christian fumbled half the contents of the medicine cabinet into the sink, but nothing stronger than Advil turned up. There was nothing useful among the skin cleansers and rejuvenating scrubs, Grecian Formula and Old Spice (seriously? What the fuck?), to fix up a mangled hand.

Okay, he relented, breathless with agony. *Maybe one little prayer, just in case.*

His grandmother was the only person of faith he never found utterly ridiculous, and she told him it was stupid at best, prideful at worst, to ask God to do something, or ask for something. You could only ask for strength and guidance, and pledge not to get upset if neither ever arrived.

Okay, God, guide me through this. Why is there eternal life, but only for him?

Oh, and some of that strength would be swell . . .

Amen.

Chapter Twenty-one

Jake came into the studio as if trying to ride out gales of thunderous applause. Eddie and Gray followed. Eddie tried to hook Esther's eyes with his, but she seemed to have drifted into shock. The others stood right where they were. Waiting for direction.

Jake crossed the room to snap up a remote and turn on the huge flat-screen TV. Flicked through channels, until he found the local news.

"... *a massacre at the Alta Vista Funeral Home in Joshua Tree, leaving four dead, and one body missing* ..."

"Woo-hoo!" Jake popped like a champagne cork. "They're playin' our song!"

Gray did not seem nearly as delighted, but he never blinked. Lighting a cigarette off his tarnished brass Zippo lighter and holding the smoke in, he looked like he'd just drunk boiling water on a dare.

"... *Funeral services for popular local cable televangelist Jacob Connaway, whose shocking murder last weekend provoked controversy when he was found in the desert outside Riverside County* ..."

Jake leaned in, fascinated. Finally, recognition! This was better than a mirror, bigger than his own show. Everyone else watched, too, as crime scene footage from both the desert and the funeral home took turns across the screen.

On the TV, a grizzled, fiftyish, hard-assed cop made the most of his close-up. The text crawl labeled him as *SHERIFF BILL LeGRANGE* underneath.

Gray wheeled and aimed at the screen. "God, I hate that piece of shit . . ."

Jake cut him off. "Shhh!"

"This is the second batch of murders in the last three days. And the theft of Pastor Connaway's remains . . . well, let's just say that there's harsh justice to be dealt. We will find them, believe me."

Gray flicked his cigarette at the screen. "You know damned well who he's lookin' for . . ."

"Ssssh!"

Both Esther and Evangeline were sneaking glances at the sliding glass door behind them. Emmy's gaze was riveted on Jake and the screen. Mathias was looking all over the place, and taking comfort in none of it.

"A $10,000 reward has already been offered for information leading to the return of Connaway's body . . ."

"Who did *that?*" Esther wanted to know.

Emmy looked, if anything, more horrified than before. "I swear to God, I didn't . . ."

Gray's gun chopped their conversation off. Just the little click of his thumb on the safety was enough.

"Meanwhile, some local residents blame the church itself for this wave of terror, citing the pastor's history of apocalyptic statements . . ."

"Come on," Jake bellowed. "Say it . . ."

". . . and his repeated claim that he would demonstrate the truth of the Christian resurrection, by returning to life himself . . ."

"YES!" Jake howled, jumping up and down. "Do you see? Do you see why I have to make a broadcast tonight? I HAVE TO! They are waiting on this shit!"

Everyone stared, a home-invasion version of the Last Supper, and none were more poleaxed than Gray.

"I AM THE PROOF!" Jake roared, throwing out his arms and thrusting his chest out as if something in it still beat and pumped blood. "I am the Truth, and the Light! And everything I've done has just set it all up! Bang! Bang! Bang! Like a string of cherry bombs! I AM THE LIVING SHIT, PEOPLE! Just TRY to argue with that!"

Nobody tried to argue with that. And whatever the newscaster said next was lost behind it. The TV cut to video of a funeral in Iraq with thousands of irate mourners in black robes, and then rock-'em–sock-'em footage of marines laying siege to a mosque in a war-torn city somewhere still a few shades healthier than here.

Only Gray was anxious to break the spell of the moment. "So what do you want me to do now?"

Jake looked at the women. Incredibly smug, now. If formaldehyde could bring a penis fully erect, than it was doing its distillers proud.

"Put them in the holding cell."

"They'll scream."

"Let 'em scream all they want. I'll get around to 'em when I'm good and ready."

Then he turned to Eddie and Mathias. "You two stay with me."

"Okay, sweethearts." Gray peeled Esther and Evangeline off the herd with a flick of his gun barrel. The look in his eye might have given them a yeast infection. "Let's skedaddle."

Chapter Twenty-two

Gray herded the women out the sliding glass door and into the backyard. A huge, gnarled oak tree spread its bare branches out over the whole expanse of lawn, between the house and the swimming pool. The branches thrashed in the wind that roved out of the desert to beat down on the house.

Evangeline stared dourly at the padlocked gate on their right, the spiked steel fence blocking the path to the parking lot, the malformed tree looming before them, the bars on the window to the holding cell attached to the garage before them.

Evangeline's heart sank into the bubbling bile in her gut. Of all the awful surprises of the night, this was the worst yet, somehow, because it was not a surprise at all.

She feigned stumbling into Esther, tried to grab at her arms, but they remained pinned at her sides.

Esther wouldn't meet Evangeline's eyes, but she caught a glimpse of what was about to come leaking out of them, and she finally knew.

She wanted to crow, *You knew what he was, and you let him do it to you, because you thought you were the only one. Thought it was normal, thought it was love. Thought you could hold him.*

She wanted to slap Esther, turn on Emmy behind her and knock their heads together.

You thought you were special . . .

And what did she think *she* was? She had fallen for his bullshit more often and awfully than anyone here. But now she didn't feel so alone.

He had fooled them all, used them all.

Even God.

Christian's jacket was from a vintage 1970s crushed velvet tuxedo. He liked to joke that it was haunted by the ghost of John Belushi, and sometimes by Cat Stevens, which was always good for a funny bar argument.

The shoulder seam was ripped out where Jake had whipped him around like he'd caught a fish not worth hauling into the boat. Jasper's tacky blood plastered the sleeves to his arms, and he couldn't get it off without re-setting all the bones in his right hand. He almost hadn't worn the damned thing, because it looked like rain. He almost hadn't come here at all.

Bummer, dude . . . and how's your hand?

It continued to pioneer new frontiers of hurting. The Advil or two he hadn't upchucked hadn't found his hand, and no wonder. His nerves were tied in a knot. His fist was studded with blisters, swelling up and turning purple, hogging a lot of the blood he needed to think straight, but none of the pain-feeling stuff. *Come on, is this supposed to be shock? What a rip-off.*

In another of his many awesome coats, Christian was pretty sure he had a foil bindle with two and a half Vicodin in it. Probably the red sharkskin blazer . . .

God, he wasn't even drunk anymore. *I sure hope* my *wake doesn't suck like this . . .*

He didn't think about the outcome when he swung at Jake, but he'd do it again, maybe faster, and with a pickax or a Stinger missile. But he'd definitely do it again, first chance he got.

Wait, that was useful—

Cradling his right hand against his chest, he knelt down and threw open the cabinet doors under the sink. Hair spray, cologne, insecticide, and precious little else.

Then it hit him. The vintage tuxedo jacket wasn't, technically, strictly authentic vintage, since he had his tailor put in a pocket above the hip on the inside left panel, for his cell phone.

It was easy to slap his forehead, but harder to get the phone out of the pocket with the wrong hand. Setting it on the counter, he pinned it with the back of his broken hand and tried to steady it to punch in 911.

Oops. He'd turned the damned thing off before they went in to the wake. He turned it on, wincing at the retarded corporate jingle noises it made to announce to all and sundry that Christian was about to spoil the movie for the whole theater.

Come on baby, Christian silently urged, as the chirpy phone searched for service. *Give me someone real to pray to . . .*

The awkward silence in the studio stretched out and flexed its claws, as Eddie and Mathias waited for Jake to make his move.

The man of the house sauntered around the studio, tweaking knobs and fiddling with the cameras, restless. He stopped before the oversized cross, head bowed in silent contemplation, for a long minute.

Finally, he threw a cruel smile at Eddie.

"So you're fucking my wife. How *is* that? Cuz my experience is, you really have to work her hard. But once she gets going, she just never wants to stop. You know what I'm sayin'?"

Eddie glared at him, trying hard to hold it in. He couldn't hide his fear, but he wouldn't look away.

"Maybe you wanna throw a punch, now, too?"

In spite of everything he'd seen, he wanted to, very much. He would have, knowing what would happen, if it meant a chance for Esther to escape.

Not now. He didn't know this part of the house, but if he could stay upright, the chance would come. Jake might walk and talk, but Eddie would bet his left nut that this was not God's work.

That was the only hope he could hang their survival on: that sooner or later, the Devil always breaks his promises.

The storage room behind the garage was dank and reeked of paint thinner and mildew, in spite of the arid bite of the desert air. A terrible place to store anything you might someday want to use.

It was, however, a great place to store people.

The tiny, terrifying room had one door and one window, both barred, and a bare bulb light, long since burned out. All the old paint cans and ancient school desks that once filled this room had gone to the dump when Jake moved in.

The room was left barren, except for a mattress and some shackles. Even the playpen stuff was gone now.

But the big Yale lock on the outside of the door still worked.

The three crying women filed in without a fuss, but Gray ripped Esther's handbag out of her white-fisted grip as she minced into the cell.

"Oh, please!" she bawled. "Please! Let me keep my flask!"

Gray dumped out her bag, held up the sterling silver hip flask with a flowery, unreadable inscription. She licked her pretty lips, shaky and sick with thirst.

"Sure." Gray unscrewed the lid and took a deep, satisfying swig. True to form, the package might be fancy, but it still tasted like a case of the clap.

Gray toasted Esther with her flask.

Spat in it.

Then handed it back.

"Live it up. Get your little party started. Can't wait to see who wins."

Gray slammed and locked the door.

Strolling back across the lawn in the wind-whipped gloom, he smiled as he heard them tuning up, already. He certainly heard someone screaming and moaning, out there . . .

Christian's phone walked him through its wondrous array of features, then settled on its ready screen, which told him there were fewer bars available than in the depths of Mormon country.

"Shit," he hissed, but started to punch in the number.

Three Missed Calls, said an alert screen, with a chipper chirp that made his fillings jump out of his teeth.

"Come on, come on . . ."

Out of habit, he hit *Enter* to look at the calls. All from Lisa, Jasper's date for the night.

Christian sighed as he cleared the phone. He barely knew her, but Jasper's women tended to latch onto Christian if they hoped to stick around. They thought that, because he was gay, he was a reliable double agent.

Lisa was afraid Jasper was hung up on Evangeline, and didn't want to get used as a rebound. She really liked Jasper. Everyone really liked Jasper—

Wiping his eyes, he hit the 9. The 1—

Jasper's phone rang.

Loud as fuck, and right here in the room with him.

* * *

Jake pointed at Mathias. "Or hey, maybe you can gang up on me, get a little tag-team action going. Whaddaya think?"

Eddie trembled with helpless rage. Mathias just trembled. Eddie shot a glance at the kid, but his eyes were pinned to the ceiling as if it were the Sistine Chapel.

"Didn't think so. So I guess we'll save it for your confession. After Bible Boy, here."

Mathias snapped out of his trance, looking more shocked and helpless than ever. He must have thought his prayers would do something about this, like wake him up.

The silence curled around them again, not awkward, now, but a huge, predatory presence, breathing in time with the purr of the idling studio gear.

And then, muffled by distance and heavy acoustics, someone started wailing hair metal licks on an electric guitar.

Christian was dumbstruck.

Dropping his own phone in the sink, he knelt beside his friend's corpse. "Shit! Shut up, shut up—"

Jasper never turned off his phone, but even when his phone went off in the movies, people just laughed. That it sounded like Eddie Van Halen and Yngwie Malmsteen dueling over the last bottle of vodka on a transatlantic flight only made it more ridiculous. Even if they didn't know he was a boxing champ, nobody could stay mad at Jasper—

"Shit!"

The guitar solo continued, looping over and over.

"God damn it!" Jake got between the door and Eddie and Mathias, who looked ready to bolt. *Did you let him keep his phone?*

Gray appeared in the doorway. "I got it," he snapped, and jumped at the bathroom door.

Stifling a swell of nausea, Christian laid open Jasper's blazer and dug into the pockets, but it wasn't so easy with his left hand. Jasper's pockets were stuffed with a pack of Camels, lighters lifted off anyone who'd ever offered him a light, receipts, and loose cash, all of it drenched in cool, clotting blood like cranberry sauce.

In the other pocket, Jasper's phone shivered and screamed. Slimy with blood, slippery as a fish, the phone almost jumped out of his hand when he dug it out.

Cursing himself, he flipped it open.

"Hello . . . ?" A woman's voice, compressed shouting over a muddy wall of music.

"Lisa!" Christian whispered, loud as he dared. "Jasper's dead! He . . ."

"What? I can't hear you. Jasper . . . ?"

The door slammed open. Gray stepped in and showed Christian his gun. "You got less than a second to hang up that phone."

Christian hung up and handed over the phone. Gray tossed it in the toilet and flushed. Christian stood to block the sink, but Gray shoved him back down on his knees beside Jasper.

The gun brushed Christian's ear. He closed his eyes.

Chuckling to himself, Gray turned on the tap and ran cold water over Christian's phone.

Chapter Twenty-three

Jake plucked a baseball bat from the umbrella stand by the door as he strode toward the bathroom. It was unsurprisingly burnished black, with Sammy Sosa's ersatz signature engraved in white upon it, like bone peeking out through meticulously ruptured flesh.

"Get in here and watch these guys," he barked. "I wanna have a word with the sodomite."

Down the hall, on the bathroom floor, Christian could not help but laugh. "Which one?"

Gray cocked his foot to kick him, but Jake bellowed "NOW!" from the other room.

There was no mistaking the way he jumped. Not like a friend. Not like an employee. Not like a legitimate partner in crime.

Just exactly like a prison bitch.

Christian laughed some more. It felt powerfully good. It felt . . . accurate. He might be doomed, but he at least had a handle on what was going on around here.

If he had to die—as he'd always known he would, eventually, at the hands of some psycho closet case—he could at least die speaking truth to perversity.

He'd been training for this moment all his life.

"Your master's calling," he said, as Gray shuffled

glumly toward the doorway. "Take it hard up the ass once, for me."

"You'll be shuttin' up soon," were Gray's famous last words.

Then he was out the door.

Christian heaved a whickering sigh of uncertain relief. Gray would have flat-out executed him. Jake liked to play games.

Maybe there was a way out of this, after all.

The bathroom doorway was yawning, empty. Across the hallway, Jake's bedroom loomed. The only window was at ceiling height, barely deep enough to crawl through.

But the hallway was right there.

There was a part of Christian that thought *what if I just run right now? Grab Jasper's keys, and motor on out? Call the cops? Call the National Guard? Call whoever it takes to take this fucker down forever?*

It was a beautiful thought, but it was not the truth.

Jake stepped into the doorway.

And Christian got ready to die.

Even without the baseball bat, Jake would have been terrifying. He was six feet and change of muscle-bound, weight-trained, reanimated corpse-flesh: a still-handsome man-mountain that filled the doorway like a portrait barely squeezed into the frame.

And then there were his eyes: smoldering coals that flickered from black to red, then black again. They did not look real, but they were painfully expressive.

Jake smiled, and it would have been a winning smile, were it not for the red-black agitation in those eyes.

Was it shame that Christian saw there? A little homosexual panic, cutting into his godlike confidence?

Jake stepped forward, feigning nonchalance as he stepped over Jasper's body, took a lazy check-swing with the bat. "You were saying?"

"Oh, faggot, please." Christian rallied inside, whipped up his best no-nonsense smile, made a point of looking Jake right in his nightmare eyes. "I mean, I know you're the biggest swinging dick in these parts, and all the ladies just swoon, and cock-a-doodle-doo for you . . ."

"But . . . ?" Jake was bridling, no matter how hard he tried to keep that *check-how-cool-I-am* smirk etched into his face. He did not like the look in Christian's eyes, did not like being seen that clearly.

"But let's face it, sweetheart. You'll fuck anything that walks or crawls, if it'll get you what you want. You're proud, but you're not *that* proud. Are ya?"

The words stung. It was amazing to watch. Knives hadn't worked. Embalming hadn't worked.

But calling him a faggot?

Now *that* hit a nerve.

"You don't know me," Jake snarled: smirk gone entirely, body tensed to strike.

Christian just laughed. It was all he had left.

But it felt so goddamn good.

"Again: bitch, please!" Leaning into it now. Savoring those final moments of bliss. "If I kept that much secret pet man-ass in my closet, I'd have to change my name to Karl Rove . . ."

That was when Jake swung the bat.

Christian automatically threw himself backward, raised his right arm up without even thinking. A dull double-crack resounded, and the arm went all floppy as the bones inside it shattered.

Christian screamed—the good part over—sagging against the toilet as Jake brought the bat up. Utterly demolished, his right arm fluttered on the tile, leaving him wide open.

Jake hit him again. Ribs cracked and splintered in his chest, crushing the breath out of him in big, blood-misted gusts. The pain ratcheted way past unbelievable.

The bat came up again.

Then wavered in midair, as if thinking about it.

Please, Christian thought, but could not bring himself to say it.

That was when Jake started smiling again.

And lowered the bat, ever so slowly.

"You don't know me at all," he said.

It wasn't true, but it didn't matter. History was always written by the winner. The last one standing. And that would be Jake.

Christian hung in for as long as he could before keeling over on his good side, hacking up blood from deep within. One of his lungs burned and bubbled when he tried to take a breath. More deep red liquid upsurged.

Jake hovered for a long, awful moment, tapping the tip of the bat on the floor beside Christian's skull.

"And you don't get off that easy," he added.

Then he rose up and shattered the overhead light.

Glass ricocheted off the porcelain and tile, cascading down onto Christian and the floor. A couple stray pieces bit into his cheek, his useless arm. But there was nothing he could do.

"You better hope I'm wrong," Jake continued, "while you're listening to the others die. Cuz my hope is that— a couple of hours from now—you'll still be puking up your own lungs, and I'll have nothing better to do. Kinda like stompin' a bug."

Then Jake slammed and locked the door.

Leaving Christian in total darkness.

And woefully still alive.

Chapter Twenty-four

Jake stormed back into the studio, with the bat chopping the air in a blur like a helicopter rotor.

Gray shifted from foot to foot, like he had to pee. "Jake. The front door—"

"I know, I know. Take care of it. I got things to do."

Eddie felt beads of sweat break out on his forehead. A huge Rorschach moth of perspiration spread out from his back to meet the overflow from his armpits.

Jake looked from Eddie to Mathias, doing some sick math in his head before pointing. "Take the handyman."

Gray motioned to Eddie with the gun.

Eddie wanted to run, but he tried one last time to get Mathias's attention. The boy was trapped like a bird under Jake's penetrating stare.

Gray manhandled him out of the studio, but he looked over his shoulder as they left.

Still swinging the bat, Jake strolled over to Mathias, his arrogant grin back at full wattage.

"It's time to share our faith."

Gray shut the door, and the curtain closed around it like a shroud.

* * *

In the suffocating darkness of the holding cell, the women huddled by the window, watching Eddie and Gray come out the sliding glass door: Emmy craning for a peek at Mathias through the momentary gap in the curtain; Esther pressed against the glass, as if the sight of her might finally goose her lame-ass manservant into action.

Evangeline, too, was staring through the window, trying to gauge the possibilities of escape. Right now, it all rode on this Eddie guy. And, sweet mother of God, she hoped he had a plan.

Evangeline could not stop shaking. It was almost like a palsy, too much like cold turkey: all her muscles feverishly convulsing at once, from feet to fingertips to the follicles of her scalp.

She hugged herself, but it didn't help. Right up there with trying to tickle herself, in the uselessness department. The terror in her ran so fucking deep that Jesus himself probably couldn't massage it out of her.

Gray had the gun aimed at the back of Eddie's head; but since Eddie couldn't see it, he took a moment to aim it at the window and grin, as if this were the funniest thing in the world. Which, to him, it probably was.

The other women recoiled, screeching as if already shot; but Evangeline held her ground. She knew that psychotic freak wouldn't scratch his own balls without Jake's say-so.

"Fuck you," she said out loud, and flipped him a pair of fluttering birds that only made Gray yawn theatrically.

Gray slid the door shut behind him, pulled a flashlight from his pocket. Then he and Eddie moved out of sight, on their way to the garage.

Emmy quivered in the center of the holding cell,

also hugging herself. It didn't seem to be working for her, either.

Meanwhile, Esther turned away from the window and tipped the flask to her lips, took a serious tug. It was the only sensible response, and the addict in Evangeline responded at once.

"Gimme some of that," she heard herself say, almost before the thought had registered.

Esther pulled back, possessive. "There isn't much."

"I don't want much. I don't want any." Her whole body shuddered. "I just need a little, right now."

Esther looked at her knowingly, but did not nod her head, shook the flask instead. Not a lot left. That much was true.

"Please?" Evangeline said, trying to muzzle the voice inside that said, *don't make me take it from you, bitch . . .*

Eddie opened the garage door and stared into pure darkness. Gray's flashlight shone into it but only illuminated a narrow window of it at a time, casting the rest of it into murky chaos.

It was the default storage locker, full of boxes, bric-a-brac, and broken furniture: the kind of shit you kept, but somehow never needed again.

There was a fully stocked workbench, cluttered with tools that glistened in the flashlight's beam. Eddie's shadow cut across it as he stepped inside, started walking toward the back.

"Where's the light switch?"

"Right next to you," said Eddie. "But it doesn't work. I have to pull the chain on the overhead."

"Where?"

"Farther in."

"Don't fuck with me."

"I won't. Over here." Eddie raised his hand in the general direction of the ceiling ahead of him. Gray followed it with his flashlight, saw the light fixture dangling, swaying slightly in the center of the garage.

"Okay. Where's that door?"

"In the back. Keep the light up."

Eddie advanced, brought his hand up to the chain.

And somewhere inside the garage, he heard the tittering of a madwoman.

A jagged bolt of fear ran up through Gray. He wasn't sure why, but he knew it the second he felt it.

It was the feeling of being watched, very intently.

By something very powerful.

That meant to do you harm.

Gray found himself quickly backing up into the doorway, flashing the light around the room. "Who's in there . . . ?" he barked, ashamed of how his voice cracked.

Then the tittering stopped.

And the overhead light went on, swinging back and forth.

"What?" Eddie turned to look at him.

"Who was that, laughing?"

"I'm sorry . . . ?"

The swinging light kept casting wild looping shadows across the garage. He could see no one else there. Eddie just looked genuinely confused.

Swallowing hard, feeling like an idiot, Gray waggled the gun at Eddie.

"Don't worry about it," he muttered. "Let's go."

Eddie shrugged and made his way through the clutter to the back of the garage, found the door, hoisted it up with a grunt. It was solid, dark-stained oak, and looked heavy as fuck. "You wanna give me a hand with this?"

Gray shook his head. "Why would you even ask?"

"I can't carry this thing and the toolbox, you know."

"Then we make two trips. Come on."

Eddie tipped the door forward, started to drag it along. Just a little bit like Christ, and the cross he got nailed to. Gray stepped back as Eddie muscled it toward the doorway.

The light was still swinging back and forth as they left.

Chapter Twenty-five

Eddie dragged the heavy spare door out of the open garage and into the enclosed backyard. He stumbled, lurched, almost lost his grip, catching it by the knob before it crushed his foot.

Gray stood back and supervised, making a sound he probably thought was laughter.

Eddie looked anywhere but at Gray.

His eyes were not like a man's. They were flat and almost looked painted on, like the eyes of those fish in Lake Erie that sucked all the blood and guts out of real fish.

It didn't know what it was, didn't see the right or wrong of what it did. It was as God made it; but Eddie, also being as God made him, wanted only to crush it.

Unfortunately—unlike any other parasite he'd ever seen—this one had a gun; and Eddie knew that if he looked too long, with Jake's okay or not, this parasite would kill him.

Eddie felt his feet grow heavier with each step. The adrenaline rush that had flushed him with fighting spirit from the moment Jake came in the door had burned itself out, leaving him shaky and exhausted.

Seeing Esther in that cage again, like the old times he

was not supposed to notice—locked up and fighting with Jake's *putas* like a piece of trash in the drunk tank— he might have tried to take Gray, if he were not so tired, so broken.

Esther—

Eddie worked for her before Jake Connaway came along, and for her parents, before that. His feelings for the willowy, retiring beauty who haunted the big, empty house were always strong, but he never said a word. Such things were not done, and one's heart always wanted what was not to be, just to keep things interesting.

There were others, but nothing stuck. She was saving herself for Jake Connaway. She came completely out of her shell for him, turned herself inside out. She gave him his space, having Eddie install the locks in the doors cutting off the old school wing of the house for her husband's hideout. But she seemed to be happy for the first time in her life, or at least to be trying—

When he first began to notice signs of the strange new games afoot in the house, Eddie thought she was discovering herself. He did not judge, did not let himself become jealous. He was the soul of discretion, watching as Jake Connaway tore through Esther like a forest fire, leaving nothing standing of that carefully cultivated, fragile woman.

He abused her, terrorized her, and then made her beg for more when he ignored her. He brought other women around when Esther was away, or asleep, as she seemed to be almost all the time.

It was not Eddie's place to pry. There are all kinds of happiness.

Then finally, several months ago—last Memorial Day weekend—Mr. Connaway gave Eddie a healthy bonus and told him to stay away for a week. Eddie went to the Home Depot in town to get some gopher bait and varmint traps.

That was when he saw Mr. Connaway and a gray-haired stranger loading up a white Cadillac for a road trip at the Costco across the parking lot.

Eddie had never seen the other man before, and never since.

Until tonight.

He'd tailed them north out of town. When they turned onto the 40, no doubt headed for Las Vegas, he turned back and went to the house.

He found her in that room, behind the garage.

Alone, in the hot, damp darkness that somehow never admitted light through the barred windows, even in the full blaze of day.

Drugged, chained to the wall on a mattress rife with fleas, with a jug of water and a bucket. Both eyes closed over, cigarette burns on her heaving white breasts.

It was not his place, but he could not pretend this was what she wanted, anymore. He freed her with a pair of bolt cutters and led her back to the house.

She would not hear of calling the sheriff, and she would not leave Jake. Eddie did not press the advantage. He did not get her drunk.

She reached out for him.

And he sought only to give comfort.

When Jake came back four days later, he asked no questions about how she got free. He said nothing at all. Maybe he was relieved that she hadn't died.

Eddie never turned his back on the man of the house, after that.

Mr. Connaway would look at him every so often, smiling and waggling an eyebrow at their little secret. *So it's like that,* said his smile. *You let her out, but you didn't do shit. Whatever happens to her next, you're a silent partner. An accomplice.*

If she had asked, Eddie would have killed him for her. But even as Esther gave herself to him, she was still under the monster's spell. That little bit of her that she shared with Eddie, he would kill or die to protect, but he never forgot his place. He knew that if Jake had only shown her the tiniest gesture of caring, she would never have turned to him at all.

When Jake was found dead in the desert, Eddie braced himself for her to throw him away as well, but she didn't. It had begun to look like she might finally break free.

But hell's claim on Jake Connaway was not, it seemed, as strong as Jake's claim on Esther. God had taken a holiday, and let hell come to punish them. But for what?

No, he thought, redoubling his pace across the yard, closing in on the living room at last. *This is not God's work. Only the Devil could do what Mr. Connaway's done with his word.*

Eddie could pray for salvation, but in the end, he would have to be smarter and stronger than a dead man.

Chapter Twenty-six

Daniel, Mathias thought to himself, *must have felt like this, in the lions' den.*

He was trying to whip up his courage with a story from the Bible. It was the closest he could come to accepting that this was really happening to him.

Daniel had prayed for God's grace, and the lions had not harmed him. But Daniel had been sure of his worthiness of God's grace, hadn't he? If he had any doubt, the Bible had not seen fit to print it.

Maybe Job was a better story to draw from. Or Jonah—

Jake bustled around the studio, booting up the computers, warming up the cameras and firing up the lights in smooth succession, like he'd done it a million times. But he never seemed to look away from Mathias, tenderizing him with his eyes, as if a den filled with hungry lions prowled behind them.

Something Jake did made the theatrical curtains beside the door slide apart on humming tracks, revealing a massive picture window. Beyond the glass, a huge expanse of bed, a lushly appointed boudoir decorated like a dungeon with mirrors, and all arranged to display the action for a camera set up in the studio.

Mathias looked from the bedroom to the racks of tapes and disks. He thought of Emmy, and how she sometimes got choked up when she talked about her work for the church.

Jake caught his eye and winked knowingly, licked his lips and touched a key on the sampler behind the pulpit.

"I love you, Jake!" cried a swooning woman's voice. Was it Emmy?

Jake hit another key and basked in digital worship. Rapturous applause and high, panty-creaming screams filled the studio.

Mathias cowered before the green screen when the spotlight hit him. He didn't know where to go, what to do.

"So," Jake said. "Tell me about yourself."

Camera One was on a tripod, directly facing the green screen. Jake panned and zoomed in to lock Mathias in the shot.

"Come on," Jake persisted. "You love Emmy. At least that's what she tells me. And you love Jesus." Coming out of his mouth, those sweet, simple words sounded perverse. "So tell me, real quick: who do you love more?"

Mathias blinked. "What?"

"That one too tough? Okay!" The playful edge in Jake's voice was a tissue-thin veil over barbed, rusty rage. "Movin' on. So what *else* is there to know?"

Mathias had nothing. He was too scared.

Jake stepped out from behind the camera.

"Turn-ons. Pet peeves. Favorite hobby, TV show, late-night snack. It's not that hard. Just give us a little insight into who you are, so that we might come to know you, as God knows you."

Mathias stammered, but nothing came out. Not even a prayer.

Jake nodded with sad understanding, and strolled into the shot.

* * *

In the holding cell, at least Evangeline's shuddering had subsided. The few short swigs Esther wisely donated had done their little trick, and taken the edge off the edge.

But that didn't mean they weren't still going insane.

Emmy just stared out through the window—as if God's love could peel away the bars, or at least help her see through the curtain—all the while singing "Amazing Grace" not so softly to herself.

Meanwhile, Esther polished off the last of the flask, as Emmy's insufferable choir practice swelled to a grating crescendo.

"Gimme that thing." Evangeline gestured for the flask. "I'm gonna throw it at her head."

"Leave her alone," Esther said.

"Sorry," said Evangeline. "She's makin' me nuts." Then loudly, at Emmy, "Do you *really feel saved* right now? Is that how you really feel?"

Emmy kept on singing, looking up at the sky, as if that were actually going to help.

"Some people," Esther said, "still think that faith is beautiful."

"Yeah, and some people still think Jake's a prophet."

Emmy's voice cracked, but she kept singing. Esther and Evangeline locked into each other, hard.

"Well, clearly, you must have believed in *something*, or you wouldn't be here with the rest of us suckers."

"Oh, honey," Evangeline snapped. "Belief had nothing to do with it."

"Mm-hmm . . ."

Mathias hunkered down on the cold concrete floor: arms up, scooted back up against the green screen, just a little kid about to get the spanking of his life.

Jake stopped, four feet away. Mathias looked up only

as far as his shiny black shoes, the razor-creases in his blood-spattered slacks.

"Get up."

Mathias steepled his hands over his head. "No . . ."

"No?" Jake started unbuckling his belt.

"Wh—what are you doing?"

The sound of the belt slithering through the loops was like a sharp, indrawn breath.

"Spare the rod," Jake said, "and spoil the child."

He whipped the belt off, folded it and snapped it taut in his hands, relishing how the sound made Mathias jump. The buckle was a jagged metal lightning bolt of lovingly polished brass, with the letters "JC" embossed upon it. It looked heavy, and sharp enough to cut.

Mathias started to snivel harder.

"That's what the Bible says, right?" Jake continued. "And we wouldn't wanna argue with that."

Snapping the belt in Mathias's ear.

"Confess that you are a sinner."

Without hesitation, Mathias cried out, "I am a sinner. Yes. I confess that I am a sinner . . ."

"Go on."

"I am a sinner by nature, because of the sin of Adam. But through the grace of my Lord Jesus Christ, I am made clean in the sight of God . . ."

A sad smile crossed Jake's face.

"If only that were true."

Then he reared back, with terrible strength, and lashed out with the whistling belt.

Mathias's head snapped back at the sonic boom, and his face ripped open, from brow to cheek. In the time it took for him to scream, the meat-flecked metal tore loose, cracked the air and came flying back.

He brought his arms up to shield his face, so they took the next hit: belt buckle fangs slitting the palms of his hands, and breaking the small bones beneath.

It was like being punched with a razor.

Over and over again.

Mathias shrieked and dropped to his knees, then his side, as Jake continued to biblically scourge him, the way Mel Gibson did to Jesus: literally shredding him, laying open his back until glistening ribs showed through the red.

And just as Mathias began to black out from the pain, he heard Jake howling, too.

Howling a woman's name . . .

Emmy stopped singing at the sound of the screams.

"Oh my God," she moaned, covering her ears and melting into the floor. "Mathias . . ."

In the jagged bathroom blackness, Christian couldn't even cover his ears to block it out. Moving drove him insane with pain.

So he just lay there, and helplessly listened . . .

Eddie dragged the unbroken door across the pool of blood in the foyer, gritting his teeth against the sound. Gray stepped around it, but Eddie almost slipped.

"Fuck, what a mess," Gray muttered. "You'll have to mop that up, when you're done with this."

Eddie turned to him, eyes probing for some trace of humanity.

Gray shrugged. "Don't look at me, spic. Up to me, I'd be in Jamaica by now."

His gun said the rest, motioning toward the broken door. Eddie bent to pick up one end, leaving red footprints in the flickering light.

Chapter Twenty-seven

The screaming stopped, but the wind kept howling. And so did the women, turned to face each other now.

"We've got to help him!" Emmy shrieked.

"Oh, bullshit!" Evangeline bellowed back. "We can't even help ourselves! Don't you get it?"

"Listen," Esther growled, as if her voice had gravity. "If we're going to get out of here, you will have to trust me. I know my way—"

"You know your way *what?*" Evangeline clenched like a fist. "Cuz I don't see you doing shit!"

"I know my way around here—"

"I know my way around here, too."

Esther jerked as if backhanded. "You—"

"Oh, come on! I've been locked in this goddamned room a hundred times. And unless you're an idiot, you gotta know there's no way out but through him."

Esther said nothing, but her pale flesh went even whiter.

"Please don't tell me that he never did this to you."

Esther stared at the empty flask, said nothing.

Emmy spoke quietly. "I never . . ."

"Uh-huh."

"I've been to the house. Once. But never back there, in the studio. And, I swear to God, never out here . . ."

"Okay. So maybe you're a virgin, after all." Evangeline turned to Esther. "But you and I aren't. Not with Jake, that's for sure. And not all over this house."

Esther looked up, stifled fury boiling in her eyes.

"That's right. Which is to say, Mrs. Connaway: I have fucked him in your bed, when you weren't home. I fucked him in your kitchen. I fucked him in your pool."

"Stop it." Reaching the turning point now.

"I fucked Jake right in front of that fireplace, with the pictures of you and him hangin' there, just as nice as can be."

"You stop it right now!"

"And if you'd watched any of my confessions, you'd know I got fucked in that studio, too."

"SHUT UP!"

"Just the same as you—"

Esther went, tooth and claw, for Evangeline: a full-body assault, at full speed, plowing into her in a flurry of hair-tugging, bitch-slapping animal hate.

"STOP IT!" Emmy bellowed, suddenly the voice of reason. She pushed between them, desperately trying to break it up.

Instead, she found herself pickle in the middle.

Being battered by both sides at once . . .

Eddie and the broken door were twenty feet from the garage, sprinkling the last shards of twinkling glass into Gray's path behind them.

But when Esther shrieked in pain, Eddie forgot himself and everything else: dropping the door and rushing forward.

"Fuck!" Gray yelled, and took off after him.

* * *

Once Emmy hit the floor, in predictable tears, Esther was free to dig in with both hands. Enough slapping around. It was time to do some damage.

Esther seized the moment, surging forward.

Right into Evangeline's fist.

It was a vicious right hook to the eye; and the next thing Esther knew, she was down on her ass.

Evangeline towered above her, bloody-knuckled fists on her ample hips. "So what were you saying about who needs who?"

Suddenly, Eddie was calling her name, so close to the window she could almost feel his breath against the door.

"*Eddie?*" she cried back: for a moment, actually hopeful.

Then something thudded against the door, hard enough to rattle the wall, and Eddie groaned.

As the women screamed.

"Yeah!" Gray hollered, over the wind. "He came to rescue you! And NOT A MOMENT TOO SOON!"

Gray had caught up to Eddie, shoved him off balance, kicked him hard in the ass, and sent him stumbling into the door.

Gray kicked him again, so long as he was still bent over, then resumed his aim at the back of Eddie's head.

"Now pick up the door, Zorro. Let's do this."

Eddie turned to stare at him, and there was no ignoring the hate in those eyes. Searing hate, at that moment. Only barely contained.

It was a welcome reminder that, behind the blank stares and meek demeanor, there was a man who would love to tear his fucking throat out.

Esther pressed herself against the door, the better to hear what was going on outside. But no one was talking anymore.

Only the wind.

And whatever mad God propelled it.

Esther sagged to the floor, muttering to herself, "Thank God. He's still alive . . ."

And the moment she said it, the other women cringed.

She looked at Evangeline, saw Jasper's ghost in her eyes. Saw Jasper impaled and writhing.

Evangeline cast her gaze at the house, and Esther knew she was thinking of Christian: locked up alone in there, with their dead friend's body.

And then there was Emmy, so pure in her terror and ravaged faith.

So very much like a child.

For the first time, Esther felt their loss and terror as her own.

And found herself praying.

Not just for herself.

But for them all . . .

Chapter Twenty-eight

Gray's buzz was fading fast. This party was a bust, and he was sick of babysitting.

Eddie dragged the broken door back into the black mouth of the garage. Chest hitching in momentary panic, Gray stepped into the doorway . . .

. . . and glimpsed something in the back of the shed, as the light ripped the veil of shadows away.

A girl crouched in the corner, grinning. A sloe-eyed nymph, naked and ready to play.

In that instant, he thought he recognized her.

And then, just as quickly, she was gone.

"WHAT THE FUCK?" Gray aimed his gun at the spot where he'd seen her, and Eddie jumped, too.

But when the light swung back, Gray saw the same thing Eddie did.

Nothing.

"What is it?" Eddie nervously searched the shadows, looking as scared as Gray felt.

The giggling started again, high-pitched and chilling, going all the way under Gray's skin.

He stared at Eddie, incredulous. "Are you saying you don't hear that?"

"I don't—" The words *know what you're talking about* went politely unspoken.

Gray swallowed hard, felt his mind start to come un-tethered. The giggling got worse.

"Just grab your shit, and let's go."

Eddie moved to the workbench, threw some stuff in the toolbox. He picked up a big crowbar, held it just long enough for Gray to hear the little gears turning in the wetback's head.

"You just put that down right now." Gray might be going insane, but he wasn't going stupid.

Eddie dropped it with a shrug. "Okay?"

"LET'S JUST GO, GOD DAMN IT!"

Eddie headed back toward him.

While the horrible sound that only he could hear went on and on.

It wasn't until Eddie and Gray left the garage that the women in the holding cell heard it, too.

"Who *is* that?" Emmy was first to speak, but she could see the creeping fear in their eyes.

All of them could hear it, coming through the wall.

Esther shook her head, as if to clear it. Evangeline tensed, as if to fight. Emmy knocked on the wall, as if a friend might be there.

"Hello?" she called. "Can you hear me?"

Silence.

A long moment passed. Almost long enough to be-lieve they'd heard nothing at all.

Then—from *inside* the holding cell—the giggling started again.

Emmy, Esther, and Evangeline all shrieked as one, racing toward each other.

This time, as they converged, they did not fight. Just held on tight in helpless desperation, like barely teenage girls at a slumber party séance gone monstrously wrong.

"*Oh, shit. Oh, shit,*" Evangeline hissed. Emmy hugged her right side. Esther wrapped around her left.

"Who *is* it?" Esther whispered.

Emmy held them close, and prayed that it was an angel.

She could not have been more wrong.

Chapter Twenty-nine

A woman's mocking laughter filled the studio. Jake stood back from Mathias, let the wet belt slide into a loose coil on the floor.

"Shut up," he said.

He was not winded, not sweating, but his arm felt like it might just fall off, and embalming fluid oozed like tree sap out of the sutures in his scalp.

Jake rolled the life-size wooden cross into the center of Camera One's frame, dead centered before the green screen. Mathias writhed on the floor at the foot of it, bathed in blood, a welter of bruises and open, grinning wounds. Even now, the camera didn't like him too much. Sad, that not everybody had Jake's kind of charisma.

Then came that laughter again. Sultry. Psychotic. Unreal.

"Oh, Jake. Is this supposed to be impressive? Cuz it ain't."

"Put a lid on it, Lorna."

He felt her behind him, could almost smell her stale sex and cigarette breath. His hair prickled at the memories buried in his brain, but running wild in his body.

Fear is unbecoming in a dead man.

And so he turned to face her.

A demon-whore grinned at him out of the shallow

pane of shadow in the back of the studio. At the first lick of his gaze, she took root in the room, and glided into the light, bringing the darkness in a swirling wake behind her, until she hovered over him.

Long dark hair cascaded around her exaggerated features, the smile frighteningly wide. She had not rotted in the grave, but kept on partying, harder and heavier than ever.

Nothing living could be so used up, yet her eyes sparkled with immortal carnality. A longing to have him again, if only he could measure up—

"*Look how ugly you are. You never were any goddamn good.*"

"Just shut up and watch, you fucking cow. I am stronger than you now."

Mathias looked around with his good eye, but saw and heard only Jake, coming toward him again. No one else in the room.

Jake scooped him up by the armpits. "Alley oop!" he grunted, then slammed Mathias into the trunk of the cross, holding him up by his shirt.

He strapped one arm to the arm of the cross at the bicep and wrist, then the other, until they bore his weight. Mathias kicked and arched his feet, trying to find a perch on the cross, but his legs hung free, dangling in space.

Jake stepped back to admire it like one of those maddening "magic eye" stereogram pictures, frowning until it occurred to him what was missing.

Up to now, Mathias had only gotten a deluxe package version of the initiation into the inner circle of the Church of Eternal Life. But tonight was kind of special, and Mathias seemed like just the guy to test-drive the ultimate version.

Jake had to compromise on historical authenticity, but he figured the Romans would've gladly used a Black & Decker nail gun if they'd had one lying around. It made nailing the kid's hands to the cross as simple as one-two-three.

And finally, a lacquered wreath of thorns, gouging the last inch of skin off Mathias's forehead as Jake crowned him with it.

Now it was art.

Jake threw the lever on a hydraulic lift built into the base, and the cross rose up another two feet in the air. Mathias screamed with the weight of his body suspended from his scrawny arms. His hands swelled up like surgical gloves, ripening from deep red to eggplant purple.

"This is where it starts to get real, isn't it? When you're up on that cross?"

Mathias mewled. Hot tears streamed down his face, cutting streams in the crusted blood. Jake slapped him across the face to get his full attention.

"So you'll wanna answer me now, when I speak."

"Yes! Yes! I'm sorry! I—AAAUGH!" A hollow, muffled pop came from Mathias's left shoulder as it dislocated from its socket. His shoes scrambled to prop him up, and when he slipped, the knobby end of his upper arm jutted out against his bloody shirt like a cock.

"You've probably never felt closer to your Lord and Savior than you do right now. Am I right? Do you feel his suffering?"

Nodding frantically, Mathias was almost beyond hearing, beyond anything but wanting it to end.

"AUGH! Yes, I . . ."

"Good. Then pray to him." Eyes blazing, Jake stepped in behind the blinking red light atop Camera One. "Pray for him to save you. Cuz believe me, he's the only one who could."

Mathias began sniveling, on automatic prayer pilot. But he could barely get a spoonful of air into his lungs with each stabbing breath.

"Oh Lord!" he screeched. "Christ Jesus, please help me! AUGH! Oh, my God . . . !"

Jake slapped him again.

"Come on! You can do better than that!"

Mathias lurched out of automatic, looked down at Jake, saw his burning demon eyes.

And in that moment, he knew.

Knew that he was dying.

And that his moment of truth had come.

He had been raised to love the Lord, and never strayed from his faith. Not even with Emmy, who was responsible for all this. Who had led him away from his flock and down the darkened path, and dragged him to his death.

He had done nothing wrong, except loving her. He saw that now, with horrible clarity. Mom was right. Uncle Douglas was right. And he had been wrong. Oh, so sorrowfully wrong.

"I'm sorry," he whimpered; and in that moment, something broke free inside him.

In that moment of confession, he remembered that he was already saved . . .

. . . *and there was Jesus, when he closed his eyes: up on the cross atop Golgotha, framed by a blue sky rife with swarms of almost-invisible angels. It was a strong and clear-eyed Jesus—white, long-haired, and radiant—looking courageously skyward while the blood from his wounds flowed down, becoming red mist on the wind, splashing Mathias's face.*

Mathias lifted his head as well, eyes squeezed shut, as if to see what Jesus saw.

"Oh Jesus, oh Jesus, oh Jesus, please! PLEASE look down upon me, and see that I suffer as you have suffered . . ." Sobbing uncontrollably now, fighting to breathe, hardly reacting as his other shoulder dislocated. ". . . and know that my heart belongs to you! Only you, my blessed Savior! Know that my faith is true, and reach down with your blessed hands to save me from this nightmare!"

Mathias opened his eyes. Jake was looking at him with wonder, all the loneliness of hell etched into his expression.

"Please, Lord God! Let no demon torment me! I am your servant, and I know that with you all things are possible, Lord! Yea, as you can move mountains, you can move me from this hell! I believe with all that I am, Lord! *Deliver me, now!*"

Jake watched Mathias, head cocked as if the echoes of the crucified boy's prayer still rang in his ears. Like he was waiting for God to smite him.

Mathias looked around, hopeful for a moment.

The moment passed.

And nothing happened.

"So . . ." Jake purred, "how'd that work out for ya?"

A fresh terror blossomed inside Mathias.

"Cuz the fact is, that Jesus never saved anyone. Sure as hell not a little pissant like you."

It was the blackest terror imaginable.

Total abandonment by God.

Jake came closer, until Mathias's blood and tears spattered his face. Something dark bloomed like a cloud of ink just behind him, sucked at the marrow of his misery, and laughed.

Mathias could see and hear her, now, too.

"PLEASE!" he screamed, one final time . . .

. . . but when he closed his eyes, there was no Jesus to be found. Just a dead man rotting on a lonely cross, withered skin sloughing off of greasy bone . . .

Mathias tried to scream, but his vocal cords were scoured raw. A cracked, broken kazoo sound came from his flapping mouth, even before Jake put his hands on him, and steered his face toward the monitor.

Mathias's feet could not touch the floor, but his soul had reached the bottom.

On the screen, a rolling black cloudscape filled the space behind the cross. But it was not just an effect. He could not look behind him, but he could feel it at his back: a hunger of infinite emptiness, a hole in eternity being torn with the weapon of his pain, with the blood of his sacrifice.

The whole back of the studio had opened up on another dimension, ravenous and unspeakably vast.

And whirling in the void were motes and leaves that he knew were the souls of the dead.

The studio seemed to tilt, the cross to quiver, as if teetering on the threshold, awaiting only the slightest push from Jake to send him—and perhaps the whole world after it—into this nightmare black sky.

"Take a good look at yourself," Jake crooned. "That's *you* on the cross. Just like your hero. And every bit as useless to me."

The demon at his side laughed huskily. *"I love to watch a man piss himself."*

Jake shook Mathias out of his fugue, wrenched his face around to stare into Jake's eyes.

"The good news is, you get to see him real soon. Unless, of course, I squeeze your eyes out."

Jake and Lorna laughed.

Mathias screamed louder.

"Yeah, fuck it. Let's do that."

From across the yard, the ladies could hear Mathias's screams ratchet up higher . . . and the laughter of not just Jake, but a chorus of women, as well.

Christian heard it, too. Pushing with his feet and bracing his broken ribs with his good arm, he dragged himself across the floor, toward Jasper's body. The screaming had steeped him in despair, but the toxic laughter only made him push harder.

Eddie and Gray heard it all, too, as Eddie repaired a hinge that was torn off the wall.

Eddie froze, as the sound got even worse.

"Did I say you could stop?" Gray hissed.

Jake's thumbs slid into Mathias's sockets up to the second knuckle before they met bone. Blood and orb jelly squelched out and oozed down his hands, into his sleeves.

Mathias's breathless screeching built in pitch and volume until Jake punched through the bony orbits to spear the brain, then twisted his neck with an audible crack.

Emmy broke down and sobbed when the screams cut out, and the wind resumed singing outside. Esther and Evangeline retreated into their own solitary despair. Even the giggling stopped.

Christian reached Jasper, laid his head across the dead chest in exhaustion and sorrow. Blood seeped up through Jasper's shirt, sticking to his face.

He reached into Jasper's front trousers pocket. Pulled out a lighter and flicked it.

In the darkness, at least he had light.

More, he had fire.

Jake pulled his red thumbs out of Mathias's eyeholes, shook the blood off, admired his handiwork.

What a good boy am I, he thought.

The swirling blackness behind Mathias swirled like water down a drain, turned back into green paint on a wall. Jake's afterglow faded as well.

"Well, you better hope you can do better than that," jeered

Lorna, right behind him. Always at his back, whispering, twisting knives . . .

"*Oh, fercrissakes . . .*"

"*You can't even keep the Door open . . .*"

"*MOM, GOD DAMN IT . . . !*"

And just like that, he was taken back . . .

Chapter Thirty

Suddenly, Jake was back at Lorna's place: a ramshackle white-trash redneck pigsty, circa 1973. Lorna's eyes were all too human then, but pickled in whiskey and malice.

She sneered down at the whimpering twelve-year-old Jake, slapping him repeatedly. She was only half dressed in her filthy lingerie. Behind her, an ugly man was putting on his shirt.

"You make me sick, you piece of shit! Spyin' on me, when I'm doin' my business?"

"I wasn't, Momma! Augh!"

She slapped him some more. Looked contemptuously down.

"Yeah, that's why you got your pants down, in my closet, with your thing stickin' out. I guess you couldn't find your homework."

"Momma, no!"

"My God, y'all are disgusting," the ugly man said.

"And you just paid to fuck me. So get outta my house. My boy's got a cock twice as big as yours, and he's only twelve years old."

The ugly man went out the door, muttering, slammed it shut behind him. Lorna looked down at Jake with a horrible knowingness.

"Oh, honey. You just wanna know what it's like to be a man. I understand that. My own daddy popped my cherry

when I was eight. I was way too small. But you, you're nice and large."

Her face moved closer, more intimate and frightening.

"Momma, no . . ."

"Time you figured out that men are scum, and women aren't no better. It's just the way of the world, Jake. Ugly and dumb. But my God, you feel nice."

"Momma . . ."

"Time to show you how it's done."

Chapter Thirty-one

Jake opened his eyes; and if he could spare the fluid, he might have shed a tear.

It was painful to think about his past, his hellish fucking childhood. Painful to be faced with the forces that molded him: his perspective on the world, and on women in particular. To be thrown back there was to remember how horribly twisted he was, right from the root.

And to remember how hard he'd had to fight.

To become the man he was today.

Resurrecting had been weird enough; but strangely, that was hardly a surprise. Not nearly as surprising as dying: something he'd always known was bound to happen, but never accepted as his fate.

But why, in his moment of triumph, did he have to be hounded by *her*, of all people? By Lorna, who had mercifully drunk herself dead by the time he turned twenty? Who had existed only in his nightmares and deeply closeted memories for the past twenty years?

But maybe that was the problem.

When he came back, he brought them all back with him.

It was an enormous responsibility, being the Resurrected One. The one upon whom the entire bleak fate of future history depended, and around whom it all revolved.

But in his dreams, and his heart, he had always been that man. The power-giver. The power-taker. The alpha and the omega.

He could only guess that she was here to serve, and to obey, just like the rest. That as his powers bloomed, her own would recede to an acceptable background noise.

But try as he might, he could not deny that he was flustered: first by the fag and his yapping mouth, and now by this bitch, and *her* yapping mouth. It undercut his intensity, his assuredness, his dominion.

And that was not acceptable.

When the black door had opened, he had felt it inside him. Felt its power. Felt its power as his own. Known that he was the key, and that sacrifice was the twisting motion by which it was unlocked.

What he needed was more sacrifices, now. How convenient that the house was crawling with 'em.

And when he needed more, the whole world awaited.

Jake took a moment to look around the studio, reground himself in the here and now. After his broaddaylight vision of Lorna's house, the harsh play of spotlight and shadow was almost like nascent, incipient blindness.

He took in the solid walls, ceiling, floor, and its forest of TV gear. He took in the crucified boy, with the three screaming mouths in his head.

He took in Lorna, who would not stop laughing.

"Time to show you how it's done," he said.

From the back of the house, Gray and Eddie could hear Jake's booming footsteps as he stomped out of the studio and thundered down the hall.

"NEXT!" he bellowed, so loud that it seemed to shake the portraits above the fireplace. Or maybe it was just the storm. At this point, it seemed impossible to tell whether there was any difference between the two.

Gray continued to supervise—middle management with a gun—while Eddie packed quick-drying putty into the door frame, where the upper hinge had torn out.

Eddie trembled and averted his eyes as Jake strode into the living room.

Jake laughed. "Not you, Don Quixote. You got a job to do." To Gray, he added, "Bring me that little Bible girl, quick. I'll hold the fort."

Gray dropped his cig on the carpet and ground it out as he crossed the living room and slouched out the back, leaving Jake and Eddie alone beside the open front door. The wind, gusty and curious, flowed into the room and swiped at the fire, driving it back into the embers.

Eddie focused on the job at hand, the stubby putty knife that might as well have been a Q-tip, for all the good it might do him. The words *putty in your hands* flittered through his brain, and he was stung by how hideously apropos they suddenly were.

"Hallelujah, and praise Jesus!" Jake brayed in his ear. "Your work here is almost done."

Eddie said nothing, but he visibly flinched. It made Jake smile, and step closer.

"That really bugs you, doesn't it? My whole 'Praise Jesus' thing. I watch you, and I can see it just stick in your craw."

Eddie set down the putty knife, his back to Jake, said nothing.

"You're thinkin', 'Isn't it enough that this rotten bastard is ruining the life of the woman I love? Why does he have to drag poor old Jesus through the mud, while he's at it?'"

Eddie looked up at Jake, his face as carefully blank as if he were getting lectured about the chlorine levels in the pool.

But staring into those eyes, he saw something he did not expect. Beyond the bloodlust, beyond the horror, beyond the formaldehyde stench and looming danger, there was a deep well of sadness in the monster's expression that Eddie found truly satanic. Eddie always thought the Devil must be very lonely.

It was the look at a man in desperate need of confession.

Eddie found that he could not look away.

"Now I could tell you," Jake resumed, "that my daddy was a traveling preacher. A Holy Roller. And that he fucked my momma for twenty bucks, a blessing, and a jug of corn liquor, and never came back. Never even knew I existed."

Eddie listened, giving up nothing.

"And I could tell you that I ran away from home when I was sixteen, to find that son of a bitch. And when I finally tracked him down, he was this nasty old drunk, in a trailer at a farm show outside Wheeling, West Virginia.

"But God damn if he still didn't have his congregation, just waitin' to hear what batshit craziness he'd spout off next. And damned if he still couldn't make the women wet."

Jake looked away for a second, shook his head and whistled: a weird mixture of heartbreak and grudging admiration.

But when he looked back, the admiration was gone, replaced by a smoldering, wounded rage.

"And I could tell you that I when I told him my story, he called me a liar, and took off his belt, and whipped me with it until I wound up having to beat that motherfucker half to death . . ."

Eddie tried to maintain his emotional neutrality; but the fact was, it really was a horrible tale. And it made perfect sense, in the context of Jake.

Perhaps weirdest of all, Eddie could tell that for once Jake was actually telling the truth.

Suddenly, all the years of wondering how this guy had become such an absolute piece of shit clicked into place. And while it did nothing to excuse his crimes, it went a long way toward explaining them.

Jake caught Eddie thinking, and nodded his head as if to say *yep, that's how it happened.*

Eddie found himself nodding along.

"But that's not the point of my story," Jake said.

He leaned in, confiding, as if they were almost friends: the boss sharing a hot stock tip with the help. And for a moment, Eddie was almost sucked in.

Then he eyed Jake's thumbs, hitched casually in his big black leather belt.

Which was caked in blood and bits of skin.

"The point is," Jake continued, "I learned a lot that day. But the biggest thing was . . . well, let me put it this way . . .

"The thing about Jesus is that you can get away with just about *anything*, as long as you invoke his name. You can start a war. You can burn a witch. You can hang a heathen. You can bang anybody you fucking want. You can milk the poor for everything they've got, and give the rich a cheap way to look like saints.

"All you have to do is say the magic J-word, and you give them hope they can't get anywhere else."

Eddie just listened, not even nodding. Every word out of Jake's mouth might as well have been a cockroach.

"Faith doesn't move mountains of anything but bullshit. *Will* is what makes it all happen, Eddie. If you have the will, you can control your own reality. I'm living proof of that, right?"

Scraping the eyeball crust out from under one thumbnail with the other, Jake let his face cloud over, genuinely troubled by these hard truths.

"I'm not trying to say this is how the world should be. It's just the way it is."

Jake's thumbnail popped wetly out of its rotten bed and dangled from his thumb by a streamer of pus.

"And you can tell yourself all you want that the good guys always win, and the meek will inherit the earth. But that's not the way it fucking works. You know it. And I know it. Right?"

Eddie closed his eyes and sighed: not with contempt, but with utter despair.

"Am I wrong," Jake pressed, "or am I right, on this particular point?"

Eddie did not want to answer, did not want to open his eyes. But Jake stepped closer, close enough to touch; and he would sooner cut his own hand off than suffer Jake's hands upon him.

So he opened his eyes; and the sight made him shrink back, shrivel into himself, as if Jake's gaze alone was giving him cancer.

Jake's unblinking eyes were dry as hard candy, but they pulsated red, as if swollen with thick neon blood that blazed bright as the fireplace.

And inside them was a glistening, eternal damnation.

Eddie seemed to see himself falling, sucked out of the windows of his own eyes and plummeting into the bottomless, ravenous fires of hell that waited inside Jake. You would burn forever there. You would never stop burning and falling.

I am the gate, he heard Jake's voice echo inside his head, though the undead lips were not moving. *On the right hand is the fire. On the left hand lies the dark.*

And I am in the center.

Where the darkness burns.

For a moment, the room behind Jake seemed to vanish completely, and in its place, a black billowing void full of screaming vapors, full of nothing at all . . .

None shall come unto resurrection, except through me . . .

. . . and that was when Eddie broke his gaze from Jake's, and turned his back.

The second the spell broke, Eddie collapsed against the door frame, panting. Every sweat gland opened up and doused him like a fever, but he shivered all the way down to the veins in his bones.

Nothing short of getting sprayed with Esther's blood could have pulled such a reaction out of him. Or so he would have thought.

But seeing the fate that might await his soul was too much. Too much for any mortal man to bear.

And just when he thought it couldn't get any worse, Jake laid a brotherly, crushing hand on his shoulder.

"So that should tell you something about how your bread is actually buttered," Jake nearly whispered in his ear. "You think about that. And you let me know when you make up your mind. Cuz Judgment Day has finally come. And you might even come in handy. But believe me, you will be judged."

Chapter Thirty-two

It had been quiet for a long time now.

No screaming, no crying. *Maybe it's over*, Emmy thought. Maybe Jake saw the light, and repented. Or the devil in him had been driven out.

Emmy stared out the barred window, seeing nothing but pale walls and dark curtains. She might as well have been staring at the floor, for all the information it gave her.

But given what she'd witnessed, was there any other explanation?

Jake was dead for three days. Then he got up. It was not a miracle, but a mockery of the resurrection, and a desecration of the body that had been so powerful a messenger for God's word, in life.

Hell would try to undo all the church's good works like that, because that's what hell did: it turned truths to lies, and weakness to evil.

The others in the cell with her were proof of that. Whatever truth there was in their accusations, they hadn't seemed surprised by Jake—oh, by his return, certainly.

But the vulgar, violent beast that murdered that poor man, blasphemer or not, had only seemed like the one they knew all along.

The one who fooled only her.

No, there could be no other answer. Jake had a demon inside him. But the question now was, how long before he died had it hidden inside his heart?

Maybe . . . all along?

She jumped at the sound of keys, jumped again when the holding cell door flew open. And there was Gray, grimacing at them all.

Growing up, she never watched that many movies, but she always found herself identifying every new face she saw with a movie star.

This one—this sullen, rage-drunk, hag-ridden man— looked like a young Lee Marvin, who would never grow into an old one.

Gray stepped inside and smiled tightly at the terrified women. He pointed at each of them with his gun. Emmy found it easier to watch the nickel-plated eye of the weapon than the face of the man holding it. The obvious pleasure he took in their fear made her feel dirty, as if some part of her were getting raped every time he looked at her.

"Eeny, meenie, miney . . ." he recited, as if bored. "Ah, fuck it. He wants you."

The gun pointed at Emmy.

She stepped forward, dizzy, feeling like she was falling out the door as Evangeline and Esther stepped back like the runners-up in a beauty contest, both terrified and ashamed at their relief.

The door slammed shut behind her.

Gray had to push her, to remind her to walk.

Above, the moon was bloodred, peeping down through the leafy cathedral dome of the old oak tree in the Connaway backyard. The wind howling across the desert took on a throaty, panpipe tone as it blew through the eaves of the big house, inescapably spreading out before her.

So quiet. Where had everyone gone? The screaming

was so loud, and the laughter . . . had it only just ended, or was it longer?

Emmy's mother always said she had a wandering mind. *Senile from birth*, was one of the nicer ways she put it. A little devil in her head, was what she meant.

Emmy's mother saw demons hiding behind every human flaw. She believed fallen angels blew on the wind like germs, looking for homes in uncovered, yawning mouths, unbaptized babies, and all men, everywhere.

When she saw that she couldn't beat the demon out of Emmy, or the right attitude in, she'd taken shelter in her own illness.

But Emmy had found her own cure.

The Lord was, quite literally, Emmy's tether to the world. When she dedicated herself to his work, her mind ran clear and true as an alpine brook.

But tonight, prayer had only tranquilized her, helped bring her in line with the paralyzing shock. She didn't know how long they'd stood in the holding cell. Surely it must be morning soon . . .

The back door seemed miles away across the lawn, or maybe her mind made it feel that way, by packing her thoughts with distractions.

Gray tugged on her arm, almost pulling her off balance. Her feet wanted to please him, and the rest of her was so terrified of his anger, that she would have followed him off a cliff. But she planted her foot and started, feebly, halfheartedly, to resist him.

It didn't matter what he'd do to her, her heart told her. If he killed her now, that might be best.

What awaited her inside, she knew, would be much worse.

Gray hissed smoke out his nose in disgust. The leaves rattling in the breeze sounded like mindless applause.

That was when they heard the laughter behind them.

Gray whipped around and searched the shadows between the house and the garage. Crazy chuckling and muttered curses strung out of his mouth; he reminded Emmy just then of her mother, seeing and hearing demons everywhere.

Except that Emmy heard it, too.

The sound was like a spray of icy water, stretched thin on the wind, but a shock on her exposed skin, not just her ears . . . as if everywhere it touched, the wrongness of the sound raised goose bumps. It pulled her out of her shock as she cowered behind him, looking over his shoulder.

"Oh, my God . . ." She searched her mind, but no prayers came.

Gray looked at her, his face as white as his bloodshot eyes weren't. "You heard that, too?"

Emmy took hold of his arm, tears streaming.

"What is *happening?* Do you know?"

The demon laughed again. It was a lewd, lascivious woman—no, higher, giddy like a girl, or a woman abused so badly in childhood that her voice never grew up. She was playing hide-and-seek, and couldn't wait to be found . . . or she was the seeker, and could not contain her amusement at how badly they were hiding.

When Emmy used to play hide-and-seek with the neighborhood kids, she always found the best hiding place; nobody ever found her. She'd stay hidden as they gave up right away and went to play something else, stayed hidden until she wet her pants and her stomach rumbled, too proud, then too ashamed, to run for the safe place.

They should run for the safe place now.

But where was safe?

Suddenly, she wanted him to take her into the house.

But Gray was frozen, too.

Emmy stared, dumbfounded. Up until this moment, it had never occurred to her that even this vicious killer might be out of his depth.

"Don't *you* even know what's out there . . . ?"

All at once, he raised a shaking hand to slap her, looked equally stunned by the fact that he didn't. The hand just hung there as they stared at each other, searched each other's eyes for proof that they weren't going insane.

But what they saw didn't make things better.

"NO, I DON'T!" Gray howled, and the admission seemed to deflate him. "Okay? I don't know *anything!*"

His voice faltered, hand fell.

High above them, up in the branches of the oak tree, the shrill demon voice let out haunting, rollicking giggles. Such games, such *fun*, for the suffering on earth.

Emmy watched the voice shudder through him, even as she shuddered herself. Gray was just following Jake's orders. Just as she had . . .

"We have to get out of here," Emmy begged. "All of us. Even you . . ."

"Even *me?*" Gray retreated into a hateful glower. She could see that she had somehow, amazingly hurt his feelings . . .

. . . and though it hadn't seemed impossible, she suddenly felt pity for this poor, lost, frightened man. Couldn't believe that she'd forgotten even he had a soul. And was instantly ashamed.

"Oh, no!" she cried, frantic on too many levels to count. "I'm sorry! I didn't mean . . ."

"You didn't mean *what?*"

Words failed her; and without thinking, she threw herself sobbing into his arms like a child.

Gray's arm enfolded her. He was stiff, unyielding, but also shaking; and if she could have seen his eyes, she would have noted, in that moment, that he looked almost sane.

The laughter circled overhead, like a murder of mad crows. He squeezed her tighter, as if to comfort them both. She squeezed tighter in return.

Then Gray's gun pressed softly into her back; and south of his belt line, something else jabbed insistently at her thigh. His breath, stale cigarettes and something deep down gone to rot inside, came faster and harsher in her ear.

Oh God, she blurted in her head, too quick to take the small blasphemy back. He was, Lord help her, aroused.

"Please," she whispered. "Just help us. Please . . ."

Gray slid the barrel, slowly, up Emmy's back, getting some unspeakable kicks out of the contact.

The wind whistled and howled with laughter.

Gray clung tighter against her, even as he brought the gun up to Emmy's head. Barrel to temple. And chambered a round.

Emmy froze: too frightened to move, too horrified even to pray. She was no longer squeezing him, but her arms were still wrapped around him in a hideous charade of affection.

"Why?" she whimpered into his shoulder.

"Because I don't give a shit about you," he said in a flat-ironed voice. "I think you're an idiot. Come on."

Chapter Thirty-three

Christian rationed the lighter. Even if he only sparked it to check out each item he dug out from under the sink, it still burned his left thumb. *Poor baby, it almost matches the other one now.*

He lay on his left side on a wadded-up bath mat and some towels, with his ruined right arm curled up against his cracked rib cage. Blessed shock had finally set in, and the reality of his predicament had settled in, as well. Perhaps he was delirious and looking at the same things over and over, but the bathroom cabinet was a bottom-less cornucopia of household products he should have been able to make into a flamethrower or a lunar lander, if he'd been more mechanically inclined.

Jake loved his hair. Hated insects.

Christian could think of plenty of ideas, sure. He could indeed use some of the old aerosol hair spray cans and his lighter to burn the fuckers when they came for him, if he only had two hands.

He could try to make Molotov cocktails out of Jake's cologne collection, but they were alcohol based, and though their stench would make baboons impotent, it wouldn't burn too long, and the bottles were thick, tacky smoked-glass bricks, all but impossible to shatter.

He could try to set fire to the door and the exterior wall, maybe punch a hole in the drywall and pour the cologne and a couple hair spray cans inside, and lie in the bathtub, covered in wet towels. Wait for the firemen.

Or he could give himself a makeover.

Jasper would know what to do. Christian tried not to cry. Jasper always knew what to do . . .

Jake's face lit up as Emmy and Gray came in the back door. Emmy choked on her tongue, eyes swarming with hope and fear.

"There you are, my shining star! You just wait right there."

All this hostility, all this doubt from the peanut gallery, was draining him dry. Right now, he needed what only Emmy could give.

Jake swooped in on her, taking Emmy by the arm, steering her back toward the inner sanctum.

Gray waggled his gun at Eddie from across the room, but put a hand on Jake's shoulder, stopping him. "Jake," he mumbled out the corner of his mouth. "We gotta talk, man. This is . . ."

"This is not the time."

His beady eyes pinged the warning tone in Jake's voice, but he jerked on Jake's arm in frustration. "Jake . . ."

The lights flickered hard, and the walls began to rumble, as if a big cargo plane passed low overhead, or a subway car was burrowing beneath them. For a moment, the wild glare of the fireplace was the only light, but Jake could have sworn he saw the gleam of a brighter fire pouring out of his own eyes, spilling over Gray's crumpled expression, and the blank slate of Emmy's undone, empty face.

"Don't make me doubt you now. You take care of your shit. I'll take care of mine."

Gray shuddered and took his hand back like it was

scorched, turned and crossed toward Eddie with the gun cocked like he was going to brain the wetback.

Jake smiled like a bashful newlywed groom and yoked her neck in the crook of his arm.

As fast as her little legs could keep up, Jake and Emmy headed back down the hall.

Jake walked fast, half dragging her along. Emmy moved like in a dream, trying to awaken.

"Jake, please, you have to stop . . . this is all wrong . . ."

Jake's tone was soothing, but his words crashed together in her head, like a roomful of devil's advocates fighting for the mic. "Oh, sweetheart. I'm back, aren't I? Just like the Good Book said, praise Jesus. Praise Jesus!"

Stopping and folding her in arms like amorous pythons, he tenderly kissed the top of her head.

. "Yes," she whimpered. "Praise Jesus."

"Right. And right now I need you to make me look good for the cameras. Cuz God knows I gotta look good for the cameras. Jesus would want it that way."

She nodded, but he was already sweeping her along to the door.

They entered the studio.

Jake turned on the lights, dazzling her for a moment. When she stopped blinking, her eyes fixed on the towering cross parked in front of the green screen, and the all-too-familiar figure hanging from it.

Sweet, gentle, patient, faithful Mathias.

Scourged, mutilated, eyeless Mathias.

Emmy screamed.

"I know, I know." Jake took hold of and massaged her shoulders. "It looks bad. But that's only his body . . ."

Emmy went into shock, turning to ice water inside and leaking out of her shoes.

Jake held her up in his kneading hands. "Now . . . come on . . . you're not gonna do me any good like that . . ."

Jake whipped her around and slapped her. The flush of outraged blood brought the semblance of life back into her face. She blinked, tears streaming, awakening to it all over again.

"There you are. Now shut up and listen, and don't you worry about him. He's gone on to meet his maker. That's what he wanted, and that's what he got. Now you just gotta take care of me, the way you've always done. Take care of the Church of Everlasting Life . . ."

Emmy was speechless, skydiving into his bottomless eyes.

"You still believe in me, don't you?"

Emmy thought about miracles and demons, and all the subtle things she ignored, and all the shocking things she buried, that had tried to show her what Jake Connaway really was. No demon could have made her fall so hard; no devil could have twisted the love of Christ into his own sick image. What possessed Jake, seething inside the decaying shell of his corpse, had always been there.

Now it was all that was left.

Eyes locked on Jake's, Emmy involuntarily started shaking her head.

In the holding cell, Evangeline was now at Emmy's place by the window. She could see Jake and Emmy's shadows entangled on the curtain blocking the studio's sliding glass doors. "That poor little girl."

Esther's unfocused voice cracked, every syllable a whining plea for booze. "What do you think he's going to do?"

Evangeline turned to look at her clueless cell mate . . . just as Esther's soggy, stricken visage burst out of the darkness in seizures of red and blue light.

Behind Evangeline, headlights cut through the gloom of the weed-choked parking lot.

"Look!" Esther cried, rushing over and crowding her beside the barred window.

A car crawled onto the property after someone had opened the gate, rolling its roof lights as it passed by, heading around the back of the house.

A cop car.

Evangeline screamed, "Omigod! HELP!"

She started banging on the window. Esther joined her, banging on the bars with her empty flask.

But the wicked wind wailed and threw their cries back in their teeth, stealing away their screams as the cop car pulled out of sight behind the house, and switched off its lights.

Part VI
The Tale Of The
Dumb-Ass Mexican

Chapter Thirty-four

Brooding wasn't normally an unwelcome pastime for Gray, but with the way the night was dragging on—the load of bullshit housekeeping, the hour wasted overseeing this shiftless beaner on his chores—he'd had plenty of time to chew on it. Had taken refuge in it, to forget about the other shit that seemed to be trying to drive him over the edge.

Like the starving castaways in that old Bugs Bunny cartoon, whenever Gray looked at the sneaky little Mexican, he saw him slowly transform: not into a hamburger or a hot dog, but into something Gray longed even more desperately to consume.

He'd finally put together why it was that if Eddie looked him in the eye one more time, he was going to have to cut his face off and feed it to him.

Gray lurked in the doorway as Eddie put the door in place. It looked fine if you shut it, but the putty holding the upper hinge in place was still soft, and the door tilted and dragged on the porch if you opened it wide. Close enough for government work, but since they were camping out here . . .

Eddie looked around and fixed him with those sad, hangdog eyes, asking for it, giving away nothing.

It wasn't the race thing. Gray had a closetful of prejudices about the Hispanic race, but he hated them no more nor less than any other race, including his own, which was six layers of rootless American mutt.

It was his fucking eyes; and God damn, but sitting around dwelling on it, he'd had time to make the connection to memory, or drag imagination into the present.

Jake and Gray used to have all kinds of fun in Mexico.

Nobody knew Jake there, but they felt his mojo, and they treated him like a god, so long as he kept tipping. Gray swam along in his wake, bored by most of the action, but always ready to laugh at the absurdity of it all. What they lacked in wealth, taste, and refinement, the Mexicans more than made up for with their eagerness to make clowns and beasts of themselves for pocket change.

Mexicali was the only place Jake could let it all hang out like the old days, the small-time rock-star days, when they ran the string of whores in Palm Springs, of which Evangeline was the only survivor.

The last time they went down there, two years ago, they were still shitfaced at daybreak when they pulled out of the gravel lot of the Casa Delicias, where Jake always left the whores crying his name, and Gray just left them crying.

Jake had a doggy bag sucking his dick for the ride home, and the bitch had a cigarette lit in her claws as she worked Jake's cock with her tongue while he tried to steer his brand-new Hummer H2 without spilling the fifth of fine agave tequila they shared.

She burned him; the cherry must have broken off her smoke and fallen under his scrotum in his boxers, because he went berserk. Dumped the tequila in his lap and kicked the toothless skank out of it. Gray was not glad to have her crawl over him, kicking them both like a jackrabbit with her sandals, which had Goodyear white-wall tires for soles.

The Hummer swerved across the main drag, spooking chickens and chicle-peddling urchins, and sideswiped a line of parked cars.

The Hummer H2 may have been a fat-ass pussy yuppie bastardization of kickass military hardware, but it coasted down the line without stalling, ripping doors and crumpling frames on Detroit's and Tokyo's finest like a .30-06 rifle bullet through a line of beer cans.

Jake slewed to a stop sideways on the main drag. Gray looked for cops and saw nobody but a hot dog vendor ("Now with more dogs!") out on the street. The *federales* all knew him down here, respected him as a Gold Circle Club visitor, but most of the cars had California and Arizona plates.

Jake looked around for only the blink of an eye before he put on his shades, threw the H2 into Drive, and cocked that smile Gray had learned to love.

"I'm not letting this shit ruin my day," he said.

Jake threw the whore out by her hair, peeled out, and made a run for the border.

They left Mexicali on a side road to a checkpoint where the two customs guys could be counted on to wave them through. Big fans of the show, and of the whores they often dropped off. *You can't take them with you*, they always said, *but we'll always hold them for you . . .*

Everybody knew how the game was supposed to be played, except for this one dumb, fucking *patrulero*.

Not four miles from the border, this shitty old white Datsun sedan came dusting up to their bumper. Jake waved him on to pass, but floored it.

The sedan flipped on a pitiful single blue light, and a siren that might have been a cranky parrot with a bull-horn.

Jake ran another two miles before he decided, *fuck it*, and pulled over.

"How much cash you got?" he asked.

Gray patted himself down and found only two hundred, the dregs of an eight ball of crank and a glass pipe. "Fuck this guy. We gave at the office."

Then this bowlegged old taco-bender came scraping up to the Hummer like Slowpoke Rodriguez's granddad. Gray could barely see his sweat-stained brown *béisbol* cap over the driver's-side windowsill as Jake haggled with him.

The highway patrolman explained in choppy English that they were speeding, and he heard they had some trouble in Mexicali, and they needed to come back to sort it out.

Jake offered him a pig-choking wad of cash and told him, in serviceable Spanish, that it would be best for everyone if they could not be caught before they crossed the border, and were never seen in these parts again.

Gray got out of the Hummer, dropping into fine, chalky dust up to his shoelaces, like powdered bone. Unzipping and digging his shrunken cock out to piss, he wondered for about the thousandth time since Friday why they came down to Mexico.

The Founding Fathers were no dummies when they drew the line right here. Everything south of the border was rotten from the ground up.

Gray came around the hood of the huge SUV at a casual stroll, but the highway patrolman didn't even look at him. He just kept chewing Jake's ear off in that sorry-as-hell, hangdog tone. They would have to come back to Mexicali, no matter how much *mordida* they gave him. He was terribly sorry. He knew the legal system in Mexico was corrupt, but somebody had to pick up the pieces, and they'd been caught red-handed making a mess, and most of the victims were their fellow Americans, and didn't they feel bad, coming down here, and behaving in such a way as to give Americans a bad name?

Gray came within arm's reach of the old *patrulero* before he even took any notice, but Gray stopped dead when the highway cop looked at him.

Those eyes. So sad and tired and red rimmed, caked with dust . . .

They knew what he was going to do. They didn't care. They'd seen this stupid fucking movie so many times that they didn't even blame him for what was about to happen. They almost wanted it . . .

Gray unstuck himself from the tar pit in those eyes and wound up with the empty tequila bottle, cracking it across the beaner's sunburned forehead so hard the bottom flew off across the road. The old man dropped like he'd been waiting for the cue, curled up on his left side on the cracked blacktop.

Jake clapped and hooted, fired up the H2, but Gray couldn't just walk away.

That motherfucker looked at him like he was a germ, a mindless thing destined to offer him a communion he'd come to pray for. It was funny, for a second. *Losers commit suicide by cop. Cops commit suicide by Gray.*

But the geek didn't just want to get killed. He just knew how it would all play out—maybe because some higher power would reward his meek acceptance of death in the middle of the road he wasted his life guarding, or maybe because it would just be as neat an end to his meaningless life as any.

Whatever the philosophy behind it, Gray wasn't anybody's puppet. If the guy wanted to die, Gray would let him do it himself . . . after he saw himself in the mirror.

Gray finally jumped in the Hummer and tossed the bottleneck out into the desert. The *patrulero* was still breathing when they left. Gray only cut off his ears and most of his nose, and stuffed them in his mouth.

Five minutes later, at the border, they'd been having problems with the phones all morning, and only a skeleton staff out on the road to take Jake's cash with their eyes closed.

They were as good as their word on one thing. They never went back to Mexicali. Jake went down a couple times by himself, and nothing happened, but Gray couldn't go anywhere, from Tijuana to Matamoros, without seeing the *patrulero*.

Not that the geek was out there, of course. Even if he survived long enough to be found and was stitched back together by the Aztec witch doctors, he doubted the fucker was still out on patrol.

But whenever he got drunk enough, or tweaked for more than a couple days, things started to get blurry. What used to be a pleasant masking of the unbearable seediness of reality now became an unsettling game. Faces ran together when they kissed or danced, soul-shadows licking out at each other, feeding on vital essences, while he sat alone. They blurred and melted, and usually, they just turned into pigs, what fun to watch, but now, their noses and ears disappeared, and they all seemed to look at him like they knew what he'd done, and what he was going to do, and none of it was worth resisting.

Like they—all of them, everyone but Gray—knew how it would all end.

He got in trouble, bad trouble, whenever he tried to party in Mexico. He saw things, and tried to stab or shoot them. Jake thought it was hilarious at first, but finally stopped taking him when he went down.

He would give anything to go back and kill that fucking *patrulero*, to erase that mocking uncertainty that he was still out there, or whatever demon looked out of his mangled face, which was unkillable, though he would gladly try.

*   *   *

Now, he saw it looking at him out of Eddie's eyes, and he found himself painting the rest of the picture: a bushy Pancho Villa mustache, instead of Eddie's pencil-thin shit stain; the gray-whiskered jowls, the melanoma-spotted, deep brown complexion; the wheezing, dripping hole below and between his droopy, apologetic eyes. The restlessly chewing mouth, occasionally opening wide enough for the cartilage-wad of an ear to peek out.

Gray wanted to see it and lose himself in those eyes and everything behind it, right here and now, fuck Jake, fuck this whole charade . . .

Because it was so much easier to contemplate killing Eddie than to deal with the ghost that laughed at him, whenever he went outside.

Part VII
God's Law

Chapter Thirty-five

Eddie heard the cop car—saw the telltale spray of tri-color light painting the gloom of the front yard in patri-otic red, white, and blue—but he kept sporting his best poker face. He'd passed up a dozen even chances to plant the claw of his hammer in Gray's forehead or chest, as he seemed to lapse into a daydream whenever Eddie stood still to finish the door.

He would do nothing to excite this psycho fuckhead, until he was sure he could live through it.

"Oh, boy . . ." Gray sprang into ten-cups-of-coffee alertness, ducking in the doorway. "Don't do anything stupid. I can turn this place into Baghdad in five sec-onds flat."

Eddie figured this for a conservative estimate. He hammered the pin through the middle hinge, affixing the door.

"Just wave and smile," Gray growled. "Shut the door. And come with me."

Eddie tugged the heavy oak door into the jamb. He had to force it into place; the top hinge was sagging out of the frame. Oh well, you get what you pay for . . .

Dropping the hammer into the toolbox, Eddie hus-tled ahead of Gray down the hallway to the studio.

Eddie threw open the door, Gray right behind him.

Jake hovered over Emmy. Both whipped around at the sound. Mathias dangled from the cross behind them.

Eddie averted his eyes, but could not unsee it.

"We got cops," Gray said.

Jake looked groggy, as if Emmy had hypnotized him. Under the hot studio lights, his face appeared to be melting. "How many?"

"Just one car. But . . ."

"Okay, okay, lemme think for a second . . ."

Eddie couldn't stop staring at the crucified Mathias. He started shaking, bushwacked by the horror. Emmy looked like she was ready to bolt. And she couldn't stop crying.

"You stay right here!" Jake hissed at her. "You hear me? You move so much as a muscle, you make so much as a squeak, and you don't wanna know what's gonna happen."

He got up in her face. She cringed away from the heat of his stare. "You believe *that*, don'tcha?"

Emmy nodded. Musical pattering of fluid on concrete, as she lost control of her bladder.

Jake stood upright, spine popping like dud firecrackers. "I'll get Esther. Don't fuck this up." His mind still seemed miles away, Eddie noticed, but maybe it was miles ahead.

Gray herded Eddie back to the living room. Jake went out the sliding glass door and stomped across the lawn to the holding cell.

Leaving Emmy alone in the studio (*not alone, no—*) too terrified to move.

Chapter Thirty-six

Out in the big dirt parking lot, Sheriff LeGrange nosed the cruiser in behind a huge classic Cadillac, parked, tamped a plug of Red Man into his cheek, got out and looked around as if the cameras were still rolling.

Deputy Peet ran a quick radio check, grateful for somebody to talk to. The old man had run himself ragged when Pastor Jake's hunky corpse turned up naked in the desert: taking his meals at his desk and sleeping—or trying to—on a cot.

His dumpy, spinster daughter finally came in to the station to take him home this morning, but he returned before dinner, croaking for a dragnet when he heard the first calls about the funeral home massacre on his bedside scanner.

Nothing had come of their search of Apple Valley; but within hours of the case going out on the database, San Bernardino PD tipped them that the good minister's car had been found this morning, parked in a visitors' lot in a condo complex. SBPD forced entry into an empty unit after a nosy neighbor ID'd Connaway from a photo, and reported sounds of fighting, three nights before.

Some personal effects and evidence of the deceased minister, including several pints of his blood, turned up in the condo, which belonged to a Sugar Sutherland, a.k.a. Joelle Stainback, twenty-three, waitress, dancer, and sometime Internet porn talent, originally of Riverside.

Riverside Sheriff's chipped in the news that the trailer of Margaret Stainback, fifty-four (unemployed), burned down night before last; the two bodies inside had been tagged as Sugar and her mother.

Of Sugar's live-in boyfriend, Frankie Petrasino, twenty-six (surprise! Unemployed), no sign so far, leading the hunt to focus on him.

Peet wasn't the only one who connected the dots and figured Frankie stabbed the minister for jocking his girlfriend, torched his special lady at Mom's place, then lit out south. But all of that was just news headlines, no more savage or inhuman than the typing, or the sober serif font that related them.

She saw the funeral home carnage with her own eyes.

She hardly knew Lew Oliff, the Unitarian minister whose face got ripped off, but she got sick in the women's room ("No girl deputy of mine ralphs in front of the boys," he'd warned) until she'd rediscovered yesterday's breakfast.

She was only a deputy, and young, and a girl to boot, but she knew no angry boyfriend would carry a grudge this far.

Sheriff LeGrange was still hopped-up on the adrenaline rush of playing the grizzled bulldog of the law on the news. Peet would have kidded him about it, but he hadn't said ten words since they left the chapel.

The wind whipped all around them as they convened.

LeGrange screwed his Stetson down on his head. "Lord, it's an ugly night."

They checked out the parking lot, noted the sacrilegious bumper stickers on Jasper's truck: FOCUS ON YOUR OWN DAMN FAMILY and IN CASE OF RAPTURE . . . TAKE YOUR SHITTY CAR WITH YOU!

"Does that look right to you?" he asked.

Peet shook her head. "Want me to call those plates in, quick?"

"I'll tell ya right now, that one's Jasper Ellis. And what he's doin' here, I don't know. But check out the others. See what we got, before we go in."

"What about that thing?" she said, nodding at the massive white Cadillac half hidden behind the house.

"If I'm not mistaken," said LeGrange, "that belonged to the deceased."

Chapter Thirty-seven

Jake opened the holding cell and thrust a big paw inside. "Esther. I need you, baby. Quick."

Esther stumbled back, but Jake had her by the arm and snatched her out of the cell, marching her briskly toward the back door.

"Okay, honey, you know the drill. Just put on your game face, and send 'em off smiling."

Her heart thudded triple-time against her chest. "I can't . . ."

"Look, we don't have time to argue . . ."

"Jake, I . . ."

"*Please don't make me have to kill them.* Cuz if I do, I just might not able to stop . . . oh, holy Christ, what happened to your face?"

In the light from the back door, the ripening shiner had already begun to disfigure her cheek. Esther threw a glance back at the holding cell.

"That's great. That's just great . . ." Then he chuckled abruptly, and stroked her hair. "Well, at least they won't blame this one on me . . ."

In the studio, Emmy knelt before the cross and wept.

Mathias's feet dangled free. One of his brown Bass

work shoes had fallen off, and lay on its side like a cap-sized boat in a red pond. Jake's huge footprints splashed droplets of blood up the walls, and tracked gore to and from the cameras, then out the door.

It's okay, then, see? she tried to tell herself. *It's part of the show—*

When Emmy's mother left the Baptist church where she married Emmy's father, she called them all fools. They suffered her outburst; everyone knew she was not well. "God knows all! Sees all! Who's saved, who's damned, it's all in his book!" Their struggle against the Adversary was futile, because God knew the future, and none of them would pass muster.

Emmy stayed with her, cared for her, until the end. When she went out looking for a cause, she wanted to give herself to God in a way that would speak for those left out of everyone's book.

Jake had seemed to tap into the innate Christ in all people, even the lost. When she heard fallen women talk about him, about how his words "put them up on the cross with Jesus," they spoke in awed whispers, sharing a secret as breathlessly mysterious as sex.

Emmy knew about sex, of course, but she was still a virgin. Mama was wrong or lying, what she said about Daddy, and Mathias had never pressured her.

In her heart, there was an empty cross; and in those dreams—the hot, troublesome dreams that made her sick with guilt—she saw Jake on the cross. He was naked, and uninjured. Perfect.

In the dreams, he reached out to her, and he flew away with her on glorious white wings.

A stupid dream, even before . . . this.

Mathias had painted the base of the cross with bloody skid marks as he kicked with his stocking foot. Slowly, head swimming, she pulled herself upright.

Tears streaming down her face, sobbing softly as she

took stock of his wounds, she kissed her palm and tried to touch every one. She couldn't take them back—but oh, how she would—so she tried to take their pain into herself.

Out front, the sheriff couldn't say just why, but he approached the door warily, with his head on a swivel.

Behind him, Peet probed the yard and the dark windows with her flashlight, feeling a little chill as the beam picked out the creaky swings clanking in the gusty wind.

Growing up in town, the kids told stories about the Weirdo School; but aside from giving out blue popcorn balls for Halloween, they never lived up to the legend.

Tonight, though, there was no denying that the place felt far weirder than all of those stories combined.

LeGrange spat tobacco juice in the shrubbery and knocked. The heavy door rocked against the jamb, hanging lopsided and loose. Peet noticed it, too, threw him a questioning glance, her hand automatically hovering over the grip of her revolver.

He flashed her a look that said *hold tight*, but it was clear he was ready to go in, too.

Then a woman's voice from inside chirped, "I'm coming!" and both of them eased up one smidgen. But only one.

Even without Jasper's body, the living room was a nightmare tableau: blood and shattered glass everywhere, furniture in disarray, and monsters on every side.

Esther's eyes nearly swooned at Eddie as she crossed the living room. She felt giddy with relief that he was okay, but now her hands started shaking badly. She could do this, she could get through this, but she needed a drink first. Like that scotch on the counter.

Jake handed her the bottle with an eye-rolling sigh, the long-suffering husband of the functioning alcoholic, then stepped to one side of the door and blew her a kiss.

The stench of him queasily recalled the pickled cow's eye she had to dissect in junior high biology. She had never forgiven her father for that.

Esther took a good swig, went to set the bottle on the table, then remembered that it was on its back not four feet from the door. Disorientation had her so fucked up that she almost dropped the bottle before stopping herself, taking one more swig, and setting it down on the bloody carpet, where it promptly fell over and spilled.

Three pairs of eyes were staring at her—Jake, Gray, and Eddie—only one of them sympathetic. But all of them were saying, *for Christ sake, quit fucking around!*

So she forced herself forward, wrenched herself upright and poised. She had done this so many times before that pretending everything was all right was more than second nature. It had become a way of life.

Eddie and Gray stepped back from the door like a precision drill team, giving her access. Eddie's expression was flat and tense, but his eyes were full of love and fear.

Then she opened the door and stepped out on the porch, smoothly pulling it shut it behind her: smile practiced and genuine, hands clasped together tight.

"Sheriff? Deputy?" she said. "How may I help you?"

At her back, the door settled in its frame. Jake, Gray, and Eddie were totally silent, but she could feel them listening hard. She also smelled weed-killer.

"Just checking in, Mrs. Connaway," Sheriff LeGrange said. "We know this is a terrible time . . ."

"Well, thank you, Sheriff. I appreciate your diligence, but . . ."

"I see you've got company."

"Oh, yes." Nodding, whipping up a wistful smile. "I have some friends over. We were out back, watching the storm." She gave them each a meaningful glance. "I think you can understand that I don't want to be alone."

"But there's no problem."

"Oh, no!" Brightly. "Everything's . . ."

"Ma'am," the woman deputy interjected. "How did you receive that bruise on your face?"

"Oh!" Esther gave a little laugh, though her stomach was starting to plummet. "I—it's been a rough week. I've had a little too much to drink, if you couldn't tell already, and, well, I slipped and fell into the counter, just fifteen minutes ago."

It seemed like a reasonable enough explanation. Certainly, it had flown before.

So why were they looking at her like that?

"I really should put some concealer on it, don't you think?" she continued, just a bit giddily. "Or an ice pack, if I were smarter. And I will, when we're done talking. It's just been a terrible . . . what?"

LeGrange could have been a cigar store Indian. Peet wrinkled her nose and looked around for the source of the stench.

Neither one was buying the bullshit.

Only then did Esther start to panic.

And that was, of course, when the screaming began . . .

Chapter Thirty-eight

The following things went down very quickly: feeding each other, as the hellwind fed the flames of Judgment Day.

First, there was Emmy, reaching up on her tiptoes, touching her fingertips to Mathias's lips. She was almost done sobbing, almost done saying good-bye. But she was also nearly out of time.

"Forgive me," she whispered. "Please forgive me for bringing you here."

She lowered herself unsteadily, dragged her fingertips along his bloody chest, and steadied herself there, before turning to kneel in prayer . . .

. . . and the demon was there, directly before her: greasy-eyed, leering, reeking of sex and decay.

"So you like my son," the demon hissed, running horrible hands down the length of its body.

Emmy shrieked, her worst nightmares confirmed.

And before she knew it, she had run straight past the cackling demon and into the curtained sliding glass door. Clawing at the curtains, still shrieking.

Then parting them, and running out into the yard . . .

* * *

The cops were now on red alert. Guns out. All hesitation gone.

"Time to tell us what's happening," LeGrange said. "Now."

Esther wanted to warn them. She really did. But her mouth wouldn't work, and no words would come out.

Evangeline heard the crazy, whooping sobs just outside and leapt to the window just in time to see Emmy running past. "Wait! HELP!!!"

At the front door, the cat was out of the bag.

"Fuck this . . ." Jake said.

Eddie tried to say, "No . . ."

Jake threw open the door, shoved Esther aside, and stepped outside, red eyes flaring.

"Someone lookin' for me? Cuz I'm right here."

The cops reared back at Jake's approach: Peet in alarm, LeGrange in something like awe.

Peet dropped into shooting stance, aimed carefully at the dead center of Jake's chest. "Stand down!" she hollered . . .

. . . just as Sheriff LeGrange dropped to his knees, chanting, "Oh dear God, sweet heavenly savior . . . !"

Peet's jaw dropped. "Bill! What the fuck?"

Jake loomed over LeGrange—wrathful, yet amused— and reached for his face, as if to take him by the hair.

Peet shot Jake three times in the chest.

Each impact clearly stung him, but did not knock him back a single step. No blood came from his wounds. Packing foam floated out of the gaping exit wounds in his back.

Less in terror than despair, Esther screamed.

Jake staggered, but did not fall. He started laughing.

And the sheriff continued to pray.

* * *

Emmy ran around the front of the house, past the wood-pile and chopping block, to the front yard. The light from the porch spilled out across the front lawn to touch the abandoned playground. She braced herself to run through it, when something like lightning struck three times, gunshot thunder right on its heels so loud it almost knocked her on her behind.

Now she froze. Hidden on the edge of the light, unseen by Jake or the police, unable to speak or to scream, or even to breathe.

Watching, as if none of it were real . . .

Peet turned and ran for the cruiser. The dead man shambled after her, audibly popping stitches, but gaining a yard on her with every stride.

Training told her to turn around and shoot, fire over her shoulder; but there were bystanders behind him, and three shots to the chest hadn't even made him bleed.

Jake swiped at her. She dug in and threw herself forward, goosed by the pain of a hank of her hair ripping out of her head in his stinking claws.

She threw a wild glance behind her and saw LeGrange, still kneeling, now angled toward them as he took a careful marksman's stance.

Thank God, she thought, pouring everything she had into the ten yards between herself and the cruiser's open door. The shotgun was there, and if that didn't kill this son of a bitch, it would at least cut him in half. Let him chase her with a bifurcated spine, scuttling like an accordion crab. See how goddamn scary he was then.

Nine yards now, and closing. She could feel him falling behind, could almost feel LeGrange drawing a bead on him. The sheriff was an excellent shot, especially under pressure; and even with the wind howling as it was, she was willing to bet her partner could take out Connaway's legs from there with no problem.

Six yards now, each thudding heartbeat racing her feet to the all-American strobing light show's source. She was so close she could almost smell the leather interior, hear the radio chatter, taste the cordite of her shotgun's imminent muzzle flash.

Then LeGrange fired at last. Aim perfect, as always.

And her chest blew open from behind.

The impact and wet, meat-spackled momentum carried her another five feet before her legs locked, then buckled entirely. She dropped to her hands and knees, moaning and squirting, reaching out as if to find her badge, her name tag, the missing bits of her heart and lung.

Slowly, fighting for every inch, she sank down on her belly in the dry grass and bloodied dirt, still desperately crawling forward.

But the five-yard line now seemed a mile away.

And the footsteps were almost upon her.

The little girl had spunk. You had to give her that. Even as he dug a toe in her ribs and kicked her over, there was fight in her dying eyes.

Jake turned, took a look behind him. Eddie and Gray had joined the crowd: Eddie wrapped around Esther, as if to protect her; Gray jumpy and grim, about to go off on another of his bitchy amphetamine fits.

He looked back down at his hot cop-eroo. She knew she was dying, too. Still, she sucked in razored breaths, pushing gouts of blood out of her chest in anxious arcs, so she could try to tell him he was under arrest. Or a motherfucker. Or whatever.

Now faithful Sheriff LeGrange approached, Old Testament adoration in his eyes, the revolver in his hand quite forgotten.

Jake stared down at Peet, then knelt beside her. Shushing her, with sympathetic eyes.

"I got a funny feeling about you," he said. "Like you got a little something. Like you might be back, too."

LeGrange came up beside Jake, also dropped to his knees.

"All praise toward the Resurrection, Jenny," he said. "We will meet on the other side, in glory."

Jake whistled. "Now that's a true believer. Gimme your gun."

Without a twitch of hesitation, LeGrange handed it over.

Jake aimed it at LeGrange's head.

"Do you believe that if I pulled the trigger right now, your life would not be over?"

"I do."

"And would you devote your life—both here and hereafter—to serving the One True God?"

"I would."

"Then pray for her to join us. Amen."

Jake turned and shot Deputy Peet right in the heart.

"See you soon."

Part VIII
Lisa And The
Resurrection Rangers

Chapter Thirty-nine

The ribbon of road cut a yellow-lined stripe straight through the desert darkness. And thank God for that. Because even with his high beams up, Big Keith's headlights had their work cut out for them, slicing through the whipped-up particulate wind.

It wasn't a full-blown sandstorm yet, but it was enough to buffet the monster truck's cab, and fill the air with the steady crackle of the great Ford F-700's paint job getting eaten away, granule by granule, as if nibbled to death by gnats.

Jasper's would-be date for the night—the lovely Lisa Fontana—was riding shotgun, in every sense of the term: hunched up in the passenger seat, loaded twelve-gauge at her side. Her dark-tressed angel face was not so sweet at the moment—all fierce, set features, and frightened eyes—and her short, stacked body was definitely not dressed for the occasion.

She had gone out tonight in the hope of romance—or at least bodacious sex—and had dolled up accordingly. So there was a whole lot of leg showing between her black pumps and her short, tight skirt; and a whole lot of slender midriff above that, before the protuberant halter top kicked in.

Which meant that part of her felt like an action-vixen in a Russ Meyer/Quentin Tarantino film. An equal-to-larger part felt like an idiot.

And the rest of her was a little too freaked out to worry about stupid shit like that.

Lisa looked at Big Keith, who was true to his name—a whopping six foot seven inches of muscle draped in old, fading biker-and-prison tattoos—then snuck a peek at the speedometer. From where she sat, it looked like they were barely pushing seventy.

She wanted, of course, to go much faster. But he'd made the extremely good point that, unfortunately, they couldn't.

The "Murdelator"—which was the ridiculous, obligatory moniker he'd chosen for this steroidal automotive nightmare, pushing the limits of street legality—was a giant pickup truck suspended high atop 55-inch Michelin radials, with 2.5-ton military axles required to keep those babies rolling.

It was built for lugging a dozen men to a work site, loading shit up, putting on occasional shows, and terrifying every other driver on the road. That, and getting ten miles per gallon.

But it wasn't built for speed.

The good news was, they weren't likely to be pulled over for speeding, and detained by inquisitive cops. Which was something they did not want to happen. Especially not with a shotgun in her lap.

The bad news was self-explanatory.

"So what do you think?" she asked. "Ten minutes?"

Big Keith shrugged, helplessly glanced at her legs. " 'Round about. Fifteen, at the worst."

Lisa groaned. It seemed too much like forever, and an awful lot like too late.

Big Keith nodded, grimly sympathetic, visibly resisted the impulse to pat her on her knee. "Honestly, darlin'? If you heard what you thought you heard, fifteen minutes isn't gonna mean shit."

"I know," she said; and the second she said it out loud, the implications came crashing down again. She was ashamed of the quaver in her voice as she added, "And if not—"

"Let me put it this way. Either there's a situation, and we have to deal with it. Which we will, if we have to. Believe me . . ."

"I know." Fiercely nodding.

". . . or nothing happened, and you get that nice hot date you've been dreaming about."

Lisa allowed herself to laugh, a welcome emotional port in the storm. "I guess I made *that* pretty obvious, huh?"

"I'd say you got it just about right." And this time, when he looked her over and whistled, the little twinkle in his eye made it clear how much he was rooting for Jasper, not himself.

She smiled. "Thank you, Big Keith. You're a gentleman *and* a wolf."

He chuckled. "It took me a long time, but that's about the best I've figured out how to be."

She laughed, and his eyes went back to the road. But she kept watching him, appraising him now, much harder than she'd ever felt the need to do before.

Up until tonight, he'd just been the enormous, scary-looking guy at PJ's Pub who liked to throw darts. They'd never exchanged more than a handful of howdy-dos and random bar-jabber, most of it raucous and harmlessly risque.

But that was before tonight, and the murders, and that terrifying call.

Now, suddenly, he was the only backup she had.

Which made him, in a weird way, the most important person in her world.

"So you're sure you know where we're going, right?"

"Shit, kid. I'm almost sixty years old. I threw eggs at that fucking place in high school, back in 1971."

"That was way before Jake, right?"

Big Keith snorted. "Waaaaaaay before Jake. That nitwit didn't show up until, what? Three years ago?"

Lisa shrugged. "I guess last year was the first I heard of his show."

"You ever actually try to *watch* that worthless piece of . . . ?" He floundered for a word more descriptive than *shit*, couldn't find one, let it go. "Swear to God, the only people dumber than him would be the ones who actually fell for his crap."

"I gather you're not a Christian."

Big Keith grinned and shook his head. "Then you would gather wrong."

Lisa's eyebrows went up. "You're kidding."

"No, I am not. And that's why people like him make me so sick to my goddamn stomach."

Big Keith stepped just a little harder on the gas, appeared to steel himself.

In the rearview mirror, Lisa caught a glimpse of distant headlights. The only other lights on the road.

"You might've gathered, from the looks of me," he said, "that I spent some time in prison. Did some shit that I'm not proud of. If I could take it back, I would."

Lisa nodded. "I know the feeling."

"You done some time?"

"Nope." She grinned. "I pretty much always got away with it."

He laughed out loud. "Well, you're still young. Give it time. You'll get hammered eventually."

"I didn't say I never got hammered."

"Fair enough." He laughed again.

"Just that I never went to prison. But you were saying . . ."

"I was saying, there's not a whole lot of saints in there, although you might meet a couple. And all of them were sinners first. So the Bible is very popular."

"That's what I hear."

"It gets passed around a lot, like cigarettes and larceny tips and AIDS and the Koran. But out of the batch, that was the one that spoke to me."

Lisa nodded, looked back at the speedometer. Surely at least a minute had passed.

"And I gotta admit, I always had my problems with the whole Jesus thing. The big one being that I was *never* gonna be like Jesus, any more than I was gonna be like Einstein, or Steve McQueen. You know what I'm sayin'? *I was never gonna be great.* I was always gonna be this big dumb asshole who never did anything right."

"Wow," Lisa said.

"Then one day, I was reading Matthew 27—the crucifixion scene, in all its mockery and horror—and all of a sudden something hit me, the way it must have whacked St. Paul off his horse.

"And let me say, just so long as we're at it," he continued, clearly on a roll, "that St. Paul was NO FUCKING JESUS, okay? He was just another asshole, like me."

"But . . ."

"No. There's no real 'but' about it. He was an asshole. I was an asshole. We had a lot in common.

"But as for me, what happened was: I'm trying to find myself in the crucifixion scene. Trying to figure out where I fit in. Am I Jesus? No. Am I one of the people standing around, crying and lamenting? Well, maybe. Although—knowing me—I woulda died trying to kill those stupid fuckers. But evidently, that didn't happen."

"Wow," Lisa repeated, having nothing to add but her full attention.

"And that was when it hit me: I didn't try to stop the fucking centurions because I *was* one of the fucking centurions. And if it wasn't me, it was someone just like me."

She was amazed to watch a tear slide down his cheek.

"I was one of those ignorant goons that got paid to nail him down, then hoist him up, then stand around and laugh about it."

"Oh, I don't think so . . ."

"I don't think so, either. I *know* so," he said, and shot her a glance that carried all his soul behind it.

It shut her mouth faster than a sock to the jaw, though there was no violence in his eyes. At least not for her.

"And that was what Jesus gave me," he continued. "Just like he did for those dumb-ass Roman soldiers who, by the end of it, came to see the light.

"All of a sudden, I realized that *I didn't want to be that guy*. Couldn't be that fucking guy anymore. Couldn't bear it for one more second.

"Which is to say: Jesus made me want to be a better person. Not perfect—cuz that was never gonna happen—but maybe just good enough."

"Yes."

"Do you know what I mean?"

"Yes, I do." One tear of her own was rolling, too.

"Good enough to deserve to be here, on this beautiful planet, with all of God's gifts all around me. Good enough to know enough to help other people, given half a chance . . ."

"Exactly . . ."

"So that when I die, I don't have to crawl before the Lord like a grub on its belly, begging for forgiveness I never even tried to earn."

"Amen," she said, wiping away the tear.

"Amen, indeed." Wiping away his own. "That's why pissants like Connaway are the lowest of the low. He's not a real televangelist, and he's sure as hell not a real Christian.

"You know what he is? He's a cable access cult leader, with this batshit battalion of resurrection rangers that spend half their lives lazin' around on their fucking couches, thinkin' that by throwing him money and blow jobs, they're somehow gonna live forever. Which, incidentally, has less than *nothing* to do with anything Christ Jesus ever said or did.

"That's why part of me actually hopes that he *did* fake his death, like some people have been sayin'; and that he's standing there, pulling his shenanigans, when we walk in the goddamn door.

"Cuz I would gladly knock his lying ass straight out his forehead, just on general principles. Not to mention the thought of him *even thinking about* fucking with my bro."

The temperature in the monster truck cab had just gone up ten degrees, without anyone touching the heater. Lisa watched him pause, mopped a little sweat off her brow, and thought to herself *how lucky am I to have him with me . . . ?*

A half hour ago, back at the bar, it had been a different story.

The redneck crowd at PJ's Pub, on the outskirts of town, had been rowdy tonight. Nothing unusual there. Lots of loud banter and rip-roarin' laughter, poking out like rebel flags of many nations over the steady soundscape blare of George Thoroughgood, Kid Rock, and Kenny Chesney.

For Lisa, however, a hole had been blown in her good-time vibe, even before the local news came on.

It was hard not to be jealous, despite Jasper's protestations, when she learned that he was backing up Evangeline this evening. Everybody knew they'd had a thing, and that they were still just-short-of-kissing close.

But Jasper was so cool on the phone—so clearly excited about hooking up tonight—that Lisa had put that noise on the emotional back burner, trusting her own charm and bedroom skills to knock that skank out of the running. You didn't have to be a pro to fuck like one; all you had to do was connect, throw down, and give it up like you meant it.

So she was confident, if a little apprehensive, that the night would go just fine.

Then the music cut out, right in the middle of that stupid "The Devil Went Down To Georgia" song; and while that would normally be cause for rejoicing, the volume on the TV sets went suddenly up.

And the news of the "Funeral Parlor Massacre" came up with it.

Her first reaction was a generic oh-my-god-that's-so-horrible: the kind of reaction you gave to every bit of bad news that had nothing to do with you.

But as the story unfolded, her stomach sank into her knees; and she found herself trying to pull all of Jasper's cursory info into sharp relief.

Was Jasper at the funeral home? No. He said he was going to the widow's house. Was the massacre at the widow's house? No. It was at the funeral home.

Did Jasper need to know about this?

Yes, probably he did.

It was so hard not to call him up immediately. If it weren't for the fact that he'd asked her, explicitly, not to, there would have been no hesitation at all.

As it was, she watched the details pile up: multiple deaths, the original dead guy's body missing, a $10,000 reward, some mystical mumbo jumbo.

Then the segment ended, and the TV cut to a life insurance commercial. Someone hit the mute button. The jukebox kicked back in.

And her panic attack went into full swing.

She spent the next ten minutes letting various friends buy her drinks and try to talk her down, with no success whatso-ever. In fact, half of them were like no, you HAVE to call him!

Until she finally did.

And she was still kicking herself for having called from inside the bar, with AC/DC shrieking "Back In Black." Because the fact was, she couldn't be certain that she'd heard what she heard.

But the whispering hiss—just before the line cut out—sure as shit sounded like it said Jasper is dead.

She hit redial. It didn't work.

She tried Christian's number. It didn't work.

She tried them both a trillion times.

At that point, Lisa felt like she had no choice but to open it up to the floor: trying not to get hysterical as she told her friends, then the people nearby, then anyone who would listen that something was wrong at the Connaway house.

It was amazing to watch how people shrank back from her then, like she had some kind of contagious disease: a leprosy of involvement that averted all gazes, and left all backs turned.

On the far side of the pool tables, she found Denny and Steve huddled in deep conversation, their game all but forgotten. Denny was a bony-faced, scruffy-ass psycho in a dingy white I Think You Confused Me With Someone Who Gives A Shit *T-shirt. He looked much older than his forty years. The rumor was some sort of lymphatic cancer.*

But Steve was younger, and sort of cute in a beefy farmboy kind of way; and though she'd seen him flash his temper at the bar on several occasions—and heard him say some fairly out-there things about niggers, queers, and Zionists—he'd always been pretty nice to her.

They looked up, startled, as she approached, like they'd been caught in the middle of planning a 7-11 heist. And Denny's T-shirt spoke clearly for him.

But the second she mentioned the Connaway place, their eyes lit up, and they looked at each other, then back down at her tits, as if she'd just offered them blow jobs and backstage passes to a ZZ Top reunion.

Yes, they said. They would be happy to drive her. And yes, they said, they would definitely bring guns. They could leave right now, if she was ready. The sooner, the better. They were parked right out back.

And this was exactly what she'd wanted to hear; but coming from them, it suddenly sounded like the worst idea in the history of the world. Maybe it was the fact that they never once met her gaze for more than a split second. But all of her alarms went off.

When she hesitated, they started to get angry and insistent. Steve actually grabbed her arm, tried to lead her like a dog on a leash.

And just as she was about to shout for help, an enormous shadow fell over her from behind.

"I understand," boomed a voice like a white James Earl Jones, "that there might be a problem."

Steve let go of her arm so fast there was almost a ricochet effect; and Denny jumped back, his scrawny arms raised up in front of his cowering, bug-eyed face.

Lisa turned to face the giant behind her, who had inspired such fear.

"Jasper Ellis is my friend," he said. "You just let me know what you need . . ."

Lightning flashed and thunder boomed, let the wind pick up the conversation. Lisa snapped out of her reverie, back into the present, and the monster truck's cab.

Fierce light glinted in the side-view mirror, making her jump and blink. It was the high beams from a pickup truck that was coming right up on their ass; and she didn't need to read the subtitles to know that *Objects In Mirror Are Closer Than They Appear.*

She whipped around in her seat to see firsthand, was blinded anew by the high beams. Then the pickup

abruptly switched lanes, left her seeing dots as it made
to pass.

Through the dots, she saw a second pair of headlights.
And they, too, were closing in fast.

Chapter Forty

There were few things sweeter than a reason to hit one hundred miles per hour.

And with the hour of reckoning finally at hand, this seemed like the best possible reason of them all.

It had only taken a couple of minutes to scrounge up some believers: if not in Jake, then in either ten grand, some drunken mayhem, or Christ Almighty. Any one of them would do.

So there were six crazy bastards in or on the vintage Chevy pickup truck, howling through the wind like the mad dogs they were: Steve in the back, on the flatbed, careening around with Syd, Doyle, Pablo, Chuck, and a case of cheap longneck Tecate beer; Skinny Minnie, the possible booby prize, riding shotgun, so blitzed she could barely sit up; and in the driver's seat, Denny Chabert—the man with nothing left to lose—pressing that pedal all the way to the metal.

"FUCK YOU!" Denny hooted, though he knew Big Keith couldn't hear him. It was a little pregame warmup for the moment—just about to go down—when bulk succumbed to numbers, and the big man got whittled down to size.

Denny felt pretty goddamn good, all miserable cancerous things considered. He had his hands on the wheel, and a new world a-comin'. A world where remission was no longer an issue, and his skin no longer felt like it was filled with ground glass, no matter how many drugs and drinks he took.

The world that Jake had promised.

Rapture and resurrection, just over the horizon.

In all honesty, he was probably *way* too high to be driving right now, much less pushing his turbocharged Chevy into the red. But he had spent years working on that bitch, making her as badass as he'd ever hoped to be. It was the single most rewarding relationship of his life.

A hundred per was well within her comfort zone.

And, by God, he would rise to this occasion.

As he came up even with Big Keith's monster 55-inch wheels, he eased off the gas just enough to hang steady, flashing his ugliest grin; but it was like driving next to a tractor-trailer. All he could see was tires and the stepladder beneath the door.

The twin networks of nerves and cancer began to jangle in concert, fear cutting through the drugs and excitement to reactivate pain like glass through an eyeball. In his truck, Denny wasn't used to looking up at anyone. He couldn't even flip the fucker off. But he could be crushed like a beer can, anytime Big Keith wanted.

In that instant, he forgot why this was a good idea.

Then the artillery kicked in, and brought the joy back to his life.

Chuck was the first to lob an empty bottle straight at the Murderator's cab. But the wind was tricky, the sand like needles on his skin; and when his missile flew off to nowhere, like it was smacked out of his hand, all he could do was yell, "Damn!" and start laughing.

Pablo took the next shot, and it was slightly better, denting the spit-polished bed of the monster truck in a brown spray of glass and beer. The fact that it was still half full had a lot to do with how true it flew. This elementary physics lesson made a deep and immediate impression on all of them.

Doyle, of course, didn't learn a thing. He thought two empty bottles would be twice as good as one. When it didn't work, he cracked open a third and spat in his own eye: as always, far better at feeling than thinking.

That left Steve, who pulled a full beer from the case and winged it with all his might. He had a third baseman's throwing arm—trained for hurling long distances, with pinpoint precision—and he aimed for Big Keith's head.

It was an excellent shot, thrown off just enough by the wind to smash the handle on the driver's-side door.

"BOO-YAH!!!" he bellowed, throwing up his arms, the clear champion of round one . . .

. . . and that was enough for Big Keith, who muttered, "Fuck this!" and veered abruptly toward the passing lane.

He knew that an actual collision, at seventy per, would not work out so well for him. His center of gravity was a lot more precarious than an ordinary, lower-slung vehicle. He would flip before they did. And that would be very bad.

But what the Murderator lacked in high-speed maneuverability, it more than made up for with intimidation.

Big Keith couldn't see the driver's face; but from the look of shrieking terror on poor, dumb Skinny Minnie, he could extrapolate Denny's bug-eyed shit-your-pants expression with relative ease.

And when that pussy stomped on the accelerator, pushing the Chevy ahead and—for the moment—out of harm's way, it was a pure gut pleasure to watch those assholes in the back turn white as they whipped by, suddenly not so cocky.

He pulled full into their lane, missing their rear bumper by inches; and as they screeched up to eighty and beyond, he just smiled at their apelike asses, jumping up and down on the flatbed, his headlights in their squinting eyes.

Lisa started laughing in the passenger seat; and for a moment, he allowed himself the smirk of the just.

Then another set of headlights appeared behind them, less than a hundred yards back, and gaining on them like Keith was going backward.

Chapter Forty-one

Trista Gluck was no stranger to sin.

She had worked her way through hell's buffet, and stayed to lick all the plates clean, so she could look any sinner in the eye and know what they were going through.

But she knew when to say she'd had enough.

That night had come only two years ago, in a biker bar on the edge of town, where Trista, hoping only to blow a stranger for a taste of cocaine, and compulsively picking holes in her face, had first heard him preach.

Not just on his show, but in the flesh. He had waded into the deepest slough of sin and despair to rescue her, when she was going down for the last time.

Not that he'd spoken to her directly, or cast her a second glance when he came in the door. Trista wasn't much to look at even in her youth, and she'd had to party twice as hard to keep up with the guys, to be the girl ready for anything, after all the pretty ones had passed out.

Those days were long gone. Jake had addressed his sermon to a hot young thing with tits like honeydew melons and no acne scars and, more than likely, all her own teeth.

Trista had to eavesdrop on their conversation, but she was struck to the quick by the handsome preacher's words, as if they were for her alone. They owned her every failing, and forgave her; as if his piercing stare cut right through the empty vessel of the bleach-blonde slut at the bar, right into Trista's scarred, loveless heart.

She went home before last call to watch his show, and with the first golden words of his sermon, she began the first day of her new life. She took the pledge, right then and there. In Jake's name.

She's been a drunk, a drug addict, and a whore with four abortions, chronic herpes (Simplex I and II) and a crappy cot in the Joshua Tree Recovery Center to show for her misspent life. But Pastor Jake had thrown her a rope, and she had climbed out of her pit of despair, ascended into the light of grace.

To look at her these days—two years clean, and now, she ran the recovery center—was almost to see a different person. Her dentures fit so well hardly anyone could tell, and the dermatologist said the scarring might even be treatable.

But for the last three days, none of those things had mattered. Not even the love of the Lord seemed to matter.

Because he was gone. And with him, all hope.

That was thirty-five minutes ago.

When, once again, everything was changed by the hand of her savior.

The wind howled through the broken window of Trista's beat-up old Toyota Camry, almost loud enough to drown out the asthmatic scream of the overtaxed engine; but the uniquely penetrating tone of her strident voice cut through the maelstrom of noise.

"Who's smoking back there?"

She couldn't look away from the road, and her rearview mirror was knocked askew when Army got in the passenger seat, but the stink of a burning menthol butt assailed her nose like a devil's promise.

None of the lumpen cargo in the backseat made any sound. For a change.

"I *smell* it," she continued. "When the Lord calls you to testify, silence is a lie."

That one was stenciled all over the walls at the halfway house, so it got a response.

"Rudy's smoking, Ms. Trista!" Charlene bleated, a heartbeat from hysterics. "I told him put it out—"

"Rudy. We are all tempted, but his Love is the only drug we need. ISN'T THAT SO?"

They all sounded off a dutiful echo, and Rudy flicked the butt out the rear window. Some hand-slapping and whispered cursing went on in the backseat, but the four of them were packed in too tight to hurt each other.

Charlene, Rudy, Tammy, and old Mrs. Tibbs—and her blind tortoiseshell tomcat, Timothy—all wanted to come to witness the miracle, but Army had the front seat all to himself. Even if someone else could have fit in the seat with him, none of them wanted to be next to him.

Army rocked back and forth, his huge bald head knocking against the roof of the car, making the rotten foam headliner crumble and fly away on the wind. Practicing his lines, rehearsing with the knife.

Trista caught her hand digging at a scab on her forehead, and bit off her last press-on nail. She couldn't trust her hands, but she could hardly blame them. It felt like the coke bugs were back, burrowing under her skin, making her sweat through her only nice dress, despite the shivery chill in the rushing wind. But she put it behind her, threw it over her shoulder like Jake always said to do.

She didn't read too well, but she knew full well how the apostles and the early Christians were outlaws, persecuted, hated, and feared for following their savior. To do his work and spread his word, they had to break the laws of Rome.

The world they lived in was a second Rome, another Babylon of decadence and idolatry. A devil in human form—a

succubus like the platinum blonde in the bar—had silenced
Jake Connaway.

But even the Devil did God's work, as the prophet said.

Trista clamped both hands on the wheel and steered
the car out of the last hairpin turn at the top of the
mountain overlooking the town, and crushed the pedal to
the floor, heading into the two-lane straightaway that she
had driven so many times.

But this time, she would not pass by his house, as she
had, so many empty nights.

They would stop, and their actions would lay the
foundation of a new gospel.

If what the news said was true, they would be first to
bear witness; but Trista was no fool. Even if he did *not*
rise, the Church of Eternal Life would rise out of the
ashes of Jake's death.

With Trista Gluck at its pulpit.

But there would be obstacles. Up ahead, she saw the
taillights of her rivals, whipping down the road like it
was slicked with shortening as they drunkenly swerved
up around a cruising monster truck like it was standing
still.

She fought the urge to point and shriek at the first
glimpse of Denny Chabert and his pathetic wet-brained
pals: the focus of all her hatred, in that speeding pickup
truck.

But here, as in all things, she was too loaded down,
and she was falling behind.

Then the pickup slowed, as if taunting the giant.
Why, she could not begin to say. But it was clearly a sign
from God.

She stomped down hard on the gas.

The Camry's bald tires squealed on the blacktop,
Trista fighting to keep them from sliding off the shoulder into soft sand as the acceleration grappled with her
for control of the car.

In the back, her fellow apostles tried to rally their spirits with a rousing hymn, but they were each singing a different one, and Timothy yowled in his cat carrier. They knew all of Pastor Jake's songs, but they couldn't keep the lyrics straight.

To hear his heavenly message mocked as if by chain-smoking howler monkeys stretched her last nerve to the breaking point. But it gave them something to do, until they were needed.

Beside her, Army rocked harder. His meaty forehead thumped the windshield with each thrust, pumping like on a child's swing, to push the car forward.

This made her more than nervous; it scared her; but Army was more important, and she didn't want to confuse him by telling him to do anything else. If you poured too much into a shot glass, you would spill something, and Army's shot glass of a brain was filled to the brim.

Nobody knew his real name. They called him Army because he always wore ratty, ripped T-shirts from the army recruiter: BE ALL THAT YOU CAN BE, *or* AN ARMY OF ONE. *He probably never was in the army, but he must have been something, once, before he did whatever it was that broke his brain. Nobody as deeply retarded as Army could have lived to adulthood.*

His T-shirt tonight said NOT JUST STRONG, BUT ARMY STRONG, *through the carrot soup he spilled down his front when the news interrupted mealtime confession.*

Trista had made sure he understood what really *happened to Jake. The idea had come to her like a lightning bolt, divine inspiration from on high. A way to save the halfway house, which had donated more to the Church of Eternal Life in the last year than it had paid in rent and upkeep.*

A way to claim the $10,000 reward offered for Jake's murder, and make the halfway house into the church's new home . . .

Still ahead, but coming up fast, the monster truck

starting edging Denny's pickup off the pavement. It was the most beautiful thing she'd seen since Jacob Connaway's smile.

Then Denny sped up and out of the way, the leviathan sliding into the passing lane behind him.

It was as if a gateway had opened: again, for her and her alone.

The Camry almost floated above the road, the runaway car becoming a missile. They blasted by the monster truck, passing on the right, Trista waving and honking with glee.

"Thank them, on behalf of our Savior!" she bellowed, urging her passengers on.

"THANK OOO, HALF A SAVIOR!" came the resounding response of the chosen.

And only then—as she fully entered the fray—did Trista notice that there were still more headlights, far in the distance, coming up behind her.

Chapter Forty-two

Lisa watched the crazy fuckers whip by on their right; and though the shotgun was now cocked and in her hands, it didn't occur to her to actually *shoot* those stupid people.

She was more interested in blowing Steve and his pals off the back of the pickup, before they dumped any more glass in the road.

Especially now that they'd tossed a whole twelve-pack, and were picking up guns of their own.

She loved the fact that Big Keith remained cool as a cucumber throughout. Though his teeth had clenched a little when he drove over the bottles, the Murderator had barely registered the crunching. The odds on a shard of glass punching through the knobby hide of the radial tires were slim to none, but not impossible. So far, so good.

Lisa rolled down the passenger window, unclipped her seat belt, and poked the barrel out into the wind. She wasn't looking forward to sticking her head out there—spend an hour on your hair, just to destroy it in a second—but Big Keith clearly had his hands full.

And frankly, she was sick to death of feeling helpless.

"What the fuck is going ON with these people?" she hollered over the sudden upsurge in sound.

"I don't know for certain!" he hollered back. "But if I had to guess—"

"GOD DAMN IT!" Guessing the same thing, too, as the clankity Toyota sedan passed the pickup, uneasily pushing ninety.

In Keith's high beams, Lisa watched Steve and his drunken shitwits turn away from her entirely, shouting and brandishing arms.

Then the pickup took off in hot pursuit, leaving Lisa and Big Keith to lollygag after, like a tortoise racing hares.

"AUGH!" Lisa screamed, with no one left to shoot at. "How are we supposed to catch 'em now?"

"We may not have to," he said, loud enough to be heard. "Roll up the window, would'ja, darlin'? You're gettin' sand all over my seats."

Trista tried to ignore the furious honking from the pickup filled with backsliders coming up behind her, but it was impossible. Only a mile to Jake's ranch, and the bastards were drinking all the way, the road behind them littered with bottle glass and starbursts of demon liquor.

She let loose a teapot scream of wordless fury as the wets closed the distance. How dare they come to his house in such a state? They huddled around his guiding light but remained lost; to them, Jake's love was just another drug, another cheap high on a Saturday night.

They would not be saved, and they would be blasted out of their boots by the first sight of him, if he had truly risen.

She believed in him, truly and without reservation.

She would give her life, knowing he would return it to her, this night, if he could.

If he could . . .

Was that gnawing doubt the work of a demon in her head—a coke-bug infestation of the soul—or was it destiny, calling her to do its work?

"Go go go go," bawled Army. He lurched and stabbed the dashboard with his knife. In the back, old Mrs. Tibbs wet her nightgown, and the others tried to rearrange themselves to get out of the puddle.

Trista could not make the car go any faster, yet still the speedometer needle climbed inexorably higher into the triple digits, the whole car bouncing on its shocks in time with Army's spastic rocking.

"Get the blaspheming cocksuckers!" Rudy shouted in her ear, wind whistling through his deviated septum. "Run the shit-poking drunks off his road, praise his name!"

Old Mrs. Tibbs cried out, "Timothy wants to go home!"

"One of their number," screeched Charlene, "killed our savior!"

Army rolled around in his seat in a motion so violent it almost threw the car off the road. "NO!" he roared in their faces. Trista yanked on his jug ear and hissed at him to shut up, but he would not behave.

"*I DOOD IT!*" Army stabbed the roof of the car with the knife, slashing the headliner and cracking the dome light. "*I kill Jake! I KILLEDED JAKE!*"

The pickup whizzed past them, fishtailed across the centerline to block their passing. Someone in the bed of the truck stepped up and threw something shiny that whickered in the wind, straight toward her.

A tire iron.

The chrome swastika caromed off the Camry's hood and starred the windshield, momentarily blinding Trista and forcing a shriek from the peanut gallery.

Letting her cramped foot off the accelerator, she tipped the wheel ever so slightly left, then braked and juked right, and stomped the gas.

The pickup lurched hard to block her, but she still might have passed them, had she not recognized one of the assholes in the back.

"Pablo?" Trista squinted at the wind-warped faces of the redneck posse in the back of the pickup truck. She recognized Doyle, Chuck, and Steve, and their faces lit up as they recognized her, leering down from their perch as the Camry limped alongside them.

But she only had eyes for Pablo—the cocksucker who gave her herpes—and the cut-down twelve-gauge shotgun in his arms.

He blew her a scabby kiss and fired almost straight down into the open window of the Camry. The spray of buckshot peppered the roof and door panel. Trista reflexively cringed away, throwing up her left elbow to catch the lead pellets that missed her face.

But her hands still gripped the wheel.

The Camry swung hard into the side of the pickup truck, crushing the passenger-side door. The window shattered. The slut behind it turned red.

Trista couldn't see Chuck tumble headfirst off the back and into the road behind them, skull wetly dissembling on impact like an all-beef water balloon.

Then someone else in the truck threw a lit road flare, which narrowly missed Trista's head on its way to Tammy's lap, inducing squeals and clouds of noxious black smoke.

Trista did not notice the chaos in the backseat, any more than she took note of the pickup truck grinding into the Camry and trying to shove it off the road. Even the searing agony of the buckshot in her arm, cheek, and scalp only lifted her up, out of her terror and panic, and into a comfortable passenger seat in her own head.

She looked up into the sky above Pastor Jake's ranch, less than half a mile away now; and just as she stared, the roiling black storm seemed to part before her cloud-busting gaze, and a star like a compass rose sparkled down a beam of heavenly blessing on the roof of his house, just over the next rise of sand dunes framing the road.

And much closer—less than a football field's length—stood a lone billboard: the John the Baptist of billboards, shorted-out floodlights frenetically strobing across its message.

WHAT WOULD JESUS DO?

Trista gave a cry of pure joy, a rapture that made her forget all her doubts, and abandon all her schemes. Jake was a prophet, and his prophecy had come to pass.

"He is risen," she breathed into the wind.

Somehow, all of them heard, and replied, "Hallelujah!"

The pickup truck disengaged from the Camry and swerved onto the wrong side of the road. Then, even as Pablo and Steve opened up on the sedan with shotguns, the truck heeled back across the centerline to slam into them one final time.

Trista Gluck confessed her sins and felt the lifting out of her seat that meant she was heard and forgiven.

Beside her, Army still brayed that he killed Jake. The lost-little-boy look on his beefy linebacker's face was touching and creepy; he would have made a lousy Judas. But even he would be saved, and maybe even fixed. Restored to his senses.

All of them would be given back the lost lives they never knew, if they only acted with pure faith, in casting away the broken ones they now suffered.

Sure this was God's will—and more importantly, Jake's will—Trista brought the wheel down in a hard left to slew the Camry's nose sideways on the road.

And meet the charging pickup truck head-on.

The pickup truck and the sedan collided at an oblique angle on the double yellow centerline, brutally jolting the passengers in the Camry into the roof, but Trista's car was already spinning out of control on its bald tires. The kiss of her bumper off the rusty grill of Denny's pickup was just enough to send the overloaded truck into a sideways power skid.

Denny pumped the brakes and yanked on the wheel, but to no avail. The truck slid down the centerline until the Camry came back, whirling like a top, and slammed broadside into the only thing Denny had ever truly loved.

The foursome packed in the Camry's backseat were crushed against the opposing door until it gave way and dumped them into the road at ninety liquefying miles per hour.

The pickup soaked up all of the runaway sedan's fatal momentum with its formidable V-8 engine block, which bulldozed through the firewall of the cab to rest in Denny's lap, squeezing firehose freshets of body shrapnel out of his mouth, nose, and ruptured sides.

While the jolly lynch mob in the bed got tossed like beads at Mardi Gras.

Doyle popped straight up with a bottle to his lips, but landed in the path of the oncoming Camry, and was smeared across fifty yards of tarmac before the last sip of beer and teeth could cascade down his throat.

Pablo somersaulted clear of the accident and sailed through the air for a hopeful moment, only to get wrapped backward around a telephone pole.

Steve hit the soft, sandy shoulder of the road with an alcoholic's miraculous, rubbery grace: his arm bent backward under his weight as he landed, snapping at the elbow, then continuing to snap as he rolled over and over, getting punctured and torn by rocks and scrub brush, and screaming all the while.

But then the tumbling stopped, and Steve just lay there, numb and panting hard, staring sideways and upside down at the billboard's flickering inquiry.

Wondering if he could stand.

Spitting up a surprising amount of blood, but thinking, *Praise Jesus, it's a miracle!*

And watching the high beams of the monster truck, bouncing as they swerved off the road and climbed the sandy shoulder toward him like a huge, ugly angel charged with erasing God's mistakes.

The road ahead was getting worse by the second. The pickup truck and the Camry went cartwheeling down the road like Hot Wheels toys in a vacuum cleaner, spitting out sparks that Lisa's eyes told her, too late to blink, were flying human bodies.

Lisa lurched forward in her seat as Big Keith goosed the brakes. The top-heavy monster truck rocked on its gargantuan wheels, but Big Keith leaned over the wheel with a deep, furrowed frown that suddenly undid any illusion she might have clung to that they were okay.

Behind them, another car came, flashing its brights and playing at passing the monster truck on both sides at once. Big Keith looked over his shoulder at the oncoming lights, then back at the auto parts swap meet scattered across both lanes.

Finally, he seemed to notice Lisa sitting beside him, buckled into her seat, but with the shoulder leash pushed aside, to hold the stupid shotgun.

"I'm so sorry, darlin'."

Big Keith didn't yank the steering wheel at all, but the Murderator seemed to bounce up on its front left tire, staggering drunkenly across the left shoulder and onto the soft sand.

The monster truck almost revolted at the sudden change in course, but driving over cars at anything faster than a slow crawl would overturn the truck. The alternative to being rear-ended by the kamikaze on their rear was to turn into the open desert.

Big Keith's face remained screwed up in concentration,

but he almost began to crack a smile that said, *Shit, I guess we're gonna live, after all*, and pointed at the shotgun. "Maybe you should just let go of that—"

At less than sixty, the truck might have negotiated the ruts alongside the road, but a tumbleweed-choked irrigation ditch yawned and swallowed the wheels.

The rocky bank of the ditch smashed the bumper, and then the world was kicking them down the street in a can: end over end, sand and sky, sand and moon and stars . . .

. . . and then Steve, crushed like the desert's unloveliest bug on their front fender, and smeared across the spiderwebbed windshield . . .

Chapter Forty-three

Lisa's head had slammed against the dashboard and her headrest so many times that she must have blacked out, because she remembered only waking up in the truck and thinking it was so much nicer than when she went to sleep, even if the truck *was* upside down—

The tangle of cars on the road was now a bonfire.

The third speeding car must have slammed into the pileup and exploded, because the flickering firelight blossomed and cast the dunes and the smoldering cacti outside into a relief as bright as late afternoon.

Two bright spears of light jutted off the edge of the road, where a fourth car must have stopped. Maybe someone sane, here to help . . .

She tried to speak and reach out for Big Keith, but her mouth was full of blood and tooth fragments. Her arm was broken in three places and splinted against the shotgun, which was hot against her breasts. It must have gone off at least once in her arms when the truck rolled.

She tried to make her other hand find the seat belt release, but it wouldn't unlock, and if it did, she would tumble onto her head and probably break her neck. Keith would help her. Keith—

Her good hand strained out for Big Keith until she found his wet headrest. Big Keith was still there, but his face was gone.

His flannel-clad barrel of a torso still hung in its seat like a tapped keg, but the mess below (above) it looked like roadkill with sad, denim-colored eyes. They might have blinked once, when the breeze blew sand into them, but he was dead as anything Lisa had ever seen.

Lisa tried to hold down her panic, but found it already tame. She must be in shock, because none of it seemed to matter much. Jasper and Christian were close by, at a truly shitty party.

But no one would come to save them.

And they would all end up in the same place, soon . . .

Fuck that. She prodded and jerked on the seat belt release again, but it wouldn't budge. Bright white light pinned her eyes shut. She squinted and tried to say, "Somebody help me, I'm stuck," but she could barely make words at all.

A flashlight beam roved around inside the overturned truck cab, noting each glimmer of change or glass or shotgun shells sprinkled over spreading pools of blood. Through the glare, she could just make out a pair of skinny little legs tucked into white snakeskin cowboy boots, parked just beyond the thrusting hood of the upside-down truck.

Her eyes were watering from fumes. Was that gasoline? In movies, cars were flying bombs that lit up with the slightest fender bender, but it was pretty hard to rupture a gas tank in real life, wasn't it?

"Help me?" Lisa asked.

"Help is coming, sister," someone said. "Even for you sinners, he is coming."

Another light came into the cab with her then, in a torch of flaming tumbleweed tossed into the pool forming in the roof of the cab. It wasn't all blood. The gas from the spare fuel tanks bolted to the back of the cab. But they hadn't broken open during the crash.

Someone opened them.

That same someone stood beside the cab and sang a tuneless hymn until the fire inside stopped struggling.

And, like Lazarus, rose up in glory.

The first thing to catch was her hair, dangling down like Rapunzel's. The flames climbed so fast that by the time she opened her mouth to scream, her face was already on fire: flesh blackening, tongues of yellow-red blistering heat thrusting insistently up the back of her throat.

There were no words for this agony, no thoughts in her head.

All was burned clear in the cleansing, killing light.

It wasn't until her body shut down that she heard the voice, reverberating through the deeper chambers of her sentience.

And maybe it was just the last gasp of memory, the final flaming brain cell jumping like a rat off a sinking ship.

Or maybe it was truly a message from beyond, urging her like a beacon to the shore. She was too busy dying to tell.

The words were simple, and came only once.

"Maybe," it said, *"you should just let go."*

But she didn't know how. She honestly didn't.

And that was the hell of it.

Part IX
The Wisdom Of Whores

Chapter Forty-four

Back at Jake's—alone in the holding cell—Evangeline could only listen to the gunshots and screams echoing on the wind, and wonder what the fuck was going on out there.

She had screamed herself hoarse when Emmy ran past, but the poor cracked girl had disappeared around the far end of the house, flailing her arms and shrieking in hysterics.

After the last, solitary gunshot, the silence was terrifying; but she might just be in the safest place, all things considered. *Maybe it was over—*

As soon as she thought it, she rejected the hope for the wishful thinking it was. Nothing could stop him. Nobody would save them. The only hope left was to deny him the pleasure of having her, one last time—

"*This is where I did it,*" said a voice from behind her.

Cold in there, suddenly so frigid that she could see her breath. And the stink of shit and piss, like an overturned outhouse, made her gag.

Evangeline turned around. Her voice cracked as she cried out in surprise that she wasn't alone, after all.

A woman's pale face crushed into her own. Exotic

eyes of piercing jade, with no whites or irises; lush, pouting lips, marred by webs of bloodless cracks. Shivering in the meat-locker chill, she hugged the generous curves of her compact, naked body. Dry ice mist oozed from her tragic smile as she bared herself.

She was flawless, but for the smears of blood across her breasts. Only a man would linger on her nakedness, and miss the steaming slits plowed lengthwise up her wrists, to the elbows.

"I didn't know what else to do . . ."

Neither did Evangeline. She couldn't move, could barely breathe. But she couldn't stop her eyes from seeing, her nose from inhaling death.

Or her ears from hearing the soft, soft voice.

As the dead girl began to tell her tale . . .

From the moment she first laid eyes on him, she knew exactly what he was. Of all the foolish superstitions with which her grandmother tried to infect her, Natalya Lyubyenko only paid heed to the stories about money, and fat lot of good they did her.

But she recognized the eye of a witch when she saw it.

There were men in the clubs and on the street, when she came to Moscow, who could rape her with their eyes, and leave worse than disease in her purse. Some girls said they were old KGB, trained to pry out secrets without even speaking, while others said they were just dirty old men.

But Natalya wished she had listened closer to her grandmother, when they began to follow her around, and the police would turn their backs, smiling, to let them have her.

Better to get out, before she ran out of hiding places. The girls told her the game was easier there. The Troika would pay for her passage and papers, in return for a couple years of convention and Internet porn work. The men who took Russian brides were soft idiots, and the law in America wouldn't even let them hit you. Anything was possible there, the Moscow girls always said, but never why they did not go.

Natalya went to America. Even if all the rumors were lies, surely it would be warmer than Moscow.

A sweaty little Georgian man met her and the other girls at the Los Angeles airport, and took them to the "marriage agency." He called it that, and laughed.

There was no marriage, no agency. He took her to a club downtown, and she was delivered to her new "husband."

She did not even know she believed in the Devil, before she met Jake. When she first met him, she did not think he was a devil at all. Stupid girl, she thought she was falling in love.

He played the role to the hilt for the Troika broker, flipping up her lip to check her teeth, palpating her tits like bread dough, jabbing a gloved finger into her purse and sharing her aroma with his dead-eyed lackey.

But his eyes trapped her, the fire in them seeming to promise her that this was all a game, a dumb show, but there would be more games, and fun, later.

In his car—a huge white Elvis Presley dream of a Cadillac—he told her how it would be. She would have a room at a motel, and Gray would pick her up to go to work every evening.

The dead-eyed man never looked at her, but she could tell he was dangerous. Natalya was afraid to be left alone with this one, she knew his type too well. They hurt women, because they could do nothing else with them.

They stopped at the motel, and Jake left Gray in the car. He carried her over the threshold, humming Wagner, and laid her on the bed like the treasure she secretly believed she was.

No bride was ever so tenderly or so thoroughly fucked as Natalya, on that day. Jake was inexhaustible, using her again and again, coming in her mouth and ass and turning her purse inside and out with his hands, tongue, and magnificent cock. He must have drugged her, to wring such agonies of orgasm out of her. No man had ever made her feel anything to take away the shame of what she did, the sense of being used as a bicycle or a toilet is used. With Jake, she was under a spell, and she wanted only for it never to end.

But it did, and quite rudely. She awakened to find the other one, Gray, sitting in a chair, flicking ashes into the tangle of chilled sweaty sheets. Waiting for her to wake up.

When Jake took from her, he made her quiver and left her wanting only to give more, but what this one took, he kept it until it spoiled, and gave nothing back. He told her to get dressed in five minutes, or he'd beat her. Something cold and reeking of rotten fish dripped into her eye.

In the mirror, she discovered that the dead-eyed one must have masturbated into her hair, while she'd slept.

He took her to a nightclub in Palm Springs, where she sucked off rich old men in the VIP lounge; a bachelor party at a country club, where the best man fed her laxatives and made her take a shit on the groom's face; a palatial house in the desert, where she ate a queer sixtyish dowager's dusty cunt while her husband pumped his limp cock and called them filthy names.

And more, the next night, and the next. All she could stand, and more, until her only defense was to lose track of the days. And when she could take no more, when her misery had all but overcome her fear of Gray, Jake came back.

He was so sorry for what she had to do, but they paid a lot to bring her to this country, and everybody had to do a little dirty work, to catch up, in America, it's what made this country great. When she had earned her keep, she could come and go as she wished. She could make her own life. Or, if she chose, she could stay with him . . .

He stayed for only an hour, but he possessed her utterly, again, and left her floating in the afterglow of his passion. He left her with a steady supply of his passion, in little yellow capsules in a plastic bag.

They helped. If she took too many, she threw up, and played

with herself until she was raw, so out of her mind that she thought Jake sent his ghost to ravish her with her own hands. But just one a night, and she could almost fake her way through the work, could moan and coo at the sloppy attentions of the monsters who paid Gray.

For a while, it was good enough. But long before she ran out of pills, her brain stopped responding to them. Like a sponge with the last droplets of water wrung out, it would only begin to stir when Jake talked to her. He never answered her calls. Gray took away her phone. When she tried to run away at a truck stop, he beat her until she pissed blood, and gave her to a bunch of Mexican fruit pickers to teach her a lesson. They pulled the train on her in a portable toilet in an orange grove, then flipped it over on her.

Gray bundled her in trash bags and took her to the motel. He hosed the shit and piss off her and told her to get dressed in something nice. She was going to a party.

At Jake's house.

A bachelor party.

He was getting married.

Too tired to run away, she tried to open the door and throw herself out onto the highway. Gray dragged her back into the car by her hair.

She serviced many men, before she even saw Jake.

He finally came into the room, decked out in a dashing pin-striped suit, and smoking a cigar. The men circled around her. They held her hands and feet down, slathered her chafed purse with spit and Astroglide, staking her out for him like a sacrifice.

Laughing, he poured champagne down her throat before he fed her his cock. It still had another girl's stink on it, but she tried to take it in. She wanted nothing more, even after all she'd suffered, than to please him. She really believed exactly what the most pathetic, stupid johns believed—that if she just gave it to him good enough, he might lift her up and love her.

She wanted only to give him pleasure. She tried to swallow him, but his friends shoved him into her and jerked on her limbs. She tried to relax her throat, but he jabbed her tonsils and made her gag and vomit up all the expensive champagne he'd shared with her, along with the commingled seed of all his friends, all over his beautiful suit.

Jake screamed and jerked his manhood free, scraping it on her teeth. Before she could form the words in English to apologize, he slugged her in the mouth, knocking two front teeth down her throat.

Laughing, they tossed her aside and moved on to the night's next entertainment. Gray dragged her out to the storage room behind the garage. He kicked her a few times before locking her up and leaving her here.

Natalya wouldn't have gotten up and run away if the door was standing wide open, but she could still escape. Whatever Jake was, she could never get away from him and his dead-eyed familiar, not anywhere in America. Not anywhere on this earth . . .

There was nothing in the room sharp enough to cut, but Natalya was so cracked out that she thought nothing of biting into her own wrists. The first freshets of blood gurgled up her throat and tickled her nose, like warm Coca-Cola. She curled up around her arms, slurping the blood to keep the wounds open and flowing, shivering as her extremities succumbed to the chill of the grave.

When her vision dissolved in carbonated black bubbles, she thought she would be free at last.

She should have known better.

Evangeline trembled with the cold Natalya described—felt it on her skin, and down to her bones—but more than that, she felt the near-unspeakable degradation, the emotional devastation that came from being one of Jake's chosen whores.

Take away the Moscow memories, and it might as

well have been her *own* story, starting right from the very first moment she met Jake . . .

. . . and Natalya gave her a moment to reflect on her own past, every single memory a wound that would not heal. The first night he'd shown her everything that sex could be, leaving his brand in her forever. The first night she'd swallowed an old man's cum for money. The first night she'd puked on heroin, then relaxed into a pliant pincushion that every prick in the house impaled, over and over, for hours on end.

The first night she'd been gang-raped under Gray's supervision, as punishment for trying to get away . . .

I know, Natalya whispered, close. So close that they almost shared the same skin.

But Natalya was not finished with her story.

Hell was not hot. It was colder than Moscow. When Natalya Lyubyenko died, there was only cold and blackness, but she knew she was in hell, because she could hear the Devil speaking.

He sounded exactly like Jake.

"I thought these Russian bitches were made of tougher stuff," he grumbled.

"Whores are whores," barked the Devil's lapdog. "You try to get your money's worth out of them, shit always goes pear shaped."

"No, that's not right, man. They're not just things. They're human beings, with feelings and fears, and hopes and dreams. And souls." Then he laughed out loud. "And that's the part I like most. I don't know about you, but they're a hell of a lot more fun to play with than any toys I had as a kid."

"I didn't play with fucking toys. And this whore that you broke is way short of paid for."

"Forget about it. Those Russian fuckers know how whores are. Get Evangeline back on the beaners-and-bikers circuit a little harder for a month, and we'll make it up."

"*Easy for you to say. They don't know where you live.*"

Natalya could not open her eyes. She could see only the ultraviolet snowfall of light on her eyelids. She smelled stale cigarettes and spilled liquor, musky man-stink and cologne, all enhanced by the coppery perfume of her blood.

Jake said nothing for a long while, but Natalya sensed his brooding presence drawing closer, harder to ignore than the bottle caps and fingernail clippings digging into her dead ass.

Finally, he started laughing. "*Souls . . . When you save a soul, you'd have to be a sucker to just let God have it.*"

"*Jake, this church shit is going to your head, man. Seriously.*"

"*What's that supposed to mean?*"

"*Did I fucking stutter? It's a good grift, but . . . you're starting to grift yourself, if you don't mind my saying so. You're starting to buy your own bullshit.*"

Natalya felt Jake leaning down over her, felt his hot breath on her marble-cold skin. The rising note of anger in his voice was like an inflammable gas leaking into the room.

"*Bullshit?*"

"*It's bullshit, isn't it? You used to laugh about it, back in L.A. These fucks open their wallets and their legs for anyone who can save the one thing they don't have. There's no such thing as a soul.*"

"*I can see,*" *Jake replied, honey in his voice,* "*why you'd want to believe that.*"

Jake laid his hand on her. It burned.

She could not move a muscle, so she knew she was still dead. But the furnace-kiss of that hand, laid more gently on her than ever he touched her in life, would not be denied.

"*But there's nothing bullshit about belief.*" *Stroking her, slowly melting the rigor out of her flesh, combing her hair with feathery waves of his fingers. Loving her back to life.* "*Everything that got done in this world that was worth remembering, that changed the world, was done by people who believed some crazy bullshit. Gave their lives for it.*

"Maybe there is no God, and maybe there are no souls, Gray. Maybe you're right."

His hand curled around the bones of her neck and lifted her up off the shag carpet, wringing vitality back into her empty skull.

"But you take this whore, for instance. If she believed in God, then she's going to hell, which I gotta believe is even worse than pulling a wetback train with you conducting it."

"The bitch was sweet on you. So what." Natalya hadn't heard Gray move or breathe. "She didn't think it through—"

"But she believed!" Jake lifted her upright by her neck until she sat up in his arms. She felt his heart pounding against her, like a wild animal in a cage. "She believed in me, don't you see that? Not in God, but in me! She gave her life, but she gave me her soul.

"I can feel it, Gray. It doesn't just float off, if you know how to hold on to it. If they love you more than they love life itself . . . you can do miracles."

Gray cackled until he coughed and spat his cigarette into a glass. "You're losing your fucking mind, man."

Natalya tried to curse him, to speak up and prove her beloved was not a madman, but a prophet. If she could have spoken right then—if she could have said a word—how different it would have been.

Jake would have seen the power of his own hand, demonstrated in the fertile soul of her heart.

What might have grown—what might have been—if only he had looked into her eyes, and seen that he had reclaimed her from death.

But he didn't look down. His fist knotted up in her hair as he snapped her head back on her brittle neck.

"Don't you ever fucking call me crazy!"

He stood and jerked her up as if he meant to throw her at Gray. She was a petite girl even before Gray stopped feeding her, and Jake effortlessly lifted her to her feet.

I live! I am recalled to life through your grace, O

lord! *She willed herself to stand and speak, but she floated off her feet in his grip.*

And before she could part her lips to suck in a breath, he slammed her head into the glass and chrome coffee table between himself and Gray.

She lay facedown in jagged shards of tempered glass. She felt every gritty razor edge digging into her skin. But somehow, she could not move, could not react, when he stepped on her head and ground her face into the glass, like crushing out a cigarette.

There was a long silence between the two men.

"I'm sorry, man," Jake muttered at last. "I'm just tense, what with the wedding, and . . . all this."

"Forget it, Jake. It's cool."

"Right on," Jake said, clapping his hands to clear the air. He wiped his shoe off on her hair. "Clean up this fucking mess. I have to go call my fiancée, and ask her how her party's going . . ."

Evangeline's wrists and forearms were beginning to itch: not just on the surface, but deep inside the veins, the throbbing veins now so much louder than the wind as they resonated with the thundering of her heart.

She could not move her legs, or turn her head away. But her hands came up, as if idly, to drag their nails across her wrists.

Left to right, and right to left.

And the only other sound in the world was Natalya's voice, whispering the last of her secrets . . .

Natalya might have died again. She might only have gone to sleep.

But when hearing and feeling returned, it was as if layers of gauze were wrapped around her head: a balaclava filled with sizzling coals and broken glass, through which the world came

*down a long, dark tunnel she could barely focus on through the
pain.*

*She was in the trunk of Gray's car. The huge, heavy door
swung up and he reached down to drag her body out, bathed in
the deep crimson glow of his taillights.*

*Perhaps it was only dumb luck; that she had survived her-
self and Jake's callous resurrection was another peasant's daydream. As hard as their lives were, Russians were notoriously
hard to kill.*

Or perhaps it really was another miracle.

But again, it was much too little, and much too late.

She spoke. "No, please don't—"

*"Jesus Christ!" Gray dropped her and pulled a gun out of
his jacket.*

"Please . . . take me back to Jake . . ."

He shot her twice.

*She was almost grateful for the warmth when the bullets
punched through her chest and belly. She heard a loud hissing
she thought was her lungs deflating, but Gray had shot through
her and ruined the spare tire under her hastily dressed body.*

*Cursing, Gray took hold of her again and dragged her out,
dumped her onto a tarp, in which he rolled her up, and kicked
into a shallow grave.*

*As he shoveled the broken sandstone and gravel into her
hole, she wished she could scream that she was, even now, still
alive. But she knew better than to speak up.*

*Perhaps, in the grave, the magic of Jake's touch would wear
off, and she would escape this life, and go where she belonged.*

And in the fullness of time, she did go where she belonged.

Right back to Jake.

And there they were, the two of them. Doomed, and
doomed, and doomed.

Two foolish girls. Two stupid whores.

Two lost souls, sharing a common fate.

At the hands of the same master.

But there was no denying that the ugly walls of the holding cell receded with every scrape of fingernail on flesh, the itch giving way to scratch.

And the wetter it got, the easier it became . . .

Part X
At The End Of The
Night Of Judgment Day

Chapter Forty-five

Somewhere, a dog barked. Only a few miles to the north, lightning flashed and thunder like a vault door slamming, but no sounds of alarm from the surrounding homesteads. One thing you could say for desert folk—they minded their own business.

Gray ushered Esther and Eddie back inside. Jake strolled back up the path with a jaunty spring in his rigor-palsied step, smiling up at the moon as if someone up there couldn't get enough of him.

Praying and spitting tobacco juice, LeGrange dragged Peet's body toward the cruiser by the collar of her uniform and started loading her into the backseat. Normally, the sheriff kept a close watch on his emotions, but he let slip a barking laugh, every now and then, among the grunting and "God bless its" that passed for curses when Deputy Peet's dead weight slipped out of his blood-slick, arthritic hands.

Mad, rampaging joy knocked down the last barriers in Bill LeGrange. He was done enforcing man's laws. He'd been anointed to serve a higher power.

When Millie died, leaving him alone with their barnyard exhibit of a daughter, Bill LeGrange turned to drink. Not so anyone in the department noticed, but he drank himself sick before lunchtime, more days than not.

He knew he was chasing death, and sure to catch hell. No one else could understand. None could grant the kind of absolution he needed. None but Eternal Life could strike the bottle from his hand, and assure him that he'd be with Millie again on earth.

In short: *he had taken confession, too.*

He arranged Peet's hands across the blasted ruin of her bosom in a serene tableau. She might only have nodded off in the backseat of the cruiser on a long, third watch. She might just tell herself that, LeGrange thought, if she woke up—

When she wakes up, he told himself. The pastor had come back. Tomorrow, the whole world would wake up.

One by one, if need be—

Jake finally reached the front door, looked around with that satisfied leer distorting even his silhouette, and went inside.

Still huddled in the shadows just beyond the reach of the porch light, Emmy slowly came to realize that she'd gone unnoticed. Her dark hair hung down in her eyes, plastered to her face by snot and tears. *Lucky I decided to wear black, ha ha*—

Her mind still wallowed in a quicksand of panic, but she gathered herself up and crawled away, with nowhere to run. She left her shoes in the studio. Her purse was in the living room. Mathias's keys must have been in his pocket—

She bit her fingers, hard, making her whine, but clearing her head.

To see her now, to hold her again, almost undid him.

Eddie would have jumped Gray, if she were not here.

He could face the gun, and maybe even take him, with no fear for himself. He doubted Jake needed any more improvements on the house, and he knew there'd be a settling of accounts before Jake played with his women. He'd talked himself down to a silent, permanent present, awaiting only the opening.

Gray barely covered them, for pacing and staring down the door. Probably nursing a king-size case of blue balls because he didn't get to hurt anybody.

Softly, Eddie pulled Esther close and whispered, "I won't let him hurt you anymore. I swear."

She wanted to believe him. She nodded against his neck, sniffling and balling her hands up against his chest like she was looking for a secret door inside him. Her eyes kept kicking fretfully back to the door.

He took both of her shaking hands in his and said, "You don't belong to him. Not anymore . . ."

She jumped back when Jake barged in, still waxing a big shit-eating grin that flickered not a wink as he sized them up. "I gotta say, *that* worked out pretty good!"

Gray uncorked like cheap beer in a paint shaker. "Are you out of your mind? I hate that motherfucker!" Waving the gun. "Worse, that motherfucker hates *me!*"

"He's one of us now. A righteous apostle. You better get used to it . . ."

A man of destiny never looks down. Jake tripped over the toolbox, launching hammers, screws, and drill-bit cases pinging across the floor. "Oh, God DAMN it!" he howled.

A long Phillips-head screwdriver skidded against Eddie's feet. He stepped sideways to cover it without looking down.

"Fuck that!" Gray got up in Jake's face. "Jake, this shit is out of control, and you know it!"

Neither Gray nor Jake paid any attention to Eddie,

who gave Esther a look and nudged her toward the back door.

"You want to settle up accounts and off these pigs, I'm only too happy to help. But . . . what the hell are we trying to do here, Jake?"

Gray's back was to Eddie, as Eddie picked up the screwdriver . . .

"What the fuck are we waiting for?"

. . . *and buried it in Gray's back*.

The blunt nose of the screwdriver punched through Gray's blazer, but skidded down his shoulder blade, till Eddie drove it home with his whole weight. Abruptly, the seven-inch steel shaft punched through and slid in to the hilt in his right lung.

Gray screeched: a high, sharp, almost feline sound, cut off by his gun going off in his spasming hand.

Esther turned to look as she ran, screamed, nearly tripping over the end table.

Eddie twisted the screwdriver in Gray's back, ripped it free and jumped back.

Gray dropped onto his side, roaring as loud as one lung allows. He squeezed off two more wild shots in the direction of the kitchen. Esther screamed, ducking down, unsure of which quavering way to go.

Jake smiled and popped his knuckles. Finally, the party would really get started.

Eddie rushed at Jake, stepping on Gray and leaping off the moaning gunman with the screwdriver upraised in both hands like a sword.

"RUN!" he screamed.

Jake threw wide his arms, grinning like a demonic date rapist, welcoming Eddie into his embrace.

It was exactly the opening Eddie was praying for: ridiculously overconfident, completely underplayed.

Eddie aimed for the right eye socket, the brain behind it, throwing his whole body into the thrust.

Then Jake whipped one arm around and caught him by the throat in midair.

The screwdriver whickered down, raked Jake across the cheekbone, chipping off mortuary putty and makeup, nothing more. Eddie's legs kicked out, catching Jake in the shins. The monster yelped, sagging forward under Eddie's weight.

Then Eddie fell backward, straight for the floor.

And Jake came down on top of him.

Hitting the floor was bad enough. Then Jake landed, pinning him on his back, knocking the wind out of him, and straddled him hard.

Grunting, noxious fumes belched out of Jake, but he was not breathing, either. Just choking Eddie with one hand, holding Eddie's right arm down with the other.

The talon on his throat crushed his windpipe, pinched off his carotid artery. Eddie almost instantly began to see spots. Heavy leaden waters closed over his head. He could barely see Jake's snarling white-green face hovering over his own.

Groping blindly around with his free hand, trying to find something useful, Eddie caught the rubber grip of a claw hammer and seized it, striking Jake a glancing blow upside the head.

"OW! SONOFABITCH . . . !" Jake howled, while the flesh at his temple tore like moldy paper, but the only damage Jake felt was to his vanity.

The fist clamped around his throat winched down tighter, until Eddie's neck bones creaked, then jerked his head off the floor and drummed it back down.

Eddie swung again, weak, wild, but the claw end first. Jake released Eddie's throat to block the swing. It wasn't that hard; Eddie's strength was waning fast.

He gasped, bucking under Jake, wracked by painful coughing fits and an even deeper sense of loss. Jake scooched up, held down his arms, hunched over to bring his face right up to Eddie's.

Jake roared. No words would begin to capture it. None were necessary.

Eddie screamed, staring up into hell.

The sight seemed to please Jake, the way a lion must be pleased when its prey has been downed: drunk on bloodlust, ready to feed. He smiled down, baring teeth, then looked quickly around at the glistening tools scattered all around them.

Jake let go of the hammer-hand, went to snatch something off the floor to his right. Eddie swung again, one last burst of desperation. Jake easily blocked it with his forearm.

And came up with something shiny, which he waggled in front of Eddie's eyes.

It was the handsaw: just a steel grip with a ten-inch tapering blade. Jake angled it like a malformed mirror, reflecting Eddie's terror back at him in warped-out funhouse form.

He saw himself; but even worse, he saw Esther reflected behind him. She was still standing there—SHE WAS STILL STANDING THERE—mesmerized by the horror, too frightened to move.

It was as if he were dying for nothing.

"RUN!" Eddie shrieked. It was the last word he had in him.

Then the blade came down, began sawing through his windpipe.

The pain was instantaneous, the damage irreparable. Eddie still struggled, but it was just a formality now. Jerking and bucking only made the hole wider. The rusty, serrated teeth peeled back his stubbly skin and sent geysers of blue venous and bright red arterial blood up into his eyes, both in and out of his mouth.

Eddie's screams went up an octave, but soon turned

to burble and spray, as Jake kept hacking through the tough sheath of the larynx.

Somewhere behind him, Esther screamed with all her heart. But now it was just background drone. He couldn't feel her anymore. Couldn't feel anything but his own throat rasping open.

And a strange, urgent tugging at the back of his soul.

Something was calling, but it wasn't Jake. Wasn't the endless plummet. Was something else.

He felt it, and the fear began to drain away.

He looked up at Jake, and Jake began to fade. The world began to fade, or at least Eddie's handle on it. The pain. The meat. The bottomless terror and failure. All receding.

It wasn't light that enveloped him now. But it wasn't darkness, either. It was bigger than both. And it was upon him.

He gave himself over, and the struggling ceased.

For Jake, listening to Esther scream was just like opera, only way more fun, and he was beside himself with righteous glee. Her anguish made it like *two* lives, swirling down the drain and straight into him. Double the flavor, double the fun.

"Let's see YOU come back from the dead, mother-fucker!" he howled at the twitching sad sack beneath him. "Let's see YOU try . . . !"

Eddie stopped jerking and gave up the ghost; his breath came in bubbles, then not at all, and his eyes glazed over. Deader than mud.

Jake wiped his hands off on Eddie's shirt. His face was a mask of arterial war paint.

"I didn't think so. Bitch."

Only then did Esther finally run.

And, as if in afterthought, Gray finally stopped screaming long enough to get up on one elbow and take a shot at her. It missed, but spooked her away from the back door, and on down the hall.

Jake laughed as he watched her.

"NEXT!" he said.

Chapter Forty-six

Too scared to go anywhere, Emmy drifted across the backyard. Through the living room window, she saw the men fighting again, and made it across without being seen.

Emmy ran up to the holding cell window. "I'm gonna get you out of there!"

Evangeline looked up at Emmy, stunned and sleepy and guilty somehow. She waved a dismissive hand, as if to say *come back later*.

Her fingers were gloved in blood.

Natalya was beside her, whispering a desperate blizzard in her ear, loud enough that she couldn't hear anything Emmy said.

"It's too late for you. Keep going."

She was right, and she should know. Nobody ever really got away from Jake, not even in death. On the other side, there was the consolation of final and total surrender.

Evangeline's wrists were scratched and torn: she had been trying to tear them open with her fingernails, but the skin was tough with scars from her experimental period, and her nails were cracked and broken from trying to escape.

Why didn't she do it right the last time? Or any of the times before?

The answer struck her so hard and sudden that it felt like being yanked out of ice water by the hair.

She had *friends*, that was why. She had friends who gave a shit about her, and wanted nothing from her but to know she was okay. They weren't out to fuck her. They weren't out to make a buck off her.

And they sure as shit weren't some dead Russian hooker, trolling for company in the great beyond.

She had friends, and one of them was dead; but maybe, just maybe, the other one wasn't.

And here was this stranger, this dumb little Jezoid, offering to help her from outside the door. Somebody who didn't even like her—probably hated her—taking the time to try and save her. And why?

Because that's what good Christians do, she thought to herself. *They try to help other people.*

At that point, the spell was broken.

The moment she stopped digging, the cold euphoria wore off. The shameful pain rolled up her arms and shocked the breath out of her. Her fingers tingled with blood loss, the pins and needles of death setting up shop.

Coming out of the shadowy corner of the cell, alone, she tucked her wrists into her armpits.

"Is Christian still alive?"

Emmy tugged at the locked door, hyperventilating. "I don't know!"

"Well, get me out of here," she said, "and let's find out."

Chapter Forty-seven

Out front, LeGrange sat behind the wheel of his cruiser with the door hanging open. He was on the radio, checking in. Screams and shooting came from the house. Another heathen converted.

"Yeah, Sandy. The wife's in shock," he said. "Needs some Valium and a shrink, not the cops."

"Copy that," said Sandy, the dispatcher. Jewish, but he forgave her tonight. They would all awaken to the same faith. "It's a hell of a thing, after losing her husband like that . . ." Her menthol-scratchy voice went vague, like it always did when someone talked in her other ear.

"Sheriff, we got a 911 call . . . need you and Peet to go check out Joey's Cabaret on Kearny, ASAP . . . There's a man down . . ."

At the sound of her name, LeGrange looked back at Peet.

Still dead.

Agnostic, of lapsed Catholic parents. Strict vegetarian. Never could get his head around it.

Damned, though, if the stink of the shit in her britches didn't stink a mite less than the average death-dump.

LeGrange wanted to tell Sandy to round up the boys, have them load up all the prisoners in the holding cells in the bus, and bring them here to share in the miracle, but he was getting ahead of himself.

Surely, the Lord must have new orders for him. And he would serve . . . unto death, and beyond.

Halfway down the strobe-lit corridor, Esther tried the laundry room door, threw it open . . .

. . . *and a voluptuous, used-up demon-whore reached out for her, cackling as she beckoned from just within a throat of swirling blackness, stuffed to choking with wailing, damned souls.*

Esther screamed, kept running, the laughter pursuing her.

Gray hawked and spat out a gob of dark, half-congealed blood. Jake got up, pulled his friend up by one hand, ignoring his tremors and curses, and started down the hall. Gray was almost delirious with pain, but he could walk.

"Come on. You can do this."

Gray limped down the hall, trying to light a cigarette. "Augh! Fuck!"

Esther reached the end of the corridor, and Jake's door. She balked at touching it, then raced into her own bedroom, slammed the door and threw herself against it, turning the flimsy lock in the knob that he'd broken half a dozen times before . . .

Breathe. Breathe. You're alive.

But you're not very bright, are you?

The only windows were narrow slits, ten feet above the floor.

She looked at her bed, her closet, her pretty things, her refuge from Jake. The only other door led to her bathroom.

Behind her, the footsteps, the hyena-barks of pain and insane anger, were coming closer.

Esther retreated into the bathroom and locked the door, turned on the flickering light.

Again, no escape but those narrow windows, far above. So stupid, so helpless. He tried to save her, told her to run . . .

She whimpered, trapped, spinning round and round.

She stopped, caught by an inkling of salvation.

She threw open a cabinet, pushing aside the Clairol color kits and the huge Tupperware chest of prescription pain relievers, digging to the back.

Where a bottle lay waiting.

From the depths of Jake's domain, they heard the sudden pounding and caterwauling of Evangeline's fag. It sounded like he was trying to beat through the door with his bare hands, although where he'd gotten the fortitude for that was another of tonight's great mysteries. Jake and Gray paused in the corridor, listening to Christian's noise.

"Would you just kill him now?" Jake snarled. "I gotta take care of something."

Gray mopped blood off his chest. "Dude, I've got a big-ass hole in me. We gotta do something . . ."

"I will take care of you. I swear it." Jake looked sincere, but Gray felt his stomach go all squirrelly. "One way or the other. Now go."

Gray staggered—gun ready, and grimly determined—toward the bathroom where Christian continued to bang. He loved Jake. Would die for him, and not ask to come back.

But he wasn't sure, just now, that he was looking at his friend anymore.

Looking over his shoulder, he stepped into Jake's office.

And walked right into the giggling demon.

He recoiled and bit his tongue to keep from shrieking.

He blinked and rubbed his eyes, but she was still there, leering out of the dark, peeking at him around her tiny, baby hands.

"Jake had you kill me, too. Right in the head. BOOM!"

She whooped and shook her baby-fat body at him, gyrating with gales of laughter, black blood squirting from the hole in her forehead.

"I DON'T EVEN KNOW WHO YOU ARE!" he bellowed, as much in pain as terror.

"Oh, you will," she said, giggling harder. *"Just wait till the rest of YOUR demons show up!"*

Gray aimed at the crazy bitch, but she was gone. The mocking laughter only got louder, as did Christian's bang and wail.

He continued miserably down the hall.

Chapter Forty-eight

Now was certainly not the time for a drink; but when *is* the proper time for a nervous breakdown?

Esther swigged from the vodka she had stashed. She wasn't even trying to escape anymore. Just drinking and silently praying on her knees, in the center of the room. She never really thought she was free of Jake; it hadn't even begun to sink in that he was gone, and then he was back. So it hadn't even been much of a change at all.

She was weak, no argument here, and the drink was not making her stronger. Only more flexible, more able to absorb it, maybe sleep through it altogether. Maybe she did not deserve to be saved, but she didn't deserve to suffer, either.

Because she was weak, and she'd been through too much already.

Was all of this her fault? Should she have seen it in his eyes, that first time? Should she have listened to her father, who never told her what to do, once in her life?

When he swept her off her feet, going away with the rock-and-roll preacher had seemed like rebellion against everything Mom and Dad stood for. It was not that he treated her as an object. She only tolerated that because she believed she could see the beast inside him, even when he was on his best behavior; and with her father's selfless hippie healer dedication, she thought she could heal it.

And how it felt when he fucked her had, naturally, nothing to do with it . . .

When he loved her, he turned her inside out, unzipped her very soul. But it had only been so much stuffing to him, incidental garbage in the way of whatever he was looking for in her, in all the other women she refused to believe came after her . . .

A wrecking ball tore down the bedroom door and swept through her room, overturning furniture, dumping drawers, and smashing her mirrors.

"ESTHER!" it roared.

"He really did love me," she murmured, and took a last gulp of vodka. "Oh, Eddie . . ."

Jake kicked down the bathroom door. It flipped off its hinges and landed squarely before her. She screamed, dropping the bottle, and scuttled back against the toilet.

He held up a pair of handcuffs, waggling them like a leash. *Wanna go for a walk, girl?* He smiled, but his eyes were like burning plastic. In a face that was starting to rot in earnest and separate from the bone, it was the only part of him she recognized.

Jake dragged Esther down the hallway by her hair. She cried out in pain and despair, but put up little other resistance. "The thing you don't seem to understand is that you belong to me. Just ask God. He'll tell ya."

They followed the long smeared track of blood from Evangeline's friend all the way back to the living room, where Eddie's dead body lay supine on the shag carpet, arms stretched out on a cape of deep burgundy.

Esther wailed and took a swing at Jake.

The blow barely mussed his hair, but he cut a grotesque pantomime, as if she'd mortally wounded him.

"He takes note of betrayal, believe you me. He's like Santa Claus and the 'naughty' list with that shit."

Jake flipped open one shiny steel cuff and held it out like the fanged mouth of a rattlesnake.

"Not like me . . ."

Chapter Forty-nine

Gray staggered up to the bathroom door where Christian was still pounding. If only everything tonight were this simple. Pointing the gun, he walked up to the door, thumbed the safety off, and started firing.

From inside, Christian yelped.

The banging stopped.

As Gray reached for the knob, he noticed that he'd stepped in a puddle. The sissy must've flooded the place. His sense of smell was hardly the best, what with a lifetime of smoking, one working lung, and a night with an embalmed guy. But he smelled alcohol, and not the fun kind.

He turned the lock and opened the door.

Something small and metallic hit the floor on the other side. Blue flames squirted out from under the door and devoured the puddle he stood in.

Gray jumped back and pumped three more rounds through the half-open door. His shoes, socks, and trouser legs were sheathed in fire.

Even as he yelped, danced, and batted at them, the flames began to die out. Fed on rubbing alcohol and cologne, they were nothing more than a distraction—

He looked up just as Christian spilled out the bathroom door and pointed something at him.

An industrial spray can of insecticide.

A cold mist engulfed Gray's face in liquid agony. His eyes stung, teared up, seemed to melt down his face. He sucked in a breath and promptly gagged on the flavor, felt his lungs turn brittle and wither like dead flowers.

The awful tingling weakness spread out into his limbs, robbing him of his last reserves of strength. Suffocating, blind.

But damned if that bitch was getting past him.

He heard Christian in front of him, aimed and fired, charging, then instantly tripped over Jasper's dead body.

Shards of glass punctured his knee, and more bit into his shoulder and face when he sprawled in the chunky glass from the broken cologne bottles, the razorlike light bulb shards.

Gray heard crunching glass behind him, over the sound of his own screaming.

Grunting in sudden pain, the faggot kicked him in the ass, thanked him for an enchanted evening, and slammed the bathroom door.

Chapter Fifty

Christian limped into the studio. The fog of shock was all but worn off, and he could vividly feel every broken rib fragment grating against the walls of his chest with every movement.

It was all he could do not to scream at the top of his lungs, but that would hardly help with the pain. And even if he couldn't find anybody, he was pretty sure he wasn't the only one left. He had to find Evangeline. They needed to get the fuck out of here before he passed out—

"Oh dear God," he said.

It just slipped out. It didn't mean anything. What else would he say, upon seeing an eyeless, crucified boy?

The dead kid, Mathias, looked like a prop. Its skin had a marbled gray pallor that made it tough to think of as human flesh. The cameras pointing at it all had blinking red lights. He was taping this, recording the death . . . and then what?

It was heartbreaking, true enough, but all the sight made Christian think of was that he had to find Evangeline. Now.

That, and some serious Vicodin.

He heard the banging of metal on metal or stone. And screams.

Shuffling across the studio to the sliding glass door, he heard Evangeline screaming. He tore the curtain aside and tugged the door open, wincing at the pressure on his ribs.

Sweat broke out on his forehead. If he didn't lie down, he was going to pass out. If he didn't do something to save his friend, he might as well lie down and die.

That was no choice at all. He kept going.

At the holding cell, Bible Girl was trying to smash the lock on the door with a rock. And getting nowhere.

"Try the garage!" Evangeline yelled.

"What, for keys?"

"No, get a goddamn hammer!" Christian yelled, surprising them both, and praying that Emmy knew enough not to hug him right now.

Chapter Fifty-one

Jake hauled Esther's limp form over to lie beside Eddie's body. Driven into a frenzy by her passivity, he pushed her to her knees, and ground her face in his open throat, holding her by the back of her head as if he meant to drown her.

She screamed into her lover's mortal wound and flailed at her undead husband's unyielding arm. If she held her breath, she could black out. Maybe she could drown. She could deny him that little bit, at least—

When he tired of this game, Jake grabbed one dainty wrist, twisted it behind her, and slapped a cuff on it. Her face came up slathered with blood, coughing up inhaled blood and vodka vomit.

She gasped for air, and blew it all out as loud as she could. "NO!"

"*No?*" He paused, as if genuinely puzzled. "Guess you should have thought of that before you spread for him, huh?"

Yanking her cuffed arm away from her breasts, Jake slapped the other cuff around Eddie's wrist.

"And now you're gonna stay with him, just like this, until you rot."

LeGrange came in the front door, observing, hat in hand. Esther screamed up at him.

"PLEASE!"

He looked at her like she was dirt, then turned devotedly to Jake.

"Lord, you said . . ." He bowed his head, overcome by stage fright in the face of his cable-access savior.

"What? Speak up!" Jake demanded.

"You said that . . . on the Day of Reckoning, even those whose bodies had been burned or buried would rise, in spirit, to return to the faithful . . . ?"

"Yeah, sure, all that shit's totally gonna happen. But in case you hadn't noticed, there're nonbelievers in the temple. Thieves trying to steal what's mine."

"Forgive me," LeGrange fumbled. "How may I serve you, Lord?"

Jake pointed out back. LeGrange picked up the fireplace poker where Christian dropped it, as he crossed the room, impervious to Esther's pleading, and went out the back door.

Jake grinned malevolently down at her, then turned to the roaring flame.

Chapter Fifty-two

Emmy came running with a hammer from the garage. Christian leaned against the door, talking to Evangeline. "We're gonna get you out, okay?"

Evangeline reached a bloody hand out through the bars to touch his face. Her fingertips felt like dry ice. "Oh God, Christian . . ."

Evangeline held on to him as Emmy took the hammer in both her pudgy little hands and started banging on the lock. In her haste, she just swung faster and wilder with each stroke, almost braining Christian. Each bang was as loud as a gunshot, but she seemed to be doing little else.

"Give me that." Christian took it from her and, struggling to hold himself steady, banged on the cheap sheet metal flange holding the lock onto the door frame.

Three strokes and it broke.

Evangeline popped out the door, hugged Christian, making him grunt in pain. "Never so happy to see a cop in my life—"

Christian struggled to turn around in her arms. He only caught a glimpse of the big man in khaki and a cowboy hat coming up the yard toward them.

But Emmy recoiled in fear. "Oh, no . . ."

Christian hobbled out to meet LeGrange, who strode

across the lawn like he was late giving a ticket. Swinging at his side, Christian only barely noticed, was the wrought-iron fireplace poker.

"Thank God!" Christian wheezed. "Officer . . ."

"Shut your fucking mouth."

LeGrange laid into Christian with the poker. Christian turned away and raised the hammer, but the iron rod clipped his undamaged arm above the wrist, snapping the bones clean through his skin.

Christian bowed over his ruined arm just as LeGrange kicked him in the balls hard enough to flip him on his back, then resumed savagely beating him with the poker.

Frozen for a fatal instant by the betrayal of a man in uniform, Evangeline and Emmy could only stand and scream at Sheriff LeGrange to stop.

But that wasn't going to happen.

Chapter Fifty-three

Jake was kneeling in front of Esther and Eddie, transfixed by the roaring hellfire, the oversized family Bible laid out before him. A miasma of noxious fumes curled up from his suit and his sick, sallow skin. He was barely aware of them as he tore sheaves of onionskin pages out of the New Testament and offered them to the fire.

Every so often, he took up a Buck knife and cut off some of her hair, added it to the blaze. She feigned unconsciousness, squeezing her eyes tight and biting back screams as he turned to cut off something more substantial from Eddie's face.

The hungry red flames seemed to feed on something much more volatile than paper, hair, and flesh, and bloomed up from a place much deeper than the hearth. Like an infinity of fire, stretching down into a bottomless pit.

Something danced in it, feeding the fire forever without ever being consumed.

It spoke to him.

Suddenly, despite the fire, the living room became as cold as a tomb, as if a door had opened on the Arctic. Esther opened her eyes again and looked around. The last dregs of vodka still in her stomach curdled and agitated for escape.

The lights slowly went brown and died out, until only the unearthly fire lit the room, the walls of which now receded into blackness.

She looked, and she saw them.

Three naked women appeared out of the shadows, forming a triangle around Jake and his victims. Fluttering, twitching as if they were unstuck in time and space, and ridden by a dozen warring appetites.

Their eyes, fixed on Jake, were mirrors. They sneered and dripped venom that turned to smoke and flies. But when they spoke, it was with one voice.

"This is the Night of the Great Transformation. This is the end of the world you knew."

Jake quivered. "I'm ready . . ."

"This is the Night of All Souls, in revelation. The death of all lies, in the face of what's true."

Jake threw the rest of the Bible into the fire. "Hallelujah!"

Esther saw the demons all too clearly now as they converged on Jake, and she began to go out of her mind.

They were not demons, she told herself, but ghosts. The ghosts of his women: the one who scarred him, and the harem of hapless whores on whom he vented his awful wrath. Hollowed out by their vices until they served only hell, they taunted him with their spectral nakedness, gyrating lewdly and convulsing as in a Saint Vitus' dance, as if jolts of orgasm and strands of barbed wire ran through their nerves.

Their mercurial, ever-shifting faces betrayed the pure desolation of human hearts that might once have saved themselves from this. But Jake's Furies descended on him only to urge him to greater cruelty, wider wakes of torment and devastation.

This was not revenge. This was not justice.

This was evil rewarding evil . . . and where was God?

Beneath his notice now, Esther started crawling toward the back door, dragging the inert concrete of Eddie's body, not trying to escape, only to get away. The handcuff dug bloody ruts into her wrist. Eddie's empty olive face stared at her, minus the random plots of skin and scalp that Jake had carved off. Twin, blood-rimmed mouths hung agape, asking her why he threw her away.

Jake and the demons laughed at her, but were content to let her crawl away.

At last, he had everything he needed.

Chapter Fifty-four

Half blind and still picking glass out of his face, Gray staggered out into the backyard.

Drawn by the sound of Christian's screams like a moth to a streetlight, he fought the pain and weakness that were dragging him down. Even before he staggered out onto the lawn and saw them, his brain pulled him forward with the tantalizing image of Sheriff LeGrange kneeling over Christian, beating him.

There is a magic moment in every fight when the combatants slip out of the deadlock of evenly traded blows, and one ascends, while the other submits, or simply breaks down.

To witness that moment, when the victor ritually drinks his victim's courage as totally as if he'd literally pried out and devoured his heart, is to feed on the spray of energy released in the delivery of the deathblow. Professional sports is as much designed to maximize and lay bare that mysterious transaction, as it is to preserve the lives of the contestants.

In the front of Gray's mind as he hobbled over to the horribly uneven match were two things: pure, simple disgust with how this evening had spun out of control, and the overwhelming need to clean house.

In the back of his mind—unexpressed in words, but driving his unsteady stride more than any sense of duty or love—was the idea that if he could get into this limousine wreck before that magic moment, on this night of all nights, he could devour them both, and be made whole.

Sometimes, you just had to believe in miracles.

"LeGrange," he said. "Your zipper's down."

The sheriff looked up from his work, his eyes a hundred thousand years away. Christian mewled on the red grass, but thrust up a twisted arm to swat at the sheriff's leg. Still alive, still a fighter.

Gray shot LeGrange dead-center in the forehead. The sheriff dropped flat on his ass beside the queer, then flopped on his back, Stetson pushed down over his face like he'd just laid down for a siesta.

Christian looked acidly up at him with his one intact eye, stuck out his tongue, and sprayed fragments of teeth and blood-threaded spittle as he blew a ripe raspberry.

Gray took aim and fired.

"NO!" Evangeline shrieked, tackling Gray, but not before his shot put a hole where Christian's heart was.

Then his legs tied in a bow and dumped him under the pummeling, blood-crusted fists of the kamikaze whore.

Emmy whimpered and covered her eyes, but still leapt up to run back to the house.

Evangeline's broken fingernails dug into Gray's scalp and raked his face, searching for his eyes. Rolling and batting at Evangeline, Gray threw out his gun arm and fired.

The wild bullet hit the wall just in front of Emmy, who squealed and ducked into the studio.

Chapter Fifty-five

Emmy ran through the studio with her hands up like blinders, sliding into the hallway in her stocking feet, looking for a place to hide. The bathroom and bedroom doors flanked her, both open, but hardly inviting. The bathroom door was scorched, and puddles of blood and broken glass fanned out into the hall. She smelled Old Spice and overcooked bacon.

She froze and hugged herself when she heard Jake's pounding footsteps, rounding the turn at the far end of the hall. She stifled a scream and ducked into his bedroom, realizing too late that there was no exit, and never would be.

Jake thundered down the corridor. The walls seemed to shake with every step. There was almost no point in hiding. If he didn't find her, he'd bring the house down on top of her.

Esther did not stop to cry as she dragged Eddie around the back of the house, but her breaths came in exhausted sobs, and tears blurred her vision. After desperately racing to get around the corner of the house, she had collapsed beside Eddie. It would be vintage Jake to let her run just far enough away to think she was safe—

to kid herself he'd let her go—before he reached out and slapped her down again.

She tugged the chain between their cuffs because she could not bring herself to touch his body, and her cuff had gouged bloody ruts in her wrists, fringed with ruffles of shredded skin.

But even as she pitied herself, she felt boiling self-hatred scald her from the inside out.

She couldn't even bear to look at what Jake had done to Eddie's face and scalp, the patchwork of flayed muscle and exposed bone that had smiled at her and promised to protect her from her husband.

He had given his life for her, and she'd failed him. She could do nothing for him now, but she could try to honor his sacrifice.

But she couldn't do it like this.

Esther gripped Eddie's lukewarm forearm. It was slick with blood, but she dug her nails into the meat of his arm to get traction and slide him a little farther down the path that led to the side yard.

The chopping block was there.

And the ax.

Evangeline kicked Gray in the balls so hard he threw up and dropped his gun, then brought his head down into her ascending knee, smashing his nose. He bellowed as he tumbled, but kicked her legs out from under her. She hit the dirt on the flat of her back, utterly out of breath.

Gray crawled on top of her and brought the bubbling ruin of his nose in close enough to drip on her. For one, terrifying, breathless moment, she thought he was going to kiss her, or bite her lips off.

He brought his head down blindingly fast and hard, smashing his forehead into the bridge of her nose. Fireworks burst, supernovae exploded and somewhere, a band was playing. Laughing crazily, Gray kept time by knocking his skull into hers, again and again.

The world went wavy, but instinct made her fight back with all she had. She lashed out with her jaws and caught Gray's broken nose in her teeth. Feeling broken bone and cartilage gritting between her teeth, she bit down.

Jake entered the studio, did not see Emmy. But at the far end, behind Mathias and the cross, *the blackness had swallowed the green screen wall entirely*.

This was a very good sign indeed.

"I am sooooooo ready," he said, addressing the void. "So ready to take command. So ready to show what I can do. What I *will* do, now that I know who I am."

He threw his arms wide, emulating Christ on the cross; and not for the first time, he thought how fucking easy it was to look like you wanted to give the *whole wide world a hug* when your hands were nailed as far apart as they could possibly go, to either side.

His lovely model, Mathias, was also demonstrating the pose. Only he was just dead. Not resurrected.

And frankly, Jake didn't know if *anybody* else was getting back up. But he sure as hell had. And that made him kinda special.

The most special person on earth.

The human race had waited over 2,000 years for someone to come back from the dead. Millions of them had their bet on Jesus, and a couple of other billion were probably hedging their bets, just in case their own personal choices might turn out to be wrong.

There were maybe four, five hundred people in the Inland Empire, tops, who had their bet on Jake.

And they would be rewarded now.

His innermost circle, expanding outward in glory.

Gray and LeGrange were the first line of defense—one utterly loyal, the other utterly faithful—and the fact that they hated each other could not be more convenient.

But there would be more, as cable access led to CNN, and CNN led to Al Jazeera, and Al Jazeera led to whatever the fuck they watched in Russia, or China, or Japan.

Once his show was back up on the air, it would just be a matter of hours before everyone, everywhere knew his name. All over the world, they would fall to their knees.

For this was the message the blackness brought him: that he was born to lead, to carry that dark torch, put an end to the false light forever and ever. That he had been right about this all along, and that Christ had *always* been wrong.

That virtue was not turning the other cheek, but banging it from behind, then making it beg for more.

Two thousand years of wishful thinking on the part of the useless and meek, finally getting put right tonight.

And he was just the man to do it.

"You're welcome," he said. "My will be done, on earth as it is in heaven."

It was at that moment that Jake came up even with the two-way mirror, saw a sight that both surprised and delighted him. Like a treat from the psychotic God that truly ran the show.

He saw little Emmy cowering in his bedroom. Turning this way and that, in search of nonexistent refuge. And then finally, like a child playing hide-and-seek, lying down and sliding under the bed.

Jake laughed, blew a kiss to the billowing blackness. "Oh, this is gonna be great," he said.

There was a special camera on this side of the mirror, reserved for such special occasions. He turned it on, hit record, and adjusted the angle to his total satisfaction.

He wasn't gonna want to miss a second of this in playback.

Time to convert his first Christian, and show itsy-bitsy Emmy what life was really all about.

Gray and Evangeline grappled in the dirt, pounding the shit out of each other, both fighting for their lives, neither of them coherent enough to remember their own names.

She gave as good as she got, socking him in the throat and kidneys where he slapped and scratched her neck and her breasts, clawing at the wounds on his back and face when he let down his guard to hit her. Long after they lost the strength to land punches, they rolled across the lawn with their hands battling, hers to get at his face, his to get around her neck.

The outcome was anything but certain until Gray pinned her down and punched her square in the face, then took two handfuls of her wild red hair and bashed her head into the ground so hard that her eyes shook like dice in a cup.

He had beaten her down. She was too groggy to do more than wave her hands in the air and moan, "Fuh-fuh-fuck you." Gray retrieved his gun and tried to lever her upright by her hair, but they were both way too fucked up to stand.

Esther was just angry enough, just crazy enough with pain and frustration, to go through with it.

With her own cuffed arm, she dragged Eddie's wrist onto the block. The chain was just a little more than four inches long, too short to trust to her aim. Her hand shook when she picked up the small hand ax, tears streaming down her face. This would be easier with the big ax; but only, of course, if she had two hands free . . .

That was why she always let men do everything for her, she suddenly knew, why she could only resist Jake when someone else agreed to be her crutch. She was terrified of taking her life in her own hands, of screwing it up.

"I am so sorry . . ." she said.

Then she brought the ax down, again and again.

From under the bed, Emmy watched Jake's boots slowly walk into the room, felt the gentle brush of trapped air as he closed the door. She was holding her breath.

"Oh, Emmy, Emmy, Emmy," he crooned. "Little bundle of faith. What will it take to make you mine again?"

She was utterly still, completely terrified, watching the boots keep walking.

"You think I don't know how you feel. What you need. But you're wrong. I know."

The boots stopped in front of her face. Pointed toward her. She almost swallowed her hands, trying to hold the scream in.

"Time to know you like God knows you. From the inside out."

All at once, Jake rolled the bed out of the way, leaving her exposed on the floor. She shrieked.

He laughed, and moved toward her.

Eddie's severed hand lay on the chopping block. The bloody handcuff dangled from her wrist.

No one was watching. She was free to run, to save herself, like Eddie had told her to.

She thought about it for a moment.

From inside, she could hear Emmy screaming.

She watched the racing black clouds in the tortured night sky, wondered where she could run to. And how she would face herself when she got there.

Esther dropped the little ax.

And picked up the big one.

Chapter Fifty-six

Jake pulled Emmy from the floor. She came up clawing and screaming, ripping meat off his cheek.

"AUGH! NOT THE FACE, YOU BITCH!"

He whipped her around, drove her back, and *slammed her into the two-way mirror:* the back of her head shattering the glass and leaving a jagged hole.

She went blank as a rag doll, and Jake spun her around: facing the mirror, her ass to him.

She could see it all, horribly reflected in the shattered glass.

Gray manhandled a punch-drunk Evangeline into the studio by her hair, prodding her and spanking her ass with his gun.

"JAKE!" he called out, but got no response. He thought he heard one of his master's bitches whining somewhere nearby, but he didn't want to know.

Something had gone sour with their little miracle, and Gray had a sinking feeling that the worst was yet to come. One thing was for certain: this party was a fucking bust.

All he could do was guarantee that nobody was leaving.

"Jake! I'm gonna punch this bitch's ticket . . ."

He had to grab the doorknob with his gun hand.

Evangeline barely knew where she was, but he kept an eye on her as he threw open the door.

A towering shadow fell across the threshold. Before he even turned to look, Gray gagged at the stink of blood and excrement: outhouse-foul, but so much fresher than Jake that he figured his friend must've taken a shower.

"Jake, where do you want this bi—"

Gray swallowed his tongue.

It wasn't Jake.

It was Jasper Ellis. Grinning. No longer dead.

Or maybe still dead. But no longer down.

"Shhh . . ." Jasper hissed, holding one mischievous finger up.

Then he punched Gray's front teeth all the way down his throat, threw a wink at the stunned Evangeline, and kicked Gray's inert body out of the studio doorway.

"You comin'?" he said.

Jake heard the commotion in the hallway, but couldn't see. It pissed him off.

"KEEP IT DOWN OUT THERE, GODDAMIT!"

Through her shock, through the hole in the mirror, Emmy saw the camera aimed at her face. Also saw Mathias, still dangling lifeless on the cross behind it. She noted the jagged shards of mirror, razored stalagmites directly below her throat.

Behind her, Jake lifted up her skirt, pulled down her panties, and bared her ass.

Very softly, through the brain-fog and terror, she began to pray.

As effortlessly as taking out the trash, Jasper dragged Gray out to the middle of the studio floor by his limp arms; then, dropping the left like a dead catfish on the concrete, he took hold of the right and bent it backward at the elbow till it snapped.

Gray awakened and wailed. His legs kicked spastically and his other arm came up to fend off Jasper, but the dead man caught it and trapped it.

Evangeline stared, unbelieving, uncertain who was the greater threat. Jake's baseball bat jutted from the umbrella stand to her left, and she scooped it up instinctively, swaying.

"Jasper . . . ?"

He smiled warmly at her, caught her staring at the gaping hole in his chest, the ruptured lobe of lung hanging down the front of this shirt like a fleshy necktie.

"Gimme a second, honey," he said. "I wanna make sure this fuck stays down."

Snapping Gray's left arm with the same clinical detachment, Jasper shook his head at Gray's tactless mix of begging and cursing to get him to stop. Gray's pulse practically jumped out of his neck; he banged his head on the floor and gnashed his teeth on his tongue to fight off unconsciousness, but every movement only drove him to more outrageous fits of agony.

"I'm sorry, man." Jasper took Gray's left hand in both of his, gently shaking the arm like a masseuse does, to work out the tension, but wringing tortured howls from Gray. "This isn't about hurting you, honest to God it's not."

Beginning with his trigger finger, Jasper broke each finger at the second knuckle. Still smiling as he did it: not with evil, but with anger and purpose. "We can't solve our problems by killing each other anymore. We have to find a new way . . ."

Evangeline looked away. "Jasper, what happened to you?"

"Well, fuck," he muttered, oddly low and thin. No breath. Louder, he added, "I guess I got killed."

"What . . . what was it—?"

"It hurt." Jasper dropped the ruined hand, a curled-up

claw the hue of an eggplant. "But you know what? Right now, *it's not so bad!*"

Gray fainted dead away; only labored breathing escaped his devastated grill.

Evangeline used the bat as a cane, to steady herself, trying not to step in any of the lakes of blood. Her eyes crept up the cross, bearing unwilling witness to the worst thing she'd ever seen. Repulsion and awe battled for her sanity.

There was nothing she would not put past Jake, nothing he would not do to satisfy his titanic ego, and his endless appetite. When he came back, she was the least surprised: it was only natural that he would ignore the laws of nature, just like he flouted all the others.

But looking at Mathias, she had to adjust her idea of Jake, and what he was capable of.

While the skinny boy was flayed and mangled to a degree that would have made the Romans puke, the extremity was of a ritual nature that betrayed a sense of purpose. He was not just trying to wallow in his own cruel whims one last time, or even to drag his victims back to hell with him.

Jake did not seem to totally understand it, himself, but she had no doubt that he must have succumbed to his own bullshit. Having come back from the grave, he must really think he could raise the dead.

But he could not have meant to bring Jasper back, could he?

She passed Mathias and looked at the sliding glass door, still ajar from when Gray dragged her in here by her hair.

Nothing was holding her here. She could run away, but she would never escape, unless she saw it through. She tried to take her own life tonight. Out of her mind at the time, but the thought of what he almost made her do shook her to her core.

She was going nowhere, until they stopped that moth-erfucker cold.

She turned to survey the room, looking for some sign, some sense of what was supposed to happen tonight. A row of monitors showed a continuous feed of Mathias, still as a portrait.

A big flat-screen TV on the wall behind it played a cable news show. The talking heads were red faced, shouting, pretty much like always.

The other monitors showed snow, but the last screen played what she took at first to be one of his home movies.

Until she realized that it was another live feed.

And the weeping girl facing the camera was Emmy.

"No . . ."

Picking up Gray's pistol where Jasper tossed it, she shambled toward the mirror. Almost tripping over cables and her own treacherous feet, she could barely see the real Jake and Emmy for all their doubles.

She had to drop the bat and use both hands to lift the gun up and aim it at the one true Jake.

"Stop," she moaned, but could barely hear herself. It was like she watched a movie, unable to change the channel with the remote in her hand.

It only clicked and clicked and clicked, every time she pulled the trigger.

Emmy saw Evangeline through the hole in the mirror, pointing a gun and mouthing a silent word over and over.

But there was no salvation there.

Behind her, Jake unbuckled his belt, dropped his slacks, and massaged his cold, dead member. She caught a glimpse of Eve's apple of temptation, gray and sickly, jutting out between his knuckles in the mirror's reflection.

There was no temptation there. No lust for him left.

Only fear and revulsion.

It had never been Jake that she loved. She realized that now. He was the worst kind of deceiver: the serpent, shamelessly quoting Scripture, interjecting himself with a swaggering grin between Christ Almighty and her own foolish heart.

In the end, there was only Jesus. Her lord and savior. Her light in the darkness. Her solace in woe. Her life everlasting.

In the end, that was the only choice that mattered.

She closed her eyes, and opened her soul . . .

. . . *and there he was: her beautiful Jesus, so strong, so pure, so suffused with light. He stood before her, looked her straight in the eye, and there was no withering judgment there.*

Just total compassion. Total forgiveness. And total under-standing.

As he opened his arms to her.

For Emmy, there was no hesitation. Only shimmering clarity, and utter relief.

She let go of the wall, hoisting herself upward and throwing wide her own arms, as if they were wings.

She felt herself hover for one long microsecond: in defiance of gravity, the ugly weight of the world.

Then her body fell, no longer needed.

And the glass cut her tether.

As it sliced through her throat to the bone.

Chapter Fifty-seven

"HOLY SHIT!" Jake stepped back from the spritzing body, watched it dangle and twitch, impaled at the neck.

It wasn't just shock. It was the fact that he was *robbed*: robbed right at the moment of truth, with his dick still hanging out.

It reminded him grimly of Frankie and Sugar: the last time he'd been cock-blocked by death. The memory was not a pleasant one.

It made him recall what it was like to be afraid.

He stared at Emmy's untapped ass, no longer attractive in the least, and instantly checked his boots to see if they got any on 'em. Madness and vanity had long since trumped any ennobling human response, so pity was out the window.

He wanted to laugh, but it just wasn't funny. In fact, it was fucking repulsive.

Then he saw something even more repulsive.

Himself, in the two-way mirror.

Jake stared, horrified, into his own reflection: his embalmed flesh scratched and oozing, his mad eyes, his stabbed and bullet-ridden body.

"Oh, no," he moaned, suddenly realizing how badly this would play on TV.

He vainly tried to put some of the ragged flesh back up over the wounds on his cheeks. It flopped back down, as if ashamed to be a part of him.

"No!" Trying again, as if his will could force a better outcome.

Floop went the meat.

Mouth closed, he could see his own teeth.

Jake turned away from the mirror. This was fucked. This was thoroughly fucked. It was one thing to come back from the dead, quite another to *look* like you just came back from the goddamn dead!

So what was he supposed to do? Shellac his head? Steal somebody else's? All his life, he'd relied on his good looks to get him through the rough patches, of which there were many.

Now he *was* one of the rough patches. He looked like Keith Richards being run through a cheese grater.

Jake wasted another full minute of eternity, locked in frantic self-pity. Then he heard the sound of glass and plastic shattering from the studio.

And through the hole in the two-way mirror, he saw Evangeline, using his own baseball bat to smash his computers into rubble.

Chapter Fifty-eight

Jake blew into the studio from the hallway door, still buckling his belt, charging right by Jasper and Gray. He had eyes only for the destruction of his legacy, and the records of his miracles.

Evangeline whirled and smashed the camera that had recorded Emmy's death. The decapitated tripod skated off into the far corner of the studio, while the camera itself sailed into the picture window directly above Emmy's corpse, splintering the heavy plate glass and flinging cascades of razors into Jake's bedroom.

"STOP!" Jake screamed.

"FUCK YOU!" she screamed back.

Looking for another target, Evangeline turned to the row of monitors, but stopped when her eyes registered what was on the TV screen.

And Jake, amazingly, stopped as well.

On the huge, silent flat-screen monitor, a frantic anchor with tears in his eyes tried to read the news, but his mute mouth moved in the round, frozen expression of a shaken but faithful man singing a hymn.

The supertitles crawling across the screen said it all: *The Dead Rise: President Declares "Judgment Day!"*

Both of them stared as the TV cut abruptly to a scene

in a war-torn Iraqi city, and the shattered dome of a mosque, painted in livid red and purple by a smoke-stained sunset. A blinking caption announced that the footage was *LIVE* as a shrouded, still-dead man was carried from the mosque.

At the head of a procession of walking corpses.

Some were robed followers, devout beyond the grave. Some were Iraqi, and even American, soldiers.

All were peppered with shrapnel and gunshot wounds.

All were gray and green with decay.

And all were throwing out open arms to embrace and beg wisdom and mercy of the panic-stricken American soldiers who were, even now, trying to mow them down.

But mowing them down wasn't working.

Would never work again.

Because the rules had forever changed.

The TV cut back to the weeping news anchor, while a whirlwind of images from around the world played behind him in seeming slow motion.

But the point had been made.

Evangeline started laughing.

"Oh, you asshole," she said.

"What?" Jake muttered, distracted, eyes still locked on the footage of the rising, walking dead.

"You thought this was all about you," Evangeline continued, light dancing in her eyes. "You *always* think that it's all about you."

"Shut up . . ."

"But it's not. And it never was." She laughed again. "You're just another narcissistic fuck."

"Shut up!"

"Don't you get it? God didn't pick you. GOD PICKED EVERYONE!"

On the cross, Mathias awoke, lifted his ravaged head, and wailed like a baby on fire.

"NO!" Gray screamed, and tried to get up. "NOOOOO!!!" Still alive, but only for the terror and pain.

Jasper shook his head, stepped on Gray's right thigh and grabbed it at the ankle, twisting brutally counter-clockwise till every bone and tendon popped.

The left leg went next, cracking backward like a giant Alaskan king crab's, pointing straight up in the air at the obliterated kneecap.

Gray shrieked and blacked out. Mathias's scream went on and on. On the TV, a dead man wept.

And Evangeline could not stop laughing.

Suddenly, she was not alone in this.

Cancerous shadows oozed up out of the corners of the studio: Jake's demons, converging and circling around him like cackling carrion birds.

They laughed and laughed, glutted and drunk on all the devastated pride they'd stoked, all the pain they'd harvested from Jake's insane quest.

It was clear, in that moment, that they'd known all along. Were just egging him on, building up to this moment.

Jake's gaze went from the demons to the screen, every last drop of embalming fluid draining from his cheaply mummified face.

Watching his dreams die, one by one.

"And you know what else?" Evangeline howled. "Nobody wants to see your STUPID FUCKING SHOW . . . !"

He came at her, and she swung the bat.

It was aimed straight at his face. Reflexively, he lifted his right arm to block it, was stunned when it connected.

He did not expect his forearm to shatter. But it did, flapping awkwardly in his sleeve.

Jake bellowed, more in disbelief than pain.

Evangeline raised the bat again.

Then his other hand shot out to seize her by the throat. Lift her off the floor.

And squeeze.

Evangeline's eyes and tongue bugged out, all blood flow to her brain cut off. It sucked the strength out of her next swing, which barely cracked his ribs.

At which point, she began to die.

"YEAH!" he screamed, laying into the moment. It was the only satisfaction he had left: the ability to hurt someone smaller and weaker.

It lasted about five seconds.

Then the ax plowed into his back.

Esther's deliberate swing neatly severed his spinal cord, just below the shoulder blades. Instant, absolute paralysis set in. And every semblance of control disappeared.

"TAKE THAT, YOU WORTHLESS MOTHER-FUCKER!" she shrieked.

Jake's nerveless fingers lost their grip, and Evangeline's throat slipped from between them as her legs gave out, and she sagged to the floor, staring up at his frozen frame.

He dangled above her, legs locked, only standing because his wife still held the handle on the blade wedged in his back. Esther tried to yank it loose, but Jake just teetered back with the motion, almost knocking her flat.

Jasper stepped up from behind, grabbed Jake by the shoulders.

"Pull," he said.

Esther planted a foot in the crack of Jake's ass and pried the ax free.

Jake didn't collapse so much as *tip over*, like a deposed dictator's statue. Evangeline ducked out of the way just in time, and Jake hit the floor face-first.

"WHO BELONGS TO WHO?" Esther screamed.

The ax came whistling down again: biting deep into his shoulder, severing his aorta, sluicing fluid the color of antifreeze across the floor. "WHO FUCKING BELONGS TO WHO NOW?"

When the ax came out, it flipped him half on his back. Evangeline kicked him the rest of the way.

Now Jake could do nothing but helplessly stare at the mocking crowd, and his own undoing.

This time, the blade buried itself to the hilt in Jake's rib cage, carcass cracking wide open when she twisted the blade. Putrid freezer-bagged pouches of organ meat erupted, venting clouds of charnel decay.

Esther dry heaved, still bent over, weakly clutching the handle, not quite able to pry it loose. Jasper stood to her right, put his hands on her shoulders.

Evangeline, to her left, winced and dropped the baseball bat.

"Excuse me," she said. Esther looked up weakly. Evangeline's smile was grim but true. "I think it's my turn."

They locked eyes, shared a moment of understanding.

Esther nodded, let go of the ax.

The demons gathered close around Jake now, kneeling to either side of his head, the better to savor every speck of his destruction. This was their revenge, too, and their demented jackal-laughter all but drowned out the wailing of the dead boy on the cross.

Esther stepped back. Evangeline stepped forward. The wooden handle of the ax still jutted straight up, at the center of Jake's vision.

Evangeline yanked the blade out with relative ease, savored the heft, wavered only slightly as she brought it up over her head.

Jake knew where the next blow was going to land, even before it happened.

He tried to scream, but the sound was no louder than

a pilot light igniting. He couldn't see the black sludge and wriggling maggots that squirted from the canyon where his crotch used to be.

But he knew what he had lost.

Then the ax came up again.

Evangeline moved to the right of Jake, and Esther stepped forward, right between his useless legs.

As the world Jake had once hoped to rule shrank down.

To the shadow of the blade.

Falling hard, across his face.

Epilogue
Giving Up The Ghost

After the dying came the living again.

And so it was with the dawn, as it slowly broke over the slaughterhouse formerly known as the Weston-Partridge Free School and Homestead.

The storm was over, and the pale sun's groping rays seemed to find nothing moving but the shadows in retreat.

Nothing living, at least.

A shambling figure banged against the black gate, butting into it and turning round again and again. It was stuck inside a tiny loop of senseless motion, with only enough brain left to keep going.

Searching for a freedom it would never, ever find.

Sheriff Bill LeGrange had somewhere to be, but not the foggiest notion of how to get there. Glazed eyes rolling back and forth without seeing, snorting and hacking up curds of gray leakage.

He was stuck forever: banging his head absently against the bars, with nary a thought in his head.

No Millie. No Jesus. No Jake. No self.

No redemption.

But underneath, the emptiness gripped him with a

vague yet bottomless fear that he was—and always would be—in the wrong damn place.

In the studio, the volume on the TV was up. It was tuned to CNN, as it had been for the last six hours. So there was no escaping the latest coverage in the ongoing "Judgment Day Crisis."

Not for Gray, anyway. He couldn't work a remote to save his life. Which was, unfortunately, no longer an issue.

He couldn't even get off the fucking floor.

Dead now, but never more miserable, Gray helplessly stared at the yammering shitheads on the screen. Movement had been agony before he crossed over; but this was, if anything, worse. The slightest effort to either side made the bone shards in his arms and legs grind together in brain-scrambling agony.

Weird thing was, he couldn't be sure if he still really *felt* pain, or just fantasized about it. But one thing was for certain.

He was definitely in hell.

And it was worse than he'd ever imagined.

When 9/11 hit, he realized now, CNN and the rest of the news media had it easy. They could just run the same clips, over and over—the Twin Towers, going down—to hammer it home. It was an iconography of disaster everyone could understand.

But this was different, because it was coming from *everywhere*. If there was one central image, it was a dead human face, looking right at you. Only the face kept changing.

And there was no one to pin it on. No one to whom it wasn't happening. No one leering from a videotape, unscathed.

No one to blame but God. Or the Devil.

Or, possibly, ourselves.

On the TV, over the last several hours, thousands of the living and dead alike had filed past him: either crying and praying together, or fighting street to street and house to house. Reaction worldwide seemed pretty well split between the desperate urge to kill and the desperate urge to heal.

As usual, the news ran in circles around the twin poles of its circus tent: the obvious thing *everyone* knew, and the thing that obviously *nobody* knew.

The curse—and the peace—of death had been denied us. And nobody had the slightest idea what it meant.

But that sure didn't stop them talking.

Gray didn't know whether to laugh or cry as he watched Larry King and Wolf Blitzer welcome undead pundits into roundtable discussions. (A series of emergency "town meetings" were scheduled to run in the next twenty-four hours.)

It was refreshing to see them all off their talking points, shitting directly into their pants; but painful to watch them still miss the point and flail around in the clinch.

Questions like "How can we stop the dead from rising?" and "How might this affect U.S. foreign policy?" were almost as useless as the endless commercials.

Dear God, the endless fucking commercials . . .

Gray understood the function of media in crisis. When the drooling idiot-child that was the collective human psyche got awakened from its slumber, the media's job was to pat it on the head, offer it candy, and reassure it that the malls would still be open in the morning.

But he tried to remember: did the whistling ads for "Bob" and his penile enhancement keep running through Hurricane Katrina? And did they really want to say *this apocalypse is brought to you by Enzyte?*

Evidently, they did.

Oh, yes, this was certainly hell.

Mathias started wailing again. Gray turned his neck—the only thing that didn't hurt—toward that stupid piece of shit, and yelled, "SHUT UP!" for the one hundred thousandth time.

Those assholes had cut him down before they left with what was left of Jake, but couldn't pry him away from the cross he'd hung and died on. The brain-damaged bastard clung to it still, wrapped around its base, piteously whining like a deserted dog.

Every so often, he would turn to Gray, staring through the gaping stigmata holes in his palms at his passion play's captive audience. With no recognition whatsoever.

And that—beyond the pain and death—was probably the worst. To be stuck here, surrounded by retards. Endlessly bearing witness. And unable to strike back.

"SHUT UP!!!" he screamed again, unable to believe that things could possibly get worse.

Then the giggling demon returned.

"Oh, fuck me," Gray moaned.

From somewhere far off, as if the studio was an airplane hangar, he heard her delirious, unhinged trill.

"Hey, Gray! You ready to party?"

Suddenly, she appeared before him.

Suddenly, he remembered who she was.

Her name, as if anyone cared, was Crissy Nailor. She was just some mouthy jailbait bitch Jake hooked up with back in L.A., when he still had a band. She'd got on his nerves in record time; and when Jake dumped her, she'd threatened to go to the cops, so Gray was only too happy to take her out with the trash.

Some people just had to be dealt with. It wasn't personal. Why was she pushing *his* shit in?

"Oh, I'm pushing your shit in, all right," she cooed.

Demon Crissy hovered close enough that the drooling bullet hole in her forehead spilled phantom gray matter down his shirt. Her tongue flicked out and grazed his face with an icy tingling, like frostbite.

"*That's why I brought over some people,*" she whispered in his ear, then roared, "*And they JUST CAN'T WAIT TO SEE YOU!*"

Sugar was first, her charbroiled face cracked open in a blackened grin. Her eyes bubbled and ran down her cheeks, but he could still feel her looking right through him.

Frankie was next. He looked like a sandblasted side of beef jerky. Even his ghost could not recover all the layers of flesh he'd left on the pavement Gray's car dragged him down, or his pretty-boy bleach-blond scalp, which a vulture had carried away as Gray dug his grave.

Gray screamed.

There were more, many more, lining up behind. Sugar's mother. His own father. The first little boy he'd killed. Dozens of victims, from a lifetime of violence, all gathered here together to celebrate his doom.

He couldn't even count the whores.

And somewhere toward the back of the laughing crowd, he swore he saw that fucking *patrulero*, ready for a little Mexican payback at last.

"*Are we bugging you? Are we bugging you?*" Crissy howled out loud. "*We're not TOUCHING YOU!*"

But she lied. They were going to touch him plenty.

Gray's hell was just getting warmed up.

In Jake's bedroom, Emmy's body lay splayed across the bed with her hands across her bosom, and her chin tucked down over the gaping trench in her throat.

Jasper and Evangeline had lifted her off the broken glass and left her to awaken, but she slept on: her features composed and sedate, her bruised and battered body empty and unmoving.

And in the living room, the wreckage remained.

But the fire had finally gone out.

The dirt parking lot in the front yard was empty, but for Mathias's sedan. Esther's car, Jasper's truck, and LeGrange's cruiser were long gone. Only the fleeting dust devils whipped up by the rising heat stirred outside the Connaway house. Not even the decaying swing set creaked.

High above, a halo of circling vultures seemed to echo and mock the symphony of screams and terrible laughter that came from the studio.

Or maybe they just cried out in pity for the world they had inherited, where the dead would no longer lie still to be eaten.

The cruiser tooled down an empty, dusty desert road, past open land that seemed to spread forever.

In the distance stood the ever-popular billboard that invited all comers to answer the question: WHAT WOULD JESUS DO?

Beyond it, there seemed to be one hell of a pileup. Hard to tell how many, at this point. But certainly not less than a dozen.

The radio continued to squawk, a panicked voice at the other end drowning out the automated 911 operator.

"... *come in! For God's sake, somebody, please ...!*"

Deputy Peet turned down the volume, not ready to respond quite yet.

She was pale, her chest held together by the bullet-proof vest she'd found in the trunk—now that the horse was out of the barn, so to speak—and half a roll of duct tape.

Even with the A/C blasting, the vanilla-scented crucifix air freshener dangling from the rearview mirror couldn't quite overcome the sickly sweet scent of decay, already wafting off her in the quickening daylight.

Be that as it may, she had a job to do. She wasn't quite

sure what that meant anymore, but she figured she was about to find out.

If there was any order left to be preserved, she would do what she could to help that happen. That was what she'd signed on for. What she believed in.

And none of that had changed.

The closer Peet got to the wreckage, the more the dead became apparent. Mostly unrecognizable human slushies, up front, though even the severed limbs and skid marks kept twitching or crawling, like they had somewhere to go.

She slowed the cruiser to a crawl as she came up on the first wave of destruction, then pulled off the shoulder, half into the sand.

Now the moaning and screaming grew louder.

As the wreckage got vaster and deeper.

Past the twelve vehicles that had actually collided—in stages, evidently, based on the progressive ripeness of the smoke—past that, there were another fifteen cars, trucks, and vans that were merely skewed all over the road like tailgate partiers in a parking lot free-for-all.

Most of them with doors wide open.

Most of them with many bullet holes in the doors.

This was where the still-walking, still-brawling, blood-spattered dead slammed into each other and yammered and screamed, unable to let go of the nonsense that had brought them all here in the first place.

It was tragic, but there was nothing to be done. At least nothing that she could do alone. There were too many. Too many of them armed. And dead as she was, things could always get worse.

The scrawny corpse in the white snakeskin cowboy boots took a .45 shot at her head. Thank God his eyes were missing, or it might have actually hit. Then three mangled metalheads took him down by hand. Some high notes ululated, went on and on and on.

Peet looked up just in time to see the shadowed silhouette of the burned girl before her: shivering transparent on the gravel shoulder, holding up her cindered hands as she begged facelessly for mercy.

But the cruiser passed through her like the vapor that she was.

Nothing to be done about that, either.

And then—as if even God recognized the urgent need for comic relief—a huge, smoldering sasquatch of a man stumbled past and ran off into the desert, clapping his hands and whooping with glee as he chased after a blind tortoiseshell cat.

Peet shook her head, rolled her eyes, and laughed, watching his tattered army shirt flap in the breeze. It was the first laugh of her afterlife, and it felt fucking fantastic.

She didn't feel the need to radio in a report on this. The poor desperate dispatcher had enough on his plate.

But it was definitely time to check in.

"Peet here," she husked into the handset. "Hit me."

The cruiser kicked up a rooster tail of dust as it fired up its lights and sped off for the highway. There was, unsurprisingly, plenty left to do, for both the living and the dead.

And it was always nice to be needed.

In the desert, you can lose anything. Make it disappear, never to be seen again.

Maybe that was why so many of the world's great and not-so-great religions had been born there. It was more than the scorching sun, the chilling moon, the visionary madness and blinding rage that seemed to thrive in such merciless places.

The desert was full of secrets—God's, Nature's, and Man's—only some of which would ever be found.

That was certainly the idea this morning.